Praise for Rita Mae Brown's novel
Outfoxed

"Compelling . . . Engaging . . . [A] sly whodunit . . . A surprise finish . . . [Brown] succeeds in conjuring a world in which prey are meant to survive the chase and foxes are knowing collaborators (with hunters and hounds) in the rarefied rituals that define the sport."

—*People*

"A rich, atmospheric murder mystery steeped in the world of Virginia foxhunting . . . Rife with love, scandal, anger, transgression, redemption, greed, and nobility, all of which make good reading."

—*San Jose Mercury News*

"A snappy mystery . . . [Brown] does a masterly job of putting you in the saddle."

—*The Baltimore Sun*

"Original, funny, poignant, irresistible: Brown's best work in years . . . Not since Anthony Trollope has foxhunting been so vividly novelized."

—*Kirkus Reviews* (starred review)

ALMA MATER

RITA MAE BROWN

BALLANTINE BOOKS | NEW YORK

A Ballantine Book
The Random House Publishing Group

Copyright © 2001 by American Artists, Inc.

Published in the United States by Ballantine Books, an imprint of
The Random House Publishing Group, a division of Random House,
Inc., New York, and simultaneously in Canada by Random House
of Canada Limited, Toronto.

Ballantine and colophon are registered
trademarks of Random House, Inc.

www.ballantinebooks.com

Library of Congress Control Number: 2002093141

ISBN 0-345-45532-0

Cover design by Drew Pennington-McNeil
Cover photo © Claire Hayden/Stone

Manufactured in the United States of America

First Hardcover Edition: November 2001
First Trade Paperback Edition: November 2002

4 6 8 9 7 5

THIS NOVEL IS DEDICATED TO
BAD GIRLS,
BECAUSE
GOOD GIRLS GO TO HEAVEN, BUT
BAD GIRLS GO EVERYWHERE.

Sex makes monkeys out of all of us.
If you don't give in to it,
you wind up a cold, unfeeling bastard.
If you do,
you spend the rest of your life picking up the pieces.

I f knowledge were acquired by carrying books around, I'd be the sharpest tool in the shed, Vic thought as she carted the last load up three flights of stairs on a hot summer day.

Sweat rolled between her breasts. Light poured into the rooms, the windows thrown open to catch any hope of a breeze. As she placed the carton on top of the old kitchen table, it swayed ever so slightly from the weight.

"Dammit!" a voice complained from outside.

Vic walked to the kitchen window that overlooked a well-maintained yard. A small creek bordered one side of the property, a line of thick pines obscuring the view into the neighbor's yard.

Vic leaned out her window and listened to the sounds of struggle and fury. She trotted down the stairs, jumped the creek, and emerged through the pines. A young woman perhaps five feet five inches tall, blonde, her back turned to Vic, was cussing a blue streak while trying to slide an old dresser from the back of an equally old Mercedes station wagon.

"Need a hand?" Vic's low alto startled the woman.

She turned around. "You scared the shit out of me!" Her voice betrayed Pennsylvania origins.

"Sorry." Vic smiled. "I'm your neighbor. Vic Savedge. Come on, we'll get the dresser out and we can carry it up together."

"I'm Chris Carter." The woman held out her hand.

Both women smiled and shook hands.

Then Vic removed the dresser with one pull.

"How'd you do that?"

"Patience. You lost yours," Vic sensibly replied.

"Guess I did." Then she slyly added, "Anyone ever tell you you're big and strong?"

"Every day. And it doesn't get them anywhere." Vic laughed. "But in your case, seeing as how I have to live next to you for the year, I'll carry this up."

Chris struggled to pick up one end. "This thing is awkward." She blinked to keep the sweat out.

"Put it down," Vic commanded.

"Why?"

"Just put it down," Vic repeated. "You go ahead of me and open the doors."

"You aren't going to carry that up by yourself, are you?"

"It'll be easier than trying to maneuver you *and* the dresser." Vic hoisted the bird's-eye maple dresser on her back, bent over, and started up the back stairs of the Olsen house. Chris's apartment was at the top of that house just as Vic's apartment was at the top of the DeReuter house. She gladly put down her burden when she reached the top of the last flight, breathed deeply, then picked it up again and headed toward the bedroom. Chris led the way, apologizing with every step. Vic placed the dresser against the wall.

"There."

"Thank you. Really. I can't thank you enough."

"A Co' Cola would help." Vic wiped her brow, droplets of sweat spraying off her fingertips.

Chris's kitchen was graced with newer appliances than were in Vic's kitchen. She opened the refrigerator door, pulled out a cold can of Coke, grabbed a glass with dancing polar bears on it, dropped in ice cubes, and poured the soda. Then she repeated the process for herself.

"They taste better over ice."

Vic gulped hers down. "True."

"Here, you need another one." Chris popped open another can and poured its contents into Vic's glass. Her eyes met Vic's for a second. Vic had green eyes, deep electric green. Set against her black hair, her eyes could be almost hypnotic. "You have the most incredible eyes."

Vic laughed. "It runs in the family. So does the height—my mother's six-one, too." Then she studied Chris. "Well, you've got brown eyes and blonde hair and you're petite. I bet everyone tells you you're pretty, it's a beautiful combination. Do you listen to them?"

"Never. Do you?"

"No, I don't want to be known for how I look but for what I do."

"If we were both butt-ugly we'd probably feel different."

They laughed, then Vic said, "What year are you?"

"Junior. I'm a transfer from the University of Vermont. It's a good school, but I never knew how much I hated cold weather until I wound up in Vermont. Fall starts in August. I think you have to be born to it, you know?"

"I don't know. I've never been to Vermont. The farthest north I've been was to visit Cornell but it was during summer."

"Same difference. Fall starts there in August, too." She finished her drink. "Are you moved in?"

"Yes," Vic said with relief. "I'd just put the last carton of books on the table when I heard you."

"Was I that loud?" Chris's hand flew to her mouth, an unexpectedly feminine gesture.

"Uh-huh."

"It could have been worse. I could have yelled 'fuck.' "

Vic laughed again. "One of two things would have happened: Every old biddy on the street would have fainted dead or the men would have come running, hoping you meant it."

Chris wrinkled her nose. "Neither prospect sounds very appetizing." She took the glass from Vic's hand. "What year are you?"

"Senior."

"Lucky dog."

"I guess. I still have to get through it. Don't count your chickens, et cetera." She walked over to the sink as Chris washed out the two glasses. "Do you know anyone at William and Mary?"

"Not really. I fell in love with the school and figured I'd make friends."

"You're in luck. I have wonderful friends. If you're really good to me, you can meet them."

"I'm pretty damn good," Chris replied.

Well, there she was, your little sister, her midriff bulging nasty white, a pair of pedal pushers—yes, pedal pushers—tottering on open-toed wedgies that Carmen Miranda must have cast off on her way back to Brazil. I can't take her anywhere." R. J. Savedge, Vic's mother, lit up her Lucky Strike, unfiltered, and then just as quickly stubbed it out. "I am giving these goddammned things up." This was followed by a mournful "But how?" as she instantly lit up another.

"Mother, it's expensive to stub them out like that."

R. J. shot back a look, then softened. "Of course, you're quite right. I can't stand that I don't have the willpower. They taste *so-o-o* good."

People could not remain immune to the mind-numbing beauty of Vic or her mother, carbon copies of one another separated by twenty years. The difference was that Vic was still working out her style; R. J. had perfected hers.

Rachel Jolleyn Vance Savedge was R. J.'s full name. Vance, her maiden name, was the middle name she bequeathed to Vic, Victoria Vance Savedge. The Savedge women could make you forget all about the Ten Commandments or the fact that your wife might be packing a .38.

"Mother, why don't you buy Mignon some clothes?"

"Your younger sister remains in the chrysalis. I am not wasting money on a fat caterpillar who I devoutly hope—no, I pray—will emerge as a butterfly. God, I hope she doesn't take after the Catlett side of the family." She exhaled a plume of heron-blue smoke. "In that case, she'll stay a fat caterpillar."

"Mom." Vic laughed.

"It's true. Look at your aunt Bunny." R. J.'s sister was younger by two years and pudgier by fifteen pounds, although not a bad-looking woman at all.

"Too many potato chips."

"Sublimation."

"I thought you didn't believe in psychology."

"I don't, but I'll use anything to make my point," R. J. said. "She worries too much about what Don is doing."

Don was Bunny's husband, who possessed a wandering eye. The rest of him wandered right along with it.

"Maybe if I take her, Mignon will buy some clothes."

R. J. paused, cigarette glowing orange in midair. "We haven't any money, dear. Your father has lost it all again."

"Oh, Mom. I'm sorry."

"Me, too." She smiled tightly. "Thank God you earn your money. And you will marry brilliantly." She leaned across the kitchen table. "Charly Harrison."

"Mother." Vic hated being pushed, although she expected (as did everyone around her) that Charly Harrison would ask her to marry him before their senior year was over. And it *would* be a brilliant match. The Harrisons of Charles City, Virginia, had produced one president of the United States, and they luxuriated in pots of money. The Harrison money appealed to R. J. far more than their lineage. Her pedigree was equally impressive—minus the president.

R. J., a born-and-bred Virginian, knew the value of bloodlines and believed, up to a point, that breeding people was no different from breeding horses. Breed the best to the best and hope for the best. But money mattered far more than the old Virginia families cared to admit.

If nothing else, Yankees were totally honest in their pursuit of wealth. And for this lack of subtlety, of course, no Virginian could ever forgive them.

"Well, naturally, I long for your happiness, for a full and fulfilled life. And for Mignon, too. Marrying well is a step in that direction."

"You didn't," Vic put it bluntly to her mother.

"No. I married for love, and look where it got me." She smiled slowly. "And I still love your father. He gambles. Oh, it's the stock market, so that makes it somehow acceptable, but I don't see that it's any different from the boys out at Goswells betting on cocks. At least cockfighting has the prospect of being more exciting than gray little numbers."

"I have a little money put aside. I could get Mignon some clothes."

"Vic, you're a love, but no. For one thing, she really must lose this baby fat. I don't care if I have to wrap her in Grandma Catlett's old house dresses until she drops the tonnage. That ought to give her incentive. In the meantime I shall squander what slender resources are at my disposal on cigarettes and roses. I don't think my garden has ever looked so thrilling as it does this year."

The sound of footsteps on the stair landing interrupted their conversation.

Vic got up and opened the door before the caller had time to knock. "Come on in."

"I'm sorry. I didn't know you had company." Chris backed away.

"My esteemed mother. Really, come on in. Mother loves an audience. You'll be new ears for all her stories."

Chris stepped over the threshold, noticing how bare Vic's apartment was. A kitchen table, four chairs. That was all she could see.

"Mother, this is Chris Carter. Chris, my mother, R. J. Savedge, the reigning beauty of Virginia's Southside."

Chris walked over to shake hands with R. J., who, as befitted her station, did not rise but extended her hand.

"I'm pleased to meet any friend of my daughter's."

"Sit down. It's my turn to give you a Coke." Vic placed a glass filled with ice cubes in front of Chris. The cold can quickly followed. "Mother, do you want a refill?"

"No, thank you. But you may clean the ashtray."

Vic dumped the ashes, wiped out the tray, and placed it before her mother.

"Thank you, dear." She looked closely at the ashtray, round glass surrounded by a miniature rubber tire, an advertisement for Goodrich tires from the 1940s. "Did your aunt Bunny give you this?"

"She did."

R. J. turned her attention to Chris. "Don't believe Vic about this reigning beauty stuff. She's buttering me up."

"I do believe her. You two could be twins. It's hard to believe you're her mother."

R. J. smiled. "I like you, Chris."

People were usually overwhelmed when they first met R. J. Like Vic had said, she was a bit over six feet tall, perfectly proportioned, with jet-black hair and green eyes—although her eyes were a lighter shade than those of her elder daughter.

"Thank you." Chris smiled, too, and relaxed a little.

"Since we live across the river, I can pop in and out of Williamsburg with ease, a fact not always appreciated by my beloved firstborn."

"I love seeing you, Mother." Vic said it like a joke, but she clearly meant it.

"And where is Charly?"

"Practice." Vic turned to Chris. "Charly's my boyfriend. You'll meet him eventually. He's the halfback on the football team. Mom's in love with him."

R. J. was smiling at her daughter's assessment of her feelings for Charly. "Chris, how did you meet Victoria?"

"She carried my dresser up to my apartment just next door."

"Strong brute, isn't she? She used to pulverize the boys in school, even in high school. She reduced them to tears. I told her there really are better ways to wring concessions from men."

"Mother," Vic sighed.

"I suppose I should train Mignon." R. J. ground out her cigarette, smoked down to the nub. "Mignon's her younger sister—quite a bit younger, just fifteen. I couldn't bear the thought of two children in diapers simultaneously. The human animal is slow to mature. Mignon should be trained to be the family vixen since Victoria here will continue to apply hammerlocks."

She instinctively reached for her Luckies. "I can't resist these things. I swear I can't. But, it's better than if I were a nymphomaniac. My nickname is Orgy." She laughed at Chris's surprised expression. "I'm not a nymphomaniac; I don't go to orgies. It's a childhood nickname. It's better than being called Snooze or Peanut. And I could think of even worse." She patted Chris's hand, which was on the table. "I'm not your run-of-the-mill mother."

"No, Mrs. Savedge, you're not."

"And what does your sainted mother" —she paused dramatically— "*do?*"

"Puts up with me," Chris replied, laughter in her voice.

"Ah yes, I suppose all you daughters require that, since you break your mothers' hearts. Where are you from, Chris?"

"York, Pennsylvania."

"Once the capital of the country, if I remember my history."

"Yes, Mrs. Savedge, it was."

"You don't look very German. I always assume that everyone from Pennsylvania is either German or Quaker. Carter. Good English name. We have much to thank the English for, especially giving us all names we can spell—that and finally getting out of there. It would never do to have kings and queens in America. Of course, it hasn't really worked for them, either."

"Chris has transferred from the University of Vermont. I'm going to show her around." Vic was accustomed to her mother going off on tangents.

"Vic knows everybody. And if I might take some pride in my daughter, she's a good friend to have."

"Thank you, Mother."

R. J. glanced at her watch, an old Bulova that had belonged to her father. "Let me take you two girls out for dinner."

"Thank you, but I really just dropped in to see if Vic knew a good clothing store in town."

"She does, as I do. I'll drive you, although they'll be closing now.

Come on, girls. I know how much you eat at your age. I'm famished, and I've learned better than to expect any food here. Which reminds me, dear, you'd best come home this weekend, if you can."

"Yes, ma'am."

"Bring Chris." R. J. paused, casting her eyes over Vic's jeans and cutoff T-shirt. "You aren't going out like that, are you?"

"Mother, it's fine. We aren't going to church."

R. J. airily called over her shoulder as they descended the stairs, "Daughters were born to break their mothers' hearts."

There's someone just wonderful out there waiting for you. He might even be on this campus," Vic said.

"Puh-lease," Jinx Baptista said, wrinkling her nose.

Vic wrapped her arm around Jinx's waist as they walked through the quad. Charly Harrison flanked Vic's right side, his arm around her waist.

Being Vic's best friend could be a trial for a girl. Jinx bore it as best she could, having recognized since childhood that all eyes would seize upon Vic first.

"Someone intelligent. He'd have to be intelligent to keep up with you, Jinx," Charly said.

"And well hung." Vic giggled.

Jinx winked at Vic. "Your mother didn't raise you right."

"I'm not listening. I'm too sensitive." Charly's voice mocked them both.

They were strolling through campus and into town, where shops festooned in green and yellow welcomed back the students as an influx of gilded locusts each fall.

Jinx returned to the topic of the absence of men in her life. "Charly, men don't like intelligent women. I've been thinking about what you said."

"What did I say?"

"That a man would have to be intelligent to keep up with me."

"Oh." He stepped between the women to place a hand in the small of each woman's back as he escorted them across the road safely to the other side. "Well, he would."

"And I'm saying men don't like intelligent women."

"Jinx, come on." Vic rolled her eyes.

"It's true."

"Vic is intelligent." Charly said this with conviction.

"Oh, bull—you'd love her if she were as dumb as a sack of hammers."

"I would not." A tiny, indignant wrinkle crossed his tanned brow.

"You'd still be sexually attracted to her."

He looked at Jinx. "Probably. But I wouldn't love her. If she didn't have a brain, I'd get bored eventually."

"For some men, 'eventually' lasts years," Vic teased him.

"You two are scratching for a fight. Come on, women can be just as superficial about looks as men."

"That's true," Vic agreed with Charly, "but they don't have as much opportunity to exercise it."

"My mother thinks it's true what they say about women using sex to get love, and men using love to get sex. I think I agree with her."

"Jinx, since when have you ever agreed with your mother?" Vic said, punching Jinx on the arm.

"I am now." Jinx returned her attention to Charly. "Do you remember the first time you saw Victoria?"

"Sunken garden behind the Wren Building. I spent the whole next week looking for her. I asked everyone I knew if they knew her or had ever seen her."

"She could have been mentally defective, you wouldn't have cared." Jinx pretended to be horrified at his shallowness.

"Yeah, but once I found her I discovered she was bright and beautiful."

"Thanks to me. I am responsible for bringing you two together. You owe your happiness to me."

"Saint." Vic put her arm around Jinx's neck.

"Face it—if Charly and I hadn't had Physiology together, then who knows? You were waiting for me after class, and then he wanted to know me." Jinx sighed.

"If you hadn't introduced me, I'd still be out there trying to find Vic." Charly smiled.

What Jinx wouldn't admit was that when Charly came up to her before the next class, her heart had skipped a beat. But when he asked about her friend, she knew she was defeated before she'd even had a chance. She promised to introduce Charly to Vic, and she kept her promise. Jinx loved Vic, she would always love Vic, but there were times when it was hard not to resent her.

"Vic, do you remember the first time you saw Charly?"

"Sure, when you introduced us."

"Well?"

"Well, what?" Vic shrugged.

Jinx asked. "Do you remember what you thought?"

Accustomed to male attention, Vic remembered her first meeting with Charly, but it didn't loom as large in her consciousness as it did in his. She hoped that didn't show. "I thought he was a nice guy."

"Thank you." Charly smiled.

"Jinx, if you go around trying to find someone, you never will. I think it kind of sneaks up on you. You'll meet the right person."

"And he'll like intelligent women." Charly winked at Jinx.

He liked Jinx. She was cute, energetic. He had to like her. Jinx and Vic were inseparable.

They passed the Catholic church, St. Bede's, stopping to admire the large statue of Mary, the Blessed Virgin Mother, in the middle of the immaculately kept grounds. Across the street, the monsignor lived in a tidy white house where he kept an eye on St. Bede's and Mary.

"She always looks so peaceful," Jinx remarked. "Male saints never look as peaceful as the Blessed Mother."

"Because they're struggling against their own testosterone."

"If Raphael were alive, he'd paint you as the Madonna." Charly kissed Vic's cheek.

Jinx grimaced. "I'm going to throw up."

"Cynic," Charly said.

"I'll be the godmother to Vic's children. They'll need a cynic in their lives. That's probably why the BVM looks so peaceful. The kids are out of the house."

"Your mother, if she heard you . . ."

"She won't unless you tell her." Jinx pinched Vic's arm. "Which reminds me, what's the plan for the weekend?"

Vic rolled a deep breath. She hadn't yet told Charly that she needed to go home. He hated it when she missed a football game. In his defense, he attended all her lacrosse games. Vic and Jinx held the lacrosse team together each spring.

"Home."

Charly's face fell.

"Dad's lost all our money. Again." She glanced at each of her friends and then back to the serene BVM. "Mother came by yesterday. She didn't make a big deal about it, but you know it is. Last time he did this I was in seventh grade, and it was hell."

"Can you pay tuition?" Charly dropped his large hand on her shoulder, lightly squeezing.

"I did already. That sucked up most of the money I made working for Uncle Don this summer." She exhaled again, louder this time. "I've got enough for my books, but I think I need to get a job. No lacrosse."

"Don't say that," Jinx said quickly, her voice carrying a sense of urgency. "There's plenty of time before practice starts. We'll think of something."

"Hey, it's not a funeral. If I can't play lacrosse, I can't. I can't let Mom and Mignon down."

"There's got to be another way," Jinx said.

"Sell dope?" Vic suggested, raising her eyebrows.

"Mmm, not a good idea."

"Charly, you're so straight." Jinx studied the BVM's impassive, beatific expression. "I think she'd look fetching in a striped uniform."

"Prisoners wear orange now," Vic corrected her.

"Orange, well, that's bright and cheery." Jinx thought for a moment. "Maybe someone needs a researcher, some professor who lost his graduate assistant."

"Yeah, but I'm not in graduate school."

"They can make exceptions," Jinx said hopefully.

"We'll figure something out," Charly reassured her.

They walked back toward the shops. Charly kissed Vic again and then headed for class.

Vic and Jinx walked back to Vic's apartment, just around the corner from Jinx's. The two friends could never be far apart, but they couldn't room together. They'd figured out early on that they'd never get any work done.

"Jeez, there's nothing in here." Jinx looked around her friend's apartment.

"One bed, one kitchen table, four chairs, and a million books. That's all I need."

"Vic, it's depressing."

"The living room is cavernous. I don't think of it as depressing. I think of it as spartan elegance."

"No money."

"Well, yeah. Now I'm really glad I didn't buy anything. I mean after Mother's visit. I've got a little bit in reserve."

"But if we go to church sales and the used furniture stores, we'll find stuff. Not here. Cross the James into Surry County, home sweet home. I know we can find stuff over there. And then there's my mother, Princess Rat Pack. I can pry some stuff loose from her."

"Did I ever tell you you're my best friend?"

"Not often enough." Jinx sat on the windowsill in the living room, looking out the wide open windows. She sighed. "I don't care about going to the football game. I'll go home with you."

"Your mother won't be happy."

"My mother has a deep primal fear that I will not properly socialize. I don't have a date for the game, so I might as well go home and see if I can get stuff out of her once she gets over the shock of seeing me. *Her* college days," Jinx said, "were an endless round of dates, parties, dances—jeez. I'm not her. She was a beauty."

"Ah, Jinx, you're great looking."

"You've been looking at me since we were born."

"Tell yourself you're great looking. Attitude is everything."

"You've got enough for both of us. But really, my mother drives me crazy. She still thinks the purpose of going to college is to get married. I can't say that your mother is far off that, except she has the sense not to push. Plus you have Charly."

"Because Aunt Bunny pushes enough. It was different for them, I guess. You know, they still think you're only as good as the man you're with."

"We should have gone to the University of Wyoming or Montana. We stayed too close to home."

"Yeah." Vic sat opposite Jinx on the windowsill. "But it would cost a fortune to go to school out of state, and those places are really far away. I'd love to see them, though."

"We could run away." Jinx almost meant it.

"Tempting. Damn, it's senior year, and I have no more idea what I'm going to do than . . ." Vic's voice trailed off.

"We get our degrees. If our GREs are good, we can push on. Not that I much want to, but it delays making a decision," Jinx said.

"Aren't you taking the Law Boards, too?"

"Yeah. If worse comes to worst, I can join your dad's law firm."

"That's worst, all right."

Frank Savedge, a country lawyer, drew up wills and did the paperwork for land transactions.

Vic stretched out, her feet touching Jinx's thigh. "You know, I sometimes wonder if we won't wind up like our mothers."

"Yeah, me, too. The feminist movement is something that happened in New York and Chicago. It ain't here, and it's already 1980."

"Nah, when it's four-thirty in New York, it's 1940 in Williamsburg."

They both laughed at the old joke.

"That's what your mother says." Jinx got up and fetched a Coke for herself and another for Vic. In the sticky heat of late summer, nothing else could quench the eternal thirst.

"You know, I do think of running away sometimes. Funny that you said it. But I don't know if I could leave Southside. It gets in your bones."

"I could leave. In a heartbeat. And so could you. Besides, we could always come back," Jinx sensibly added, holding the frosty glass to her forehead. "We need a thunderstorm."

"Sistergirl, we need more than that."

4

Bunny McKenna, R. J.'s sister, carried an expensive pair of Leica binoculars wherever she went. When R. J. joked that her sister probably slept with those binoculars, Bunny always replied that they were more exciting than her husband, Don.

An avid bird-watcher, she'd suddenly whip the binoculars to her eyes and mutter, "Green heron." It could be quite unnerving.

On this languid September afternoon as golden light splashed over the dock at the Savedge place on the bank of the James, Bunny had already identified thirty-two different species of birds, many of them waterfowl. She also named the people in the sailboats gliding by. Each passerby earned a tart comment.

R. J. was sitting by the dock in a blue rowboat. Armed with her toolbox, she was handily replacing an oarlock.

Bunny, black binocs to her eyes, again swept her gaze down the river. "Why doesn't Francie put him on a diet?" She spied some friends out in the middle of the glistening water, the husband, Nordie, at the till of a breathtaking sailboat.

"He'd just go uptown and get a cheeseburger. Ah, I got it." R. J. lifted off the old oarlock.

"Nordie's beyond a spare tire. I mean, it's a tractor tire now. Can you imagine sex with a man with a potbelly? It would be a triumph of physics."

"No, dear."

"No what? It would or would not be a triumph or you can't imagine it in the first place?" She lowered her binoculars.

"Can't imagine sex with Nordie."

"Do you think sex is overrated?"

"Bunny, we've had this discussion before. I believe it started in 1955. The day you turned fourteen."

"I hate that. You were born in an even year and I was born in an odd one. I just hate that. 1938. Now that sounds lovely. But no, I'm 1941. And all anyone remembers about 1941 is the bombing of Pearl Harbor. It's not fair."

"You aren't even forty yet, so don't bitch and moan." R. J. sanded the spot where the old oarlock had been and then placed the new oarlock on the spot. Perfect fit.

"Some days I feel like I'm one hundred," Bunny sighed, swinging her legs over the water.

"Momma said there'd be days like this."

Both sisters then sang the tune.

"You know something, Orgy? I don't know if I want to get old. Momma Catlett has lived too long. And the Wallaces—now, they're demented. I want to go flat out, pedal to the metal." Bunny stared down at the oarlock that R. J. was screwing into place. "You are so organized. Protestants are supposed to be organized."

"Bunny, I can usually follow your conversational leaps and non sequiturs, but you are positively scatterbrained today."

"How good of you to notice." Bunny whipped her binoculars to her eyes. "White ibis. Big one."

R. J. slipped the oar into the oarlock and wiggled it around. "Not bad, if I do say so myself."

"That's what men are for."

"If I waited for my husband to do it, it would never get done. I think Frank has mowed the lawn once since we married." R. J. said this without rancor, more in the nature of an accepted fact.

Bunny wondered if perhaps men weren't wiser about these things. The grass would always be there, but a good golf game—now *that* was worth one's time.

"Donald's dependable about the chores. He always hires someone else to do them." Bunny laughed.

Don made a good living off his combined Dodge/Toyota dealership. At his wife's urging, he had quickly grabbed the Japanese dealership when it became available back in the late sixties, and it had proved a sound move. Dodge was hanging in there so-so, but Toyotas were hot.

R. J. looked up at the broad blue sky. "What is it about late afternoons? I love them so. The day has fallen into place. When I get up in the morning, I know what my chores are, but the day itself hasn't taken shape. By now it has, and the light is pure gold, golden and rich like cadmium paint. The hours seem lucky, somehow."

"I never thought of it that way."

"I wonder if every hour has its own spirit."

R. J.'s poetic musings delighted Bunny even if she couldn't help teasing her sister about them. Bunny's mind worked in a straightforward manner, rather like a locomotive. She might have ideas, cars hitched to the engine of her desire, but everything was on a track. R. J.'s mind took in everything, but she didn't order it immediately. It was as though she saw the world through the compound eyes of a dragonfly, a series of separate but related images. Unlike her younger sister, R. J. could let her mind wander. She felt no great need to prove anything.

"Who's that?" Bunny peered at a large boat under power, a Chris Craft. She put the glasses to her eyes to read the yacht club flag flying from the back. "Bahia Mar. That's in Fort Lauderdale."

"Probably on the way back down for the winter."

"Winter's a long way off."

"If we're lucky." R. J. sat down, picking up an oar in each hand. "Ready for a spin?"

"Sure." Bunny gracefully dropped into the boat, turned, and untied it.

Having grown up on the water, both women were in their element and could manage any boat with an ease that people coming to it later in life envied. Both could read the river, the currents, the temperature, the quick building of a sandbar that might be sluiced away in a mighty storm. They just knew.

R. J., tall and strong like her elder daughter, pulled them out into

the deepening water with four powerful strokes. Then she pointed the
bow downriver so they could float for a while. Bunny peered at the
shoreline through her glasses. "Blue heron. Mallard. A lot of mallards
this year, and this one's a male yellow-green bill." Without dropping
her binoculars, she asked, "So what are you going to do?"

"Same as always. Go without."

"Do you think you'll have to sell off acreage?"

"I won't let Frank do that. This place has been here since 1642,
through Indian wars and white men's wars and just about every mess
you can think of, and I'm not letting him sell it."

Bunny gently placed her binoculars on her chest. "Must have been
something once upon a time, four thousand acres."

"It's something now."

"Yeah, it is. You've still got close to a thousand acres, but I don't
know what you can do to keep them."

"I can make him sign off the deed. When we married, things were
different. I was chattel." She smiled ruefully. "What was mine became
his. That's got to change."

Bunny blinked. "Would he do it? Remove himself?"

"Perhaps, but it will be a terrific blow to him."

"And even if he did, could you keep it going? Things are changing,
honey pie. You can't make a goddamned dime farming or fishing."

"No, but I've got over a mile of shoreline and if I have to, I can intelligently develop part of it."

"R. J.!" Bunny's voice rose.

"Show me another way."

"If Vic will marry Charly, that'll bring a nice chunk of change into
the family. And I predict she will marry him right after graduation,"
Bunny said.

"We don't know what will be settled on him by his family. Some
families make the kids go out and work. And I don't think that's a bad
idea—no, I don't."

"They'll get them started at least. It wouldn't do for a Harrison to
be poor."

"Bunny, it doesn't do for anyone to be poor."

"How true." Bunny stretched out her long, pretty legs.

"And what if Vic and Charly don't want to live here?" R. J. continued. "Surry County may not hold them. For all I know they'll troop up
to Richmond. Even Washington! Charly's got to get a job."

"She'd die of boredom. She's an outdoor kid."

R. J. laughed. "Vic's happiest running the tractor or putting up
fence."

"Her idea of fashion is a red bandanna around her neck, overalls,
and a shirt. Or overalls and no shirt." Bunny thought Vic's attire most
unladylike.

"She worked hard this summer down at Don's and then on the farm
in the early mornings and evenings. She's not afraid to work. Neither is
Charly. They'll make something of themselves, those two," R. J. said.

"She's going to end up the wife of an important man. I can't picture
her slapping down shingles on a roof."

"He does seem headed that way, doesn't he? Toward some kind of
power and position. In the blood, I guess. But they're young. Things
could change. Maybe he'll wind up a rich tax lawyer."

"Boring."

"Oh, he's not boring, dear."

"He'll become boring." Bunny's voice had an acid tinge.

"Not every day can be fire and flame."

"I'd settle for once a week." Bunny sighed. "All Don ever thinks
about is the business. Jesus Christ." She trailed her hand in the water.

"Maybe we can't have it all."

"I don't want it all. I just want enough."

"Oh, Bun." R. J. picked up the oar in the new oarlock and swung
the bow around. Then she rowed upstream, rejoicing in the resistance.

"Want me to row?"

"No, you need to preserve your strength. Isn't the club tournament
tomorrow?"

"Yes, it is."

The small but lovely old country club was quite active, and at the
time both young families joined, twenty-odd years ago, it hadn't been
expensive. Their parents had been members and their paternal grand-
parents had been founding members.

"We might have to drop our membership."

"Don't do that, Orgy. Big mistake. Not only are those our friends, think of the business contacts."

"Well, I'm not in business, and Frank is a good lawyer. People know he's solid. He is what he is."

"Maybe you and I could go into business."

R. J. pulled rhythmically against the light current. She noticed creamy cumulus clouds building in the west. "Bunny, we've been over this."

"You've got to do something and so do I. I want to do something . . . purposeful."

" 'Bacca."

"Tobacco is labor intensive plus all the paperwork just to keep the allotments alive."

"I do it every year," R. J. reminded her.

"I know you do the paperwork, but you don't put in much of a crop because you can't and we can't. There aren't many people left around here who know 'bacca, and sooner or later all this smoking-is-hazardous-to-your-health stuff will bite us in the ass."

"Hmm. Peanuts."

"Orgy, just keep the land in hay and timber. Trust me."

R. J. did trust Bunny, who possessed a sharp business mind. Everything Bunny suggested paid off. She read voraciously, not just about the auto industry, but about the economy in general.

All of Bunny's work benefited her husband. People knew Bunny was behind it, but still, he was the front man; he got the lion's share of the attention. She had more freedom than he did, but she felt adrift. She wanted structure, a business in her name.

"Sometimes I feel ambushed by life. Surprised. But . . ." R. J.'s voice trailed off as she glanced over her shoulder to see how she was coming in to the dock.

They hit it with a slight thud. Bunny grabbed the mooring and quickly wrapped the tie line around it. She hoisted herself out as R. J. arranged the oars.

Bunny leaned over, hand outstretched.

R. J. took it and swung herself up. Standing in the sunlight, the two of them were clearly close relations. It wasn't so much a physical resemblance, because they took after different branches of their family. It was the way they moved, their gestures, their physical comfort in one another's presence.

"Listen to me." Bunny's voice was commanding. "You don't know if Frank can make the money back. If he does, it will take years. Remember last time? You've got to go beyond what you've done before. It's a new day. Let's hope that Vic marries Charly. God knows that won't hurt. But let's go into business. I mean it. Don can give me the seed money—and he will. One, I've earned it. Two, he's still guilty about his little affairette. Three, there's a part of him that would get a kick out of seeing us succeed. Four, I'll pay him back just because I want to do that. Over time, of course. Five, Surry Crossing has been in our family since Charles the First gave us the land grant, and by God, it's going to stay in this family. Sometimes I wish I'd never left here, but Don wanted to be closer to town and we'd just married. I couldn't much see the point of being around Mom and Dad then."

R. J. draped her arm around Bunny's shoulder. "I miss them, too."

"Let's do this. Not just for you, but for me as well. Let's go into business."

"What do you have in mind?"

"A plant nursery. We've got the land. People are building houses in this county all the time. And if you ever decide to develop 'intelligently,' " —she mimicked her sister's voice— "we'll have all the nursery stock to make it the best landscaped development in Virginia."

"You're serious."

"As a heart attack."

"Maybe you've hit on the right formula this time. There's so much to think about. But the first thing I've got to do is get Frank off the deed." R. J. kissed Bunny's suntanned cheek.

Bunny pointed to a dust cloud about a quarter of a mile away. "Vic." She lifted her binoculars, catching sight of the 1961 aqua-and-white Impala convertible, top down. "Yes, it's your eldest, with Jinx. And someone else, a girl. Very blonde. Very pretty."

"Let's go greet the next generation."

"Degeneration."

"With any luck," R. J. said, laughing.

A plume of pale gray dust, atomized oyster shells, floated up toward the turquoise sky, which was the same color as Vic's '61 Impala. With the top down, hair blowing in the wind, the three occupants personified youth itself, absolute freedom allied to absolute uncertainty.

R. J. walked up the slow rise of lawn to the house, a simple frame clapboard house built in 1734. The original structure, a log cabin, was burned in 1642 during an Indian raid. It was stubbornly rebuilt, and when money poured in from England in those middle years of the eighteenth century, thanks to tobacco, the third generation of Vances built a proper frame house with large glass windows, a sure sign of affluence, and named it Surry Crossing.

Farther west past Sloop Point, Claremont Manor abutted Surry Crossing. Across the impressively expansive river, one could see from Sandy Point to Dancing Point. The vista alone was worth the generations of toil and blood.

As the Impala screeched to a halt (God forbid Vic would ever drive slowly) the doors opened, and Jinx hopped over the driver's seat from the rear.

As everyone hugged everyone else and Chris was introduced and hugged in turn, another spiral of dust could be observed accompanied by the guttural roar of a large diesel engine. The brakes squealed at the foot of the long drive, then the roar continued as the driver sped away.

"Hey. I'll be right back. Let me go pick up the brat." As Vic hopped in her car and sped down the drive, R. J. and Bunny began to give Chris the tour, starting with the enormous walnut tree planted immediately after the War of 1812.

Books under her arm, Mignon looked up to see her older sister barreling down at her. Vic pretended to steer at her and then she hit the brakes. Mignon feigned cool indifference.

"Lame," the younger Savedge said.

"Hop in, Your Weirdness."

Mignon threw her books in the back then climbed in the passenger side. "Lowness."

"Boobness." Vic spun the car around.

"You'd better not have to buy another set of tires for this, Vic. You know how Dad hates it when you do wheelies."

"Dad's not here."

They both giggled as Vic drove back to the house.

"Made an A in . . ." Mignon paused. "Who's that?"

"Chris Carter. Friend from school."

"Where's Charly?"

"Football tomorrow."

"Oh. Aren't you going?"

"No. Stuff to do here."

"Sure." Mignon's tone implied that she knew what the stuff was, which she didn't. No point in being too eager to find out, then Vic would taunt her.

Mignon came up to be introduced to Chris just as Aunt Bunny was saying, "My real name is Beatrice. If it were good enough for Dante it should be good enough for me, but Orgy, I mean R. J., has called me Bunny from the time we were toddlers. Hello, Mignon."

"Hi, Aunt Bunny."

"Chris Carter, this is my horrible little sister, Mignon Catlett Savedge. I added her middle name to make her sound better than she really is."

"Your middle name is . . ." Mignon started to say *turd* and then realized she ought not to say that in front of someone she'd just met. Well, really, she supposed a Southern lady ought not to say it at all. "Your middle name is Weenie."

"Clever." Vic pushed Mignon.

"All right, you two." R. J. gave them *the look.* "Chris, come on inside. Let me help you with your bags."

"I'll get them." Mignon knew that was her signal.

"There's just two books in the backseat of the car and a red canvas bag."

"Got it."

R. J. turned to Jinx. "Sleeping with us or at home?"

"My mother is to be avoided at all costs." The corners of Jinx's lips turned up.

"What an awful thing to say." Bunny's voice indicated the exact opposite.

"You have to see her some time if I'm going to get any furniture," Vic said.

"Come on, let me get you girls settled." R. J. pushed them into the house as Bunny headed to the kitchen to pour iced tea for everyone.

When they returned downstairs, she set out glasses and some small sandwiches she'd made. They carried everything out to the patio.

"Playing tomorrow?" Vic asked her aunt.

"She wins that damned golf cup every year." R. J. savored the sweet butter on her chicken sandwich.

"True, but does that make it any less of a triumph? Do you golf, Chris?"

"No, I'd love to learn."

"Stick around here. You'll have no choice." Bunny caught the sunlight glittering on a large spinnaker, its brilliant yellow-and-red sail billowing, and instinctively pulled her binoculars up to her eyes.

"Aunt Bunny is rarely without her binoculars," Vic explained to Chris.

"She might miss something otherwise." R. J. laughed.

"Bet she could be a detective," Mignon said. "You know, Aunt Bun, I am giving serious consideration to a profession, and I think I'd like to be a detective." Mignon adored the sound of her own voice.

"That would suit you." Vic reached for the potato chips.

"Snoop," Jinx filled in.

"I'm a snoop? Ha! Jinx, you should see what your little sister has done." Mignon rolled on. "She drilled a hole into the boys' locker room, and she's charging us a dollar to look."

Bunny winked. "Most men will show you for free."

"Chris." R. J.'s voice took on a silky quality. "What's really scary is that we're on good behavior."

Chris laughed. "I might surprise you, Mrs. Savedge."

"I hope so." R. J. smiled.

"I made JV field hockey," Mignon interrupted.

"You did that last week." Vic slapped Mignon's hand as she reached to steal half of Vic's sandwich. "If you keep eating so much you'll be a goalie."

"Goalies have to be fast."

"Yeah, well then your fat ass will sit on the bench."

"Vic," R. J. admonished.

"It's true," Vic added. "But I shouldn't have said fat ass. How about 'ample derriere'?"

"Oh, you are so funny. I mean, I could just die from laughing." Mignon fumed.

"Don't let us stop you," said Jinx, one of the family really.

Mignon, realizing she was outnumbered, tried another tack to keep the spotlight on herself. "Chris, did Mom and Aunt Bunny tell you the history of the house?"

"We did . . . more or less." R. J. added another spoonful of sugar to her tea.

"The part about why the house is painted yellow?"

"Well, no," R. J. said.

Mignon quickly declared, "In 1834, Robert Vance married a beautiful woman from Vienna, Austria, and she had some royal blood. She painted the house yellow because it's the color of imperial buildings in Vienna."

"Must have been a princess." Jinx slyly glanced at Vic.

"Yes, royal blood runs in this family." Vic's voice grew lighter. "Mignon, the Princess of Potato Chips."

Mignon glared at Jinx and Vic.

"It's really beautiful, the yellow with the Charleston green shutters," Chris remarked.

"Princess Bullshit," Vic whispered to Mignon, drawing out the word *princess* in her low voice.

"I hate you," Mignon whispered back.

"Kiss kiss. Hug hug." Vic puckered her lips, and in a flash Mignon threw a pickle in her face.

"Mignon." R. J. tried to sound stern.

"I wish it was a big fat ice cream cone. Cold strawberry ice cream going right up her nose."

Vic wiped off her face. "I don't like strawberry."

"Exactly," Mignon sang out.

"I am so grateful to my two nieces." Bunny leaned toward Chris. "They have cured in me any desire to have children."

"Cured it in me, too," R. J. said laconically.

Everyone laughed. It took Mignon a second, but she laughed, too.

Bunny checked her gold Rolex with the Jubilee bracelet. Bunny had a taste for expensive toys. "I'd better get my car." She glanced at Vic. "Honey, will you run me down to the dealership? I know your mom's got a million things to do."

"Sure, Aunt Bunny. Chris, come on. You'll see the sights and the sites. Jinx?"

"Sure, unless" —she looked to R. J.— "you need me to help you clean up?"

Mignon asked, "Where's Piper?"

"In the tobacco shed," R. J. answered. "There's a woodchuck or a fox or a skunk, I'm not exactly sure, with a burrow under the back side, and she's on patrol. And no, Chris, I don't need you to clean up, but thank you for volunteering to help, which my adorable and dutiful daughters did not do."

"Mom, I would have," Mignon protested.

"Oh, yeah." Vic pinched Mignon.

"I didn't hear you say anything."

"How could I? You were talking. Oh, how I love to come home and see my sister."

"Hateful." Mignon turned her nose up, but she obviously loved the attention.

At fifteen she carried a bit of baby fat, but it was clear to her elders that Mignon would turn into a lovely woman, perhaps not as beautiful as her mother and sister, but plenty good looking. She was impatient because she couldn't see it yet. She felt she was taking forever to grow up.

"If it's a fox or a skunk, you'll smell it." Vic stood up, picking up her plate and Chris's.

"Actually, you won't." R. J. was wise in the way of animals. "Animals can turn their scent off and on. Plus the old smoke smell is still so strong in the shed and I'm not sticking my nose at the mouth of any animal's den. What if she's got babies in there?"

"Good point," Vic responded as she headed toward the back door off the kitchen. "But too late in the season, I think."

"Mom, if you'd stop smoking, your sense of smell would improve," Mignon said self-righteously.

"I know." R. J. sighed. "I can give up smoking anytime I want. I've done it many times."

"Well, I'm not giving up my fags," Bunny defiantly stated. "A girl needs a little dosage now and then to smooth out the day. It's better than being on prescription pills like Nora Schonfeld and some others I could name."

Nora Schonfeld was the sexy younger woman Don had dallied with that spring but set aside at Bunny's urging. Urging was Bunny's euphemism. At the mention of her name no one said a word. Not one word.

After that beat of awkward silence, Vic, becoming more like her mother every day, stepped in. "You're smarter than Mom, though, because at least you smoke filtered cigarettes."

"But she smokes twice as many as I do." R. J. laughed.

"Well . . . there is that." Bunny recovered her spirits. "But I like my mentholated Kools. I like the penguin logo."

"It's all tripe." R. J. laughed again. "The plastic filters and the chemicals added to tobacco actually make it more dangerous, I swear. If you're going to smoke, then smoke a pure cigarette and be done with it."

———

As they headed toward Surry, they passed Boonie Ashley's convenience store two miles from the house. The too-small parking lot was jammed with people picking up loaves of bread on the way home—or more likely, six-packs of beer.

"Boonie is the biggest gossip," Mignon announced to Chris. She had been pointing out the sights along the way. The real historical information was interspersed with tidbits like, "Here's where Vic wrecked Dad's car."

"Men are much worse gossips than women," Bunny announced over the wind. "They just call it something else. And how they rejoice when one of them fails. Mmm, mmm." She used that special intonation among Southern women where the first "mmm" was high and the second lower.

Regiments of women could converse in Virginia without any words at all. *Mmm, mmm* could cover just about everything.

The car dealership, a mile from Surry proper, was impressive. The huge windows of the steel-and-glass main building reflected the sky and cumulus clouds. Just inside was a circular reception center on a raised dais. Hojo Haines, the twentyish, attractive receptionist presided there in command central.

A few smaller outbuildings were more traditionally sided in clean white clapboard.

The main building's floor, made of a special terrazzo polished to perfection, was dominated by three new models, two cars and one truck, each one spotlighted.

When a customer walked in the front door, Hojo, a little too good looking for Bunny's taste and a little too young, greeted them and summoned a salesperson to help them. But she had sense enough to let them browse if that's what they wanted. Hojo favored tight pants, brightly colored blouses, high heels, big earrings, and exotically painted fingernails. She was also unfailingly cheerful to the customers.

At this particular moment, Hojo was in front of the handsome main building talking to none other than Nora Schonfeld. Nora's son, a classmate of Mignon's, was with his mother.

"That bitch." Bunny couldn't help herself.

Jinx leaned over to Chris, whispering the story of Nora and Don in her ear.

Mignon's eyes widened. This might prove a very interesting trip. Aunt Bunny was known for her spontaneous reactions, in contrast to R. J., who kept a tight lid on it.

"Aunt Bunny." Vic, thinking quickly, scanned the service bays. "Nora's here because her truck is being serviced."

True enough, Nora Schonfeld's Dodge Ram, a sparkling new 1980 model, sat in the service parking lot.

"Bitch," Bunny muttered again as Vic glided to a stop at the pickup window.

The woman in the booth waved to Vic. Everyone at the dealership knew and liked the beautiful young woman. Whatever job she held over the summer she performed competently and without complaint. She had even climbed up with the roofers to help replace flashing that had not been correctly put down.

As Bunny walked to the window to get her keys, Vic turned to Mignon. "Run up there and pull Buzz and Nora into the showroom. Go on, Mignon, before there's a scene!"

Much as Mignon wanted a scene, she was delighted to be an important player in the drama. She vaulted out, hurried up to Buzz, and managed to get Hojo, Nora, and Buzz inside the building. Jinx said in a low voice, "The next closest dealer is Williamsburg."

"Yeah, it's just dumb luck she happens to be here when Aunt Bunny comes to pick up her car."

"Isn't your aunt here a lot?" Chris inquired.

"She is, but Uncle Don can usually juggle things. He's had plenty of experience," Vic wryly replied.

"Yeah, but Nora was different." Jinx quickly shut up as Bunny returned.

"Thanks, girls. I'll see you after I win tomorrow."

Bunny had recovered enough to walk to her car without buttonholing Don. She'd nail him later. As Bunny walked away, Chris noticed that she moved with the same energetic gait that all the Savedge women had; they had a little bounce. Bunny was a very nice-looking woman. Her hair was a rich natural chestnut, her shoulders were wide, and her hips not too big. She carried a few extra pounds, but by no stretch of the imagination could Bunny Savedge McKenna be thought unattractive.

She'd caught enough of a glimpse of Nora to see a curvaceous woman in her early thirties with long hair. She emitted that indescribable something that men noticed and liked, but women noticed and dismissed—studied femininity.

Bunny was pretty. Nora was sexy.

Chris looked at Vic, who had both in spades. As for herself, Chris wasn't sure what she had—but she knew she never lacked for male attention.

Mignon sprinted back.

"Good job," Vic praised her.

"Aunt Bun didn't lob a hand grenade?"

"Not yet," Jinx said, and then turned to Chris. "Welcome to Surry County."

Chris laughed. "I like it."

"Okay, Vic." Mignon sat in the front.

"Not okay. Chris, sit up front. You're the guest."

Mignon couldn't argue with that, so she climbed in the back with Jinx.

"Are you taking me to the football game tonight? We're playing Smithfield."

"No." Vic pulled out of the lot, waving good-bye to people as she did so. "Don't you have a date?"

"No." Mignon grimaced.

"What's wrong with Buzz Schonfeld?" Jinx smiled, knowing that if Mignon went out with Buzz, Bunny would pass out.

"Very funny." A pause followed. "I'm not very popular with boys." She leaned forward. "Chris, I bet you are. You're beautiful."

Chris blushed. "Thank you."

"Why don't you go with Lisa?" Jinx offered. Lisa was Jinx's younger sister, whom she didn't particularly like.

"Maybe," Mignon said without conviction.

"Come on, Mignon. You're not helpless. If you wanted to go to the game with someone, you would."

Mignon shrugged. She was a well-liked kid, but she was struggling with the hormonal surges in herself and others, sometimes taken aback at the social savagery of her sophomore schoolmates.

"Navigator to pilot," Jinx intoned. "Ice cream. You scream, I scream, we all scream for—"

"Ice cream," everyone said.

Vic turned toward town and the ice-cream parlor. As she did, the long slanting rays of the sun burnished them all bronze and the wind blew open Chris's blouse, already unbuttoned low thanks to the heat.

Vic noticed the sunlight on Chris's breasts and an unexpected lizard tongue of fire shot through her.

6

Ribbons of scarlet unfurled on the James River. The Savedges loved to watch the summer sunsets together. Sitting with their chairs in a semicircle on the patio overlooking the freshly mowed back lawn, the spot affording the best view, they chatted about the day.

Frank, genial though reserved, basked in being a man surrounded by women. He thought Vic's new friend extremely attractive with her blonde hair, lean body, and big smile. While he believed he was married to the most marvelous woman of his generation, that did not deter him from admiring others. Unlike Don McKenna, Frank never strayed from admiration to lust. He'd seen too many men undone by that. He thought beauty cruel even if the women possessing it weren't.

"—big, fat cow." Mignon wrapped up her discourse on Marjorie Solomon.

"If you can't say something nice, don't say anything at all." Vic propped her legs up on a wooden footstool, which she shared with her mother. They looked almost like twins.

"Puh-lease." Mignon rolled her eyes heavenward.

"She's right, Mignon. You don't know what Marjorie Solomon goes home to." Frank plucked a sprig of mint from his drink and chewed on it.

"Yeah?" Mignon hoped a tale of woe was about to unfold. Perhaps Marjorie was suffering from leukemia, shortly to pass from this earth, which meant they'd have to be nice to her. Or maybe her father was a closet drinker. Visions of abject misery delighted Mignon.

"She's bedridden with a hangnail," Jinx said, sucking in her cheeks, a funny face that made Vic laugh.

"Ha, ha." The little sister tossed her head, imploring her father with eyes for the real story.

"Honey, I don't know what Marjorie Solomon goes home to, but I know what you go home to." He pointed to the sunset crimson, pink, and purple with flashes of gold.

The splendor of the scene kept everyone spellbound until Mignon, having the shortest attention span, remarked, "She's probably a snob because she's Jewish."

"That's quite enough," R. J. sharply reprimanded her youngest.

"Mom, it's true. People haven't liked Jews for thousands of years."

"Jesus, Mignon, dig the hole deeper." Vic shook her head.

"Ignorant people need scapegoats. Why not pull down those who are successful? You dump your sins on them, get rid of them, and take whatever they acquired in this world," Frank evenly replied, but he was furious at Mignon.

"Dad, you're right, but at least Mignon told us what she was thinking." Vic shielded Mignon. "If she's saying it, then the other kids at school are, too. At least, this way we can talk about it." Vic turned to Mignon, who was obviously distressed that she'd upset her father. They were all quite good at reading Frank. "I'm sure Marjorie is a snot, but it isn't because she's Jewish. Think of Walter Rendell. He's the worst, and he's Episcopalian."

"I'm sorry." She was, too.

"To change the subject, Chris, what's your major?" Frank smiled at her.

"Mr. Savedge, that's a good question. I've changed it three times. I think I'll try English." She laughed, and then said, "What was yours?"

"History."

"Daddy's a Princeton man. He can't see black and orange, but he doesn't get fuzzy." Mignon tried to mollify him.

"My dad went to Colgate," Chris said.

"Good school," Frank replied.

"But it's not Princeton," Vic and Mignon said in unison.

"Family joke." Jinx filled Chris in, who figured it out anyway.

"Did you call your mother?" R. J. reached in her pocket, pulling out a small round beanbag, which she tossed to Jinx.

This excited Piper, who had given up on whatever was under the tobacco shed, at least for the moment.

Jinx tossed the beanbag to Chris, who tossed it to Vic. The bag was flying everywhere.

"I called her. She's mad at me. She wants me to come home, and I said I'd stop by tomorrow." Jinx reached up, snatching the beanbag out of the air.

"Hey," Mignon said.

"You snooze, you lose." Jinx straightened her arm, flipping it in a hook shot to Vic.

Despite Frank's financial troubles, he felt utterly relaxed in the sunset's glow, watching the small boats and larger vessels heading toward their snug ports. The sound of the water lapping the shore soothed him.

Like many extremely handsome men, he was only somewhat aware of his effect on people. Broad shouldered, tall, with a strong clean jaw—people couldn't help smiling when they saw him. He could talk with ease to both men and women. And he was going to have a talk with Sissy Wallace right now because she was tearing up the driveway laying rubber as she zoomed along.

R. J. stood up. "Sissy Wallace, full throttle."

Mignon leaned over to Chris. "Barking mad. All the Wallaces are . . ."

"Mignon, stop sitting in judgment." Frank grabbed her shoulder, squeezing it as he stood up.

"Yes, Dad." She winked at Chris.

Jinx stood up, and Vic and Chris followed. "Wonder what she did this time?"

Sissy narrowly missed one of the lampposts at the end of the driveway. She hit the brakes with a squeal, cut the engine, and slammed the door. "I shot Poppy!"

Chris froze, not knowing whether to go forward or stay rooted to the spot. If this woman was mad, might she be armed?

Vic took her hand, noticing how cool it was. "Some form of vio-
lence on a recurring basis is just the way they are. Last month her sister,
Georgia, dropped a packet of shingles from the roof, which narrowly
missed Edward, her father, who had just stepped outside. She said her
foot slipped while she was repairing the roof, but that doesn't explain
why the whole pack heaved overboard."

"He moves fast for an old man." Jinx stifled a laugh, Sissy was looking straight at her, and waved.

"Sissy can't drive either," Mignon added her bit.

"I noticed." Chris was finding her visit to Surry County even more
entertaining than she had anticipated.

Frank checked his watch and whispered to R. J. "Honey, I expect
Georgia and Edward together or separately will grace us with their
presence in under ten minutes."

"I wonder if serving them a drink is a good idea."

"Make it a double." He kissed his wife on the cheek and then
headed toward Sissy. "Sissy, now just you sit right down here and tell
me all about it." He took her by the elbow, leading her toward the
chairs.

"I shot him. I shot him," she wailed to high heaven.

Mignon said under her breath to Chris, "She puts shoe polish on
her bald spot."

"And carries a flask in her stocking." Vic wondered what she'd have
to do to help her parents.

"Support hose." Jinx thoughtfully supplied that detail.

Chris ran her left hand through her silky straight hair. "Well, I
think someone else is coming." She nodded in the direction of the turn-
off from the two-lane road to the driveway.

Even though trees sheltered the view and the two-lane road was a
quarter of a mile down the drive, in the twilight stillness they could all
hear the roar of the engine.

"I shot him in the butt," Sissy claimed. "I warned him. I fired over
his head but—"

"Poppy change his will again?"

She nodded tearfully. Before she had a chance to take her place in
the semicircle of chairs, she, too, heard the rumble of a big V-8 engine.

She stared at Chris, realized she didn't know her, and stuck out her hand. "Hello, I'm Sissy Wallace. I'm so glad to make your acquaintance even if I did fill my Poppy full of ratshot."

Vic, still holding Chris's hand, dropped it. Chris reached out and shook Sissy's hand.

"Miss Wallace, you can pick out the ratshot with tweezers." Mignon helpfully supplied this information.

"Got it to pepper the crows. If I had any sense I'd hit up Yolanda with it. Poppy lets that cow stick her head in the kitchen window. I hate that cow smell! He pays me no mind, just feeds her carrots." Sissy was recovering her aplomb. "Here comes my sister. How she has the nerve to show her face! Georgia is a hussy—oh, yes, the stories I could tell you about my sister who never has a hair out of place, all two of them."

Georgia and Edward disembarked from a big white Cadillac.

"You never loved me. You love Georgia," Sissy shouted.

"Georgia doesn't shoot me." A square-built man, fit-looking, in his eighties, sensibly replied. Hostility clearly had a rejuvenating effect on Edward Wallace.

"No, she nearly killed you with shingles."

"That was an accident," the well-groomed Georgia snapped back; her fingernail polish matched her pale pink dress. "You want everyone to pay attention to you. The world centers around your navel." Georgia pushed her tortoiseshell glasses back up on her nose.

"Don't you talk to me. I'm not talking to you."

Piper, fascinated with human irrationality, watched, wagging her tail. The golden retriever sniffed the air and raised her eyebrows.

R. J. emerged bearing a tray of potent drinks. She knew everyone's preference. Edward liked Scotch—Johnnie Walker Black, on the rocks. Georgia, pretending to partake only to be social, enjoyed a vodka martini. Sissy would drink whatever you put in front of her, but she was partial to margaritas.

The Wallaces collapsed into chairs. Frank introduced Chris to Edward and Georgia.

"So pleased to meet you." Georgia lowered her pleasant voice. "I'm sorry you aren't meeting us at our best. As you can see, we are afflicted at this moment by familial discord."

"Oh, balls." Sissy clamped her mouth shut like a turtle.

"You're the source of our affliction." Georgia's voice took on a patronizing tone.

"Am not!"

"Did I make that martini to your specifications?" R. J. handed Georgia a napkin, her own slender hands a contrast to Georgia's square fingers.

"Why, it's just perfect, R. J. Just like you, perfect. Of course, I'm not much of a drinker, so I can't really compare."

"Liar. You go to parties with a siphon." Sissy was beginning to enjoy herself. The double-strength margarita was helping.

"Mother, can I do anything to help?" Vic smiled at everyone.

"How about some peanuts and oh, there's some of that dip to go with the potato chips. Edward likes my special dip."

"Sure." Vic disappeared into the kitchen followed by the other three young women.

They could hear everything since all the windows were open.

"What's ratshot?" Chris asked.

"Little pellets. Same as birdshot, but we call it ratshot down here." Jinx pulled out a big tray from the pantry. "Napkins." She put a bunch on the tray.

"Mignon, get the bowls, will you? I can't very well serve in plastic bags."

"Can I do anything?" Chris wanted to be useful.

"Stand there and look beautiful." Vic smiled at her.

"Queer," Jinx mocked, emptying a bag of chips into one of the bowls Mignon placed on the tray.

"Takes one to know one," Vic good-naturedly shot back.

They could hear Edward booming. "Too many women. That's the trouble in my house."

"It depends on the kind of women, Edward." Frank gave him a sly glance, which had the intended effect.

Edward grunted, smiled, and leaned back in the chair for a long pull. He winced for a moment as he felt one of the little pellets that was embedded in his backside.

"Poppy, now Poppy, don't you fret. I'll carry you to the hospital if you're feeling weakish." Wrong word.

"Georgia, I've got some ratshot in my ass. I'm not feeling weakish." He looked over the rim of his depleted drink to R. J. "Pardon my French, R. J."

"I hear worse than that around here, Edward. Let me freshen your drink. It's Friday evening, and we all need to just kick back." She stood up, took the glass, and walked into the kitchen just as the girls were walking out. "Vic, the solution to this problem is to bring the booze out onto the patio."

"Yes, ma'am." Vic handed the tray to Jinx, turning to go back into the kitchen.

R. J. put her arm around Chris's waist for a moment. "Chris, there's never a dull moment around here."

Mother and daughter quickly gathered all the necessities for vodka martinis, margaritas, Scotch. Frank liked Scotch, so he was fine. He just needed a splash of soda water. R. J. rarely drank except on special occasions like her husband's birthday.

"Mom, should we put this on the coffee table or on the side table?" Vic asked.

R. J. thought a moment. "Side table. I'd better not let them fix their own drinks, in case someone loses their temper again. You keep an eye on Georgia. I'll watch Sissy and Edward."

"This is a drill." Chris laughed.

"We've done it many times." R. J. smiled as she picked up the tray with ice cubes in a silver bucket and lime, lemon, and orange rind peels in small bowls. Vic handed Chris the bottle of Absolut Vodka and Johnnie Walker Black while she grabbed the other bottles.

"Onward Christian soldiers." Vic opened the door with her foot just as Edward was pontificating.

"Women can't think straight. God love 'em, they just can't."

"I believe they say the same thing about us." Frank's tone was light. "But I bet if we all sit here we'll come up with an amicable solution."

" 'Course we will. We're men."

Chris glanced at Vic and Jinx, who bore this sexism stoically. She wondered if Virginia women believed it or if they were obedient just to get their way. Apparently those myths about the Southern belle were true. If it were up to her she'd knock the old man's teeth down his throat.

"If men are so reasonable, why do you get us in all those wars?" Georgia mentioned this without rancor.

R. J. pushed a lock of glossy black hair out of her eyes. "Georgia's got a point there."

"On top of her head." Sissy giggled as R. J. reached over, took her glass, and made her another.

"Don't be childish." Georgia scowled and then looked up at R. J. "You haven't a gray hair on your pretty head."

"Oh, yes I do. You can't see it out here. Put me under bright lights, and you'll find some."

"Georgia hits the dye pots. Her hair is a blonde not found in nature." She stared at Chris a moment. "I'm sure yours is natural, honey."

"Yes, ma'am."

The tension ebbed, the older people chitchatted about goings-on, the younger people refilled chip bowls, the ice bucket, and whatever else needed attention.

At one point, R. J. reached for Mignon. "Sugar, I thought you were going to the football game tonight?"

"I'd rather stay here with you." Mignon didn't want to miss anything, since the Wallaces were capable of explosions in a split second.

"Sure?"

Mignon smiled. "Sure."

"When I see your girls I regret not having children," Sissy said. "Don't you, Georgia?"

Georgia nodded in agreement. "Yes, R. J., you and Frank brought two lovely girls into this world. Such young ladies. And you, too, Jinx."

"Where's your young man?" Sissy leaned over to pat Vic's leg.

Vic, sitting on the edge of her chair, replied, "Football game tomorrow. We don't see much of him here on Fridays."

"We like having a young buck around, don't we, Georgia?" Sissy sighed.

Georgia paused. "Any woman who doesn't like looking at a handsome man is dead. That's what Momma always used to say."

"What was that? What did your Momma say?" Edward had never truly recovered from his wife's death thirty-four years ago; he had kept his daughters too close to him as a result of it.

"Any woman who didn't like looking at a handsome man was dead," Georgia repeated.

"That's why she married you, Poppy," Sissy cooed.

He snorted a disbelieving laugh, but he loved hearing that. He pointed his glass in Chris's direction. New ears. "My wife, Dorey, passed away on April thirtieth, 1945. She was forty-one and pretty as a picture. I tell you, honey, it broke my heart. I loved that woman and she loved me. I never have understood that." The corner of his mouth turned up in a smile.

Finally Frank, seeing his charges were lubricated, made his point. "Now I know this contretemps was over the will, and I know, Edward, your patience can be sorely tried. However, if you return to your original intention and I believe Dorey's original intention, you'll divide your estate fifty-fifty, and I think both girls will discharge their duties faithfully as regards the church and other worthy charities, won't you, girls?"

"Yes," they sang in unison.

"Bring me the papers Monday," Edward said.

"Have you destroyed your former will?" Frank asked.

"Burned it."

"All right. I'll drop by around noon."

After draining the bar dry, the Wallaces repaired to their vehicles.

Sissy opened the door to her Plymouth. "I wish Don McKenna would get a Cadillac dealership. Poppy, will you buy me a Cadillac?"

"Don't push your luck." Georgia closed the door behind her sister and walked to the Cadillac.

"I was kidding, Poppy," said Sissy, who wasn't.

Numb from the Scotch, Edward didn't wince when he shifted his weight in the passenger seat as Georgia started the motor.

"Frank, I wonder if we should let him drive home?"

"Honey, everyone knows those cars. They'll pull over." Frank laughed.

"Dad, are Vic and I going to fight like that?"

"We might now," said Vic as she put empty glasses on the tray.

"I mean over the will." Mignon couldn't imagine her parents dying, but the Wallaces were a vivid reminder that siblings will act like hyenas over the spoils.

"Everything will be left to you just as it is today," R. J. answered her, firmness in her voice.

A cloud passed over Frank's eyes as he nodded in agreement with his wife.

Later, after everyone was in bed, Chris, in the guest room next to Mignon's, had to laugh. Mignon kept slipping notes under the door. Things like: "Help, I'm held prisoner in this room." Chris would respond with a drawing or something else.

Jinx slept in Vic's room, which had two twin beds with a nightstand in between. Most of the clothes that hung in Vic's closet were Jinx's.

"What time do you want to go to your mom's tomorrow?" Vic propped up the pillows. The lights were out.

"I'll worry about that tomorrow," Jinx said. "Drives me crazy when old man Wallace talks about how irrational women are."

"Let men say and think whatever they want; then go do it your way. That's my motto," Vic replied. "I don't think Charly's going to be like that. I mean he's not that way now. He'd better not turn into a good old boy."

"Who knows? I look at my mother, and I can't imagine her young. Time really does have power." Jinx sat up. "I'm hungry."

"Eat."

"I can't. It's too late. I've got to lose ten pounds."

"Well, don't think about food."

"I'll try."

"Jinx, you know how we talk about fate?"

Both of them believed in some kind of fate or karma that determined their destinies. Over the years and in many nighttime talks, this concept evolved into a belief that everyone did have a predetermined destination, but that there were obstacles in reaching it. Plus, things happened on the way. People had choices.

"Yes."

"I was thinking, despite fate we still have individual responsibility."

"That's where honor comes in." Jinx had a vision not of honor but of chocolate cake. "How you meet your fate. See? You can either have courage or not. You can face it or run away. Just because you might not be responsible for what happened to you doesn't mean you can't act with honor."

"Ah, you see into things more deeply than I do."

"Maybe." Jinx inhaled deeply. "Chocolate cake."

"Who said anything about chocolate cake?" Vic was slightly bewildered.

"Let's raid the kitchen. I have got to get a piece of that chocolate layer cake."

"All right." Vic wasn't hungry, but she was a good sport. She slipped out of bed and threw on an extra-large T-shirt.

"Fate." Jinx put on her robe. "It's my fate to eat chocolate cake."

"You already have enough holes in your head," Vic yelled at
Mignon, glued to the backseat of the Impala.

They had dropped off Jinx, not too happy about it, at her
mother's house and were on their way to McKenna Dodge. They'd
pick up Jinx in two hours. She declared that was as long as she could
abide her blood family.

Chris closed her eyes, tilting her head back toward the sun.

"Your ears are pierced." Mignon leaped up, her lips close to Vic's ear.

"Mignon, we are not having this discussion. If you're getting your
ears pierced, Mom's taking you, not me."

Mignon now leaned toward Chris. "She is so selfish and hateful. I
bet if you had a little sister you'd take her to get her ears pierced."

"Bet I wouldn't." Chris kept her eyes closed.

"What about someone else's little sister?" Mignon was nothing if
not persistent.

Vic pulled into the dealership, parking right in front of the plate-
glass window. She grabbed a large manila envelope from the top of the
dashboard, it was full of sales figures that Aunt Bunny had inadvertently
left at the house yesterday, and got out of the car. "Mignon can cruise
the new cars."

Mignon clambered out of the car and made a beeline for the reception desk.

"Guess she's going inside to place her order." Chris laughed. "She's very bright, you know. She sent me notes all last night and some of them were very funny."

"Did that little worm keep you awake?"

"After the Wallace drama, how could I have slept?"

"Speak of the devil," Vic murmured.

Out traipsed Sissy Wallace on the arm of Don McKenna. Don's glossy curls reflected the sunlight.

"Vic!"

"Hey, Uncle Don. I was just going to drop this off for you. Chris Carter, meet my uncle, Don McKenna." She handed Don the manila envelope, which he took with his left hand.

With his right, he shook Chris's hand warmly. "Have you met the lovely Miss Wallace?"

"Last night," Chris replied.

"Girls." Sissy beamed. She turned to Don. "Just find out, please do."

"All right, Sissy. I will, and you stay out of trouble, hear?" He smiled one of those ear-to-ear grins that women found attractive.

"If I'm away from you, I'll be out of trouble." She gave a half skip to her Plymouth.

As she drove off, the three waved to her.

"Incorrigible," Don uttered through his smile as he watched her finally make it out onto the highway.

"She trying to seduce you, Uncle Don?"

"Always. Always." He let out a belly laugh. "You know what she wants? She wants me to get her a Cadillac at cost. I'm not a General Motors dealer, but she just knows I can talk the Cadillac dealer in Williamsburg or Virginia Beach or Norfolk into a brand-new Cadillac at cost."

"Where's she going to get the money?"

He hooked his thumb in his belt. "Says sooner or later the old man has to let go of some of his money. God knows he's got enough of it."

He walked the two young women into the showroom. Don, now forty-one, exuded a warmth that was irresistible. He genuinely liked people, especially women. And not just for sex—he really liked women.

"Where's Hojo?" he asked one of the salesmen.

"In the bathroom, I think. Said she'd be right back."

"Hot out there. You two like a Coke?"

"No, thanks."

"Me neither," Chris replied. "This is an impressive place, Mr. McKenna. You must be proud of it."

"Don, please. Mr. McKenna is my father." He smiled. "Thank you. We're very proud of the place. My wife helped me every step of the way."

Hojo, poured into a pair of bright orange pants, returned to her post. Saturdays, a big day at the dealership, meant all hands were on deck.

"Have you seen Mignon?" Vic walked over to command central.

"She's in the bathroom adjusting herself." Hojo smiled.

Vic noticed that Hojo's plum-colored nails now had sparkles on the metallic polish.

Mignon emerged from the bathroom, flashed her uncle a smile, and walked quickly to the car.

"Such manners. She could have come over here and talked." Vic put her hands on her hips.

"She sees enough of me, I suppose." Don waved at one of his salesmen who was heading toward his office. "I'll be with you in a minute." He returned his attention to Vic after checking the clock on the wall. "Game starts in six hours. You going to make it?"

"No, I'm here for the weekend."

"Want to bet on the score?"

"No, but I'll bet on the touchdowns." Vic smoothed her hands over her Bermuda shorts. "Charly Harrison, two touchdowns."

"Never take a bet I know I'll lose." He clapped her on the back. "You kids come on by any time."

Vic got behind the wheel. "Jeez, these seats are hot."

Chris gingerly put her butt on the cracked leather. "Head for the shade."

As they drove along, Mignon was conspicuously silent.

"When do I get to meet Charly? I feel as if I know him already, sort of," Chris said.

"Next time he comes over, I'll call you. He's a great guy. You'll love him."

Mignon leaned forward. Teasing Vic about Charly was too good to pass up. "She sleeps with him. She won't admit it, but I know they're bumping uglies."

"You don't know anything, Mignon."

"Sexual revolution. Birth control. The sixties," she sang out, her youthful voice loud.

"It's 1980." Chris laughed.

"Yeah, the sexual revolution started in the sixties and it gets better and better. I know about these things."

"Oh, and what are you doing?"

"I'll tell you if you'll tell me."

"Number one, I value my privacy. Number two, remember what Grandma Catlett says, 'Men don't buy a cow if they can get the milk for free.' "

"Gross."

Just then Vic glanced in her rearview mirror. "Mignon!"

Mignon pressed her lips together, raising her eyebrows.

"You wouldn't take me!"

Vic pulled the car over.

Chris twisted around. "Oh, boy."

"Well, everyone in school has their ears pierced. I mean, like, I am the only weirdo, chickenshit. Even Buzz Schonfeld has one ear pierced like the baseball player, what's-his-name."

"Your name is shit." Vic's face flushed crimson. "Goddammit, Mignon, Mom will never believe I didn't have a hand in this."

In Mignon's ears were two waxed strings, a tiny knot tied in each of the equally tiny loops.

Chris reached for them. "Is this fish wire?"

"I don't know what she put in there. She told me to keep moving it around. See?" Mignon tugged on the wax string, wincing as she did.

"How much money do you have in that ratty purse?" Vic reached around to grab Mignon's purse, but Mignon quickly clamped her hands on it.

"Thief." Then Mignon screamed at the top of her lungs as cars passed by, "My sister is a thief!"

"Shut up! I don't want your money, but how much have you got?"

"Why?"

"Because, you butthole, you need to buy gold posts. Otherwise your ears are going to get really infected. Wait until I get my hands on Hojo."

"She'd like that. She goes to bed with everybody, and she has the hots for you." A devilish light danced in Mignon's hazel eyes.

"Jesus, Mignon, are you having a hormonal surge or something? All you think about is sex."

"Doesn't everyone?" Chris laughed.

"Not me," Vic stubbornly replied.

"You need a wake-up call." Chris laughed even harder now.

"Yeah, I'll pass on the gold posts and buy you an alarm clock, with my, uh, twenty dollars and eighty-two cents. Wait, eighty-three."

Finally Vic had to laugh, too. "Okay, we are going to Chowder's. I know they'll have gold posts."

They drove to the new shopping center and parked in front of Chowder's, a nice jewelry store that had moved off Main Street.

Zelda Chartreuse knew the Savedges. She quickly sized up the situation.

"Not too big. I don't want to look trashy," said Mignon.

"Don't make me laugh." Vic propped one elbow on the counter while Zelda placed a tray of earrings and posts on top of it.

"What about these?" Mignon, displaying a sure touch, reached for the simple gold balls, small but very attractive.

"These will run you one hundred and nine dollars. Fourteen-carat gold."

Mignon's face fell. "Zelda, I only have twenty dollars and eighty-three cents."

"I hate you." Vic jammed her hand in her left pocket, pulling out neatly folded-over bills. She counted them out. "Okay, Mignon. Here's fifty. I need the rest for gas and lunch this week."

"All right, seventy dollars and eighty-three cents. Now these are sixty-two dollars." Zelda pointed out a pair of posts so tiny as to be pinheads.

"No." Mignon fingered the gold ball earrings.

"Honey, these silver ones are the same size. I think you're right about size. You have good taste, Mignon. You always know what looks good on you and everyone else, for that matter."

"Zelda, if she wears the silver, her ears will get infected."

Zelda noticed that whoever pierced Mignon's ears had put the holes in exactly the right places.

"I've got some money," Chris announced, reaching in her shorts pocket.

"No way." Vic grabbed her wrist. "You're the guest, and my little sister's escapade shouldn't cost you any money."

"I could give her credit. She could pay it off," suggested Zelda. "I know she will. Mignon's responsible."

"Lisa Baptista's got credit all over town," Mignon said to Vic.

"Not here, she doesn't," Zelda clarified.

"Mignon, don't buy on credit. If we can't pay in full, you're going to have to wear smaller earrings."

"Those are fly-sized." Mignon had her heart set on the ideally sized gold balls for her ears.

"Please, take my money. I owe it to Mignon for the entertainment." Chris put her money in Vic's hand, and held it there with her other hand.

A flash of fire shot through Vic. She stared at Chris, speechless.

Mignon, observing her sister's reaction, said, "Chris, we can't take your money. It's not right."

"I insist." Chris squeezed Vic's hand and then let go.

Vic dropped the money. She'd never felt anything like that in her life; white hot married to blue cold. She knew it was sexual. She knew she'd never felt that with Charly. She didn't know what to do about it and she didn't know if Chris felt that energy, too.

Mignon picked up the money, fifteen dollars.

Zelda liked the Savedges. Most everyone did. "Mignon, let's put these in your ears before it's too late and it hurts." She bent down and pulled out a bottle of alcohol from under the counter. "Chris, you keep your money. I don't want you girls telling anyone about this discount. It's our secret."

"Zelda . . . ," Vic's voice trailed off.

"Your father's been good to me. Now, let's do this." Zelda carefully wiped the back of the earring. She pulled a pair of tiny scissors from a drawer, snipping the wax threads. "Did you perform this operation?" she asked Vic.

"No. Hojo."

"Did a good job. That girl keeps me in business." She laughed. "Loves jewelry."

"She doesn't make enough money to buy your stuff," Mignon said. She winced when she tried to put the earrings in.

"Helps if you use a mirror, honey." Zelda placed a two-sided mirror before her. "Just do it fast and get it over with and then keep twirling those earrings. Put alcohol on the front and back without taking them out. In a week you ought to be fine. You look like a fast healer."

"Mignon, you don't know anything about Hojo's finances. You're the one without money, not her."

Zelda admired Mignon. "You look pretty as a picture."

"You don't have to go that far," Vic said, having somewhat recovered from the lightning strike in her body.

As they drove back to pick up Jinx, Vic told Chris that her father drew up the incorporation papers for people, wills, whatever they needed. He'd often help people who couldn't pay very much.

"Dad puts people first, money second."

"That's a wonderful quality." Chris turned around, her blonde hair shining in the light. "They do look good on you, Mignon."

Vic found herself looking at Chris. She'd look at the road and then look over at Chris. When Chris looked back at her, Vic burst out laughing. Chris laughed, too.

By the time Vic, Chris, Mignon, and Jinx arrived back at Surry Crossing, R. J. had the grill heating up and the steaks marinating.

Mignon thought she could slip past her, but R. J. knew her younger only too well. Mignon was too quiet and moving too quickly.

"Mignon, come here."

"Thought I'd fertilize your roses," Mignon replied, but observing her mother's stare, trudged over to her.

"Oh, Mignon."

8

Fortified by her Lucky Strike, R. J. recovered to check on the steaks. Bad enough that Mignon pierced her ears, far worse that she did it behind her back.

Frank wouldn't be home for supper. Since it was the Ladies' Championship at the club, he and Randy Goswell, Arnold Burgess, and Ted Baptista all took off to play at a new course near Norfolk. The boys would whoop it up.

A chastised Mignon wore her posts since Vic convinced their mother that it would be worse to remove them. The deed was done, why risk infection? Logically, she pointed out that when Mignon would turn sixteen she'd go poke two more holes in her ears. Vic reminded R. J. that Mignon made A's in school, didn't drink or smoke, and so far hadn't behaved badly with the opposite sex. Drugs weren't even mentioned. R. J. puffed on a cigarette as her elder finished her appeal.

"All right. I'm outnumbered." She drew in a breath, the tip of her cigarette a red period to her sentence. "Honey, you have a good head on your shoulders."

They both laughed as R. J. patted Vic's broad shoulder and then lightly shoved her in the direction of the dock where Jinx and Chris were watching the boats.

"Mom, why so many plates?" Mignon called from the patio.

"Regina and Lisa are joining us."

"What about Teddy and Boo?" These were Jinx's brothers, one older than Mignon, one younger.

"They're helping to officiate at the club."

"Cool." Mignon had a crush on Teddy, a senior at her high school, and she wasn't about to betray it.

"Does Jinx know her mother's coming?" Mignon carried out condiments.

"No, and since when are you so full of questions? It's rude to ask so many questions, Mignon. You know better."

"Yes, ma'am." She paused. "But aren't you glad I have an inquiring mind?"

R. J. shook her head and then shot over to the grill. Piper, when Mignon's back was turned, had grabbed a steak off the pile by standing on her hind legs and then had fled at top speed.

"Damn her." R. J. shook her head. She shaded her eyes, watching the three college girls sitting on the dock, the low sun drenching them in gold. *To be young*, she thought to herself.

R. J., not a bitter woman, endured her disappointments with equanimity. She loved Frank despite his failings, but the financial strain wore on her nerves. Sometimes, she felt old on the inside, old and tired.

Vic and Jinx flanked Chris, all of them dipping their feet into the river, the sun shining in their faces.

"Nah." Jinx shook her head.

"Why not?" Chris inhaled the heavy river scent.

"Because American men are too frightened of women in the first place. They'll never give one political power," Jinx concluded.

"Go, Piper!" Vic had just seen the dog steal the steak.

They all laughed.

"You haven't said a word." Chris elbowed Vic.

"About politics" —Vic shrugged— "I'm not very interested."

"She'll do whatever Charly tells her." Jinx knew this would provoke Vic.

"Bullshit." Jinx's barb found its mark.

"He'll run for office after a pro-football career."

Vic checked her watch. "Jesus, I forgot to listen to the game." She shrugged. "Oh, well."

"You certainly have a laid-back attitude about him," Chris said, her tone implying no judgment.

"Because Vic is so drop-dead gorgeous she can have any man she wants." Jinx sighed, wishing she were that beautiful. "Charly's a big man on campus." She used the old phrase, a light mocking tone in her voice. "But Vic is bigger in her way."

"Jinx, you're so full of it." Vic hated being singled out for her looks. After all, she hadn't earned them.

"Well, I guess she could seduce just about anybody," Chris said.

Chris flipped water over on Vic with her foot.

Heat, sweltering, uncontrollable heat, flickered through Vic's body. She stared deep into Chris's eyes. Chris winked devilishly at Vic, who smiled and then turned away.

Raised in a judgmental family, Chris had survived by nourishing her spirit of rebellion. She didn't know what she was looking for until she met Vic. Then a piece of her private puzzle fell into place. She knew she wanted to be in Vic's presence.

"We'd better read every word of the sports section tomorrow so you can pretend you listened to the game." Jinx waved, recognizing friends going by in a small sailboat.

"I'm not going to lie to him. I forgot." Vic saw the occupants of the boat waving, so she waved back. She changed the subject. "Wonder if Aunt Bunny will win the tournament?"

"She has to be pretty good to win it more than once." Chris squinted at the sun's reflection off the water.

"Aunt Bunny is good. She probably could have been a professional, but she married Uncle Don and when she was young the circuit wasn't so organized, I guess."

"Must have been a bitch," Jinx remarked.

"You take life as you find it," Vic echoed the Savedge creed.

"You think?" Chris's eyebrows shot upward. It occurred to her this was diametrically opposed to her own worldview.

"I do."

"What about changing things for the better?" Chris asked.

"You do what you can, but at some point you have to accept fate," Vic replied.

"I am not talking about fate," Jinx said. "We sat up last night and talked about fate, and then Vic made me eat chocolate cake. I'll never lose weight."

"Jinx." Vic laughed.

"You did," Jinx teased her.

"You know" —Vic turned to face Chris again, which made both of their stomachs flutter— "there we were in bed and suddenly we hear a little voice, 'I'm lonesome. I'm locked in the fridge. Save me, save me, Jinx.' So, of course we had to do what we could."

"Now you sound like your father." Jinx lifted her feet out of the river. "I once asked Mr. Savedge how he stopped that column of German tanks and he just said, 'I did what I could.' Did you know he was awarded the Distinguished Service Cross, which is the medal just below the Congressional Medal of Honor?"

"Jinx, she doesn't want to hear all this." Vic wondered if she could have done what her father did. She wanted to be brave like Frank if life tested her harshly.

"People confused the Distinguished Service Cross with the Distinguished Service Medal, which is kind of a desk-job medal." Jinx took a breath. "My dad, a looey in Korea, told me. Mr. Savedge doesn't talk about it, but the men know, I mean men who fought. They . . . I think they're different from men who haven't seen combat. Men truly respect Vic's father even if he does lose money pretty regularly."

"Jinx."

Jinx realized she shouldn't have been talking out of school. "Sorry."

Vic simply said, "Dad isn't too good with money."

"Mine is, and he's a cold bastard," Chris said this without rancor, a statement of fact, no more, no less.

"Mine's good at it—money, I mean—but he's the excitable type. Everyone tells me I take after him, and I'm not sure it's a compliment," Jinx said.

"It is. Your dad's electric." Vic smiled.

"Mother's a piece of work." As if on cue, Regina Baptista pulled up with Lisa.

"Surprise." Vic giggled.

"Goddammit!" Jinx stood up. "I'll be right back."

As she walked away, Vic and Chris laughed, then lapsed into silence looking at the river, each feeling the nearness of the other.

Chris finally said, "You have a wonderful family."

"Thank you. I'm glad you could meet everyone, even the Monster."

"She's a riot."

"Good, you can have her." Vic thought she'd melt.

"They're waving us up there." Chris swept her feet out of the water and stood up in one easy motion. She reached down for Vic who allowed the blonde woman to pull her up. For a second, Chris held on to Vic's hand.

"You're stronger than I thought you would be."

"Probably not as strong as you. Your mother said you were a brute." Chris let go of Vic's hand.

By the time they reached the patio, Regina was regaling R. J. with the vicissitudes of motherhood. "I'm telling you, Orgy, is there such a thing as ovarian recall? Can I give them back? And Lisa, don't you think for one moment that you can get your ears pierced!"

A car horn in the distance, five short toots, made Piper bark. The bug lamps gave off a citronella scent, which the bugs respected within six inches of the flame. Beyond that range they bit the bloody crap out of everyone.

Regina and Lisa had gone home after a wrangle with Jinx, who refused to accompany them.

R. J., stretched out on a chaise longue, smoking her last Lucky of the evening. She swore it was her last. Mignon twirled her new gold posts. Vic, Chris, and Jinx sat around R. J.

The tooting, closer now, was "shave and a haircut, two bits."

"Bunny's won." R. J. laughed.

Within five minutes, Bunny screeched to a halt, leaping out of her car. "Yes!" As she skipped over she held aloft her silver cup. "I retired the trophy. Three years in a row. I knew I could do it."

R. J. got up and gave her a big hug. "A victory drink?"

"I'll fix it." Vic kissed her aunt on the cheek, then she walked inside, returning with a gin ricky in a frosted glass.

"Actually, I wasn't sure I'd pull it off this year." Bunny, now seated at the end of her sister's longue, reached up for the drink. "Babs Rendell gave me a run for it. But by the sixteenth hole, I knew I had it if I could make par on the next two. She blew up on fifteen. Tricky, that fifteen." She gratefully sipped her gin ricky. "Humid tonight."

"Indeed." R. J. stretched out her long legs. "Mignon, give your Aunt Bunny your chair, please."

"Thank you." Bunny froze before dropping her rear in the chair. "What have you done!"

"Pierced my ears." Mignon acted nonchalant.

"Orgy!"

"I didn't let her do it."

"Who's the culprit?" Bunny finally sat down, placing her silver cup on the table beside her.

"I am." Mignon plopped on Vic's chaise longue. "I made Hojo do it."

"I will wring that girl's neck," Bunny fumed. "How could she do a dumb thing like that?" She held up her hand. "Excuse me, silly question."

"Done is done." Vic changed the subject back to Aunt Bunny. "What did you shoot today?"

"Seventy-one. Not bad."

"Bunny, that's wonderful." R. J. stubbed out her cigarette.

"I win at golf. You win at tennis." She winked at her sister. "Where's Frank?"

"The boys are staying at Heron Sound."

"I'd like to play that course." She held her glass to her forehead. "I wouldn't trust those men any farther than I could throw a lit cigarette, Frank excepted. The last time they hiked off, Ted Baptista bought a Porsche. Said he just had to have it." She looked at Jinx, who shrugged. "And Randy Goswell got caught with his pants down, literally, and Arnold Burgess had to protect him from his wife. She happened to drop by, which means she knows her man very well."

"I think we're better off not knowing them so well," R. J. mused.

"Well, mine is still at the club. He came over after work to help with the party. Jinx, before I forget, your brothers did a good job on the back scoreboard. Boo is almost as big as Teddy," Bunny rambled on, happy in her victory, happy in the company. "—Tommy Rendell made a little toast at the banquet that Babs might be runner-up for the cup but she was champion of his heart. Just made me want to gag."

"Another gin ricky?" Vic asked.

"No, I have to drive home tonight, although I'm sure if I wanted to get falling-down drunk, my dear sister would let me sleep it off on the porch and throw water on me in the morning."

"Wouldn't be the first time."

The corner of Bunny's nicely shaped mouth curved upward. "Oh, come on, I was still at Sweet Briar the last time I was that drunk." She peered over the rim of her gin ricky glass. "I was sick for days after, and vowed I'd never do that again. And I haven't. And I must say to your credit, Victoria, I have never seen you drunk."

"Varsity," came the terse reply.

"Speaking of that, your boyfriend was the star today."

"Forgot to listen to the game," Vic said.

"Mmm, mmm, you'd better pay attention to him. Next home game, you be there. Away games, that's okay, come on home. But the games at campus, be right in the front row." She looked out at the lights across the James, a white glow here and there interspersed with a green or red light slowly moving along the river, a boat gliding in the stillness. "If you don't take care of that boy, someone else will."

"He can take care of himself." Vic laughed good-naturedly.

"Ha. No man can take care of himself. A woman can live without a man, a man can't live without a woman." This was said with great conviction and some humor. "What do you think, Orgy?"

"They're more dependent than we are. I do think that's true."

"Marry him now. Then you can grow together. The longer you wait, the more set in your ways you become, and it's not as easy." She exhaled. "Thank God, you found a rich one."

"If you don't want him, I'll take him," Jinx said.

"What will you give me for him?"

"How about my dad's Porsche?"

"Ooh." Vic pretended this was a difficult choice.

"You all are awful, but no one is as awful tonight as Mignon." Aunt Bunny, beginning to come down after all her excitement, dropped her head back on the pillow, her hand scratching Piper's back.

"Don't you think I look older?" Mignon cocked her head toward her aunt.

"You look like a fifteen-year-old tart."

"Fig," Vic said, playing off "tart."

"Newton," Jinx added.

"Bar," Chris jumped in.

"Weiners." Mignon feigned superiority.

"Well, my dears, I'd better go home while I can. The energy leaked right out of me." She sat up and reached for her trophy. "Years from now your children will look on the huge permanent trophy in the club and see engraved there 1978, 1979, 1980—Beatrice McKenna."

"What about 1981 and 1982? There's lots of years left," R. J. said, happy for her sister.

"I hope so, but you know climbing to the top is easier than staying there. A whole bunch of ladies are gunning for me."

"Win three more years in a row so you can retire another cup. That way your fireplace mantel will be balanced, a cup on each end." R. J. rose to walk her sister over to the car.

"I'm going to bed," Jinx headed for the house.

Mignon leapt onto the vacated longue. "Let's stay up all night and tell ghost stories."

Vic wanted to sit outside and talk with Chris. She wanted to know where she went to grade school and junior high school and high school. What were her favorite books, movies, bands. What she wanted to do with her life after she graduated. She didn't know why she wanted to know these things, she just did. But Mignon would get in the middle of it and she didn't feel like being cross with her sister.

"You tell ghost stories. I'm going to bed, too." Vic rose.

"Me, too." Chris got up, stretching her arms over her head, which lifted her breasts up.

Vic couldn't take her eyes off that motion or those beautiful breasts. She had always thought boys were really stupid about breasts, focusing on one body part. She wondered why she had never noticed them before. Or why a graceful neck without an Adam's apple had never before reminded her of a swan. She felt that she had never truly seen women. She'd been blind to the beauty of half the human race. It wasn't that she couldn't pick out a beautiful woman from one less blessed by nature. It just never registered. She felt a little like she felt the first time she truly heard Mozart. She'd always thought of him as a kind of tinkling composer and couldn't understand why her parents enjoyed his work. One day, raking leaves, the radio outside tuned to the classical station, she heard the utter perfection of sound, the balance, the grace and movement, the sheer untrammeled joy of it all. The roll of the James was in harmony with Mozart.

She felt that way right now.

Jinx was already in the shower. Mignon, grumbling about how she could tell really scary stories, scary like beetles crawling out of eye sockets, hopped up behind Vic and Chris as they walked up the long stairway with a broad landing overlooking the water.

At the top of the landing Mignon hugged and kissed Vic and then hugged and kissed Chris.

"I'm glad you all were there when I got my ears pierced."

"We weren't—exactly." Vic smiled at her. "And how did you convince Hojo to do it?"

Mignon's voice rose airily. "She didn't have anything else to do."

"Uh-huh." Vic shook her head.

"Actually, Mignon, you do look good with earrings." Chris had her hand on the brass doorknob to her room.

"Really?" Mignon clasped her hands together and then threw them open, wrapping her arms around Chris's neck. "You're so cool. I'm glad my sister brought you home."

Chris hugged her back. "Me, too." When Mignon let go of Chris, Chris stood on her tiptoes and kissed Vic on the cheek. "Good night, thank you for a great day."

The kiss burned on Vic's cheek as she tried to sleep.

10

The uneven-width flooring, smooth as polished bone, glistened even in the darkness. Chris was trying to sleep. Mignon's stream of notes slipped under the door contributed to her restlessness. The memory of the sheen rising off Vic's body contributed the rest.

Unlike Vic, Chris knew she could respond to women's sexual power. It had occurred to her that she might even be a lesbian, a thought she ruthlessly shoved back into the recesses of her mind. Loving a woman didn't frighten her; people's response to it did.

She'd seen older women whom she thought to be lesbians. They didn't appear very happy to her, but if she'd thought about it, how many happy older people did she know? No one, straight or gay, likes being shoved aside. Small wonder Edward Wallace tightened his grasp on his whip hand. Money made him important. Money kept him a player, kept him young.

Chris, only twenty, couldn't fathom what the years could do. She attributed each line, each frown on a gay face, to the fact that he or she was gay. Granted, homosexuals and lesbians, despised by a few, hated by others, tolerated by some, did not expect life to be fair. Pain is pain.

One advantage of being gay, Chris supposed, was that you knew right off the bat where the pain was coming from and who was delivering it. Pain sneaked up on straight people more often than not. It accounted for their dazed expressions in their late thirties, and their frantic search for business success, the fountain of youth, or spiritual fulfillment. But at twenty, she could only see that her external choices would be severely limited if she followed her heart and her body. She knew she could force her body to do whatever she told it to do. Her heart was quite another issue.

Nor could she yet fathom the usefulness of the self-knowledge and the knowledge of society that a gay person learns.

She read Mignon's latest note. "Do you think Hojo's nails with little stars on them are cool? If you saw them, I mean."

Chris wrote back. "Hard to miss. With nails like that Hojo could pass for a really tacky mandarin. Something tells me Hojo is good at ordering takeout."

She could hear Mignon giggling on the other side of the door. She had two older brothers, and she liked Mignon, liked the idea of a sister. Sisters often seemed so close. Like R. J. and Bunny. Then, too, sisters could be of the Sissy-and-Georgia variety. The energy between sisters was so different from what she felt with her brothers—whom she did love. Defining it baffled her. She couldn't put it into words. She could only feel it. She wondered if other women felt that way; that female energy was different from male. And what did men feel? Did they tell her the truth, or did they try to protect her? Well, maybe it wasn't bad to be protected.

A fresh sheet of paper rustled as it was shoved under the door. She and Mignon had used up the first sheet.

This one read, "People say that Vic is one of the most beautiful women they have ever seen. Mom, too. I kind of feel like a donkey next to two thoroughbreds. Give me some advice. Real life stuff."

Chris propped the paper on her knees. A breeze swept in through the open windows. She scribbled in her large, neat hand, the letters slanting rightward. "Mignon, beauty is in the eye of the beholder. For starters. And you're at the coltish stage. You won't look good now. You'll look better later, if you take care of yourself. Worry about what's on the inside more than what's on the outside. That's the extent of my advice." She signed it, "The Nonauthority."

A long silence ensued while Mignon digested the response. Finally the next installment arrived with a drawing of a pig. "Are you telling me I have to lose weight?"

Chris wrote, "Yes. If you're bitching and moaning about Vic and your mother being so beautiful, do you really want to be standing next to them being less than the perfect you? Now I have a question for you. What's Charly like?"

A shooting star arched over the James, a flashing tail silver as a trout trailing behind it. Chris took it as a good sign.

Back came Mignon's note. "Charly is hot. I wish I had a boyfriend like him. He's smart, too."

Chris felt a sliver of jealousy, then dismissed it. "Mignon," she wrote, "you will have the boyfriend that's right for you. Of course, if you lost the weight, who's to say you couldn't steal Charly from your sister. (Just kidding.)"

The notes flew back and forth until finally Chris wrote, "I'm sleepy. I'll see you in the morning. Sweet dreams."

The sun's round rim climbed over the horizon. The heavy silvery mist enshrouding the river turned pink, then red, then gold. It would be nine o'clock or so before the mist lifted today, and when the sun rose above the James, the whole river would be colored bronze as that mist would reach for the impossibly deep blue sky.

Vic silently walked along the river's edge. She couldn't sleep, so she thought she'd greet the dawn, her favorite time.

When she turned back toward the dock she saw her mother—a middle-aged Venus slipping through the pale silver light, striding toward the dock.

They met and then walked to the boat, wordlessly getting in and casting off, R. J. at the oars. Because of the fog, she rowed only a hundred yards off shore. A larger craft wouldn't see her until it was too late, although she doubted anyone else would be out on the water now. If anyone was fishing, they'd be quietly drifting.

"Dreaming with your eyes open?" R. J. asked, resting her arms on the oars.

"Sort of." Vic noticed her mother's strong hands on the oars, the muscles in her forearms. Had R. J. given birth to sons, they'd have grown up to play for the Miami Dolphins or the Kansas City Chiefs.

"Great that Bunny retired the trophy. She needs it."

"Trouble with Uncle Don again? I thought that was over."

"Oh, it is, but it takes people a long time to come back. Trust broken is difficult to mend. He swears on a stack of Bibles that Nora meant nothing to him, he'll never do it again." R. J. inhaled the moisture of rich air. "Who knows, maybe he even means it. I worry about her being alone. You see, no matter what happens, I have you and Mignon. I'm better off, I think."

"Mother." Vic folded her hands together as if in prayer. "I don't know if you'd have said that when I wrecked Dad's car my junior year in high school."

"I said plenty else." She laughed, the sound enlarging as it traveled over the water.

"Guess Mignon and I are pretty expensive."

R. J. replied, "Well, that's part of motherhood, but you've worked every summer since you were fourteen. You've helped out."

"If I quit school now, I'll get most of this year's tuition back. I can go to work and help more." Vic's voice, quiet, seemed in counterpoint with the lap of the water.

"Absolutely not. Vic, you get that idea right out of your head."

Vic lowered her voice, her tone resonating, deeper. "The last time Dad lost our money, he was almost ten years younger. He's sixty years old, Mom. You forget how much older than you he is. He can't make it back. I don't think he can." She held up her hand because R. J. was ready to interrupt again. "Mignon wants to go to college. If I start working now, I can help with that, too."

"You're almost finished, Victoria. One more year."

"I can finish later. We can't lose the farm, Mom."

"Victoria, I forbid this. It's too foolish to discuss." R. J. lifted her head as a blue heron appeared out of the fog, swooping low enough to touch.

"I remember the last time, Mom," Vic said simply.

R. J. remained silent. They drifted. Fish jumped out of the water. The mist began to thin. They could see the undersides of the ducks flying overhead.

Vic finally spoke again. "If I marry Charly, assuming he asks me, I don't know if his parents will give us money for a wedding present, and I don't want to disappoint you."

"You won't disappoint me. And of course he'll ask you to marry him and his family will make your life very comfortable."

"You think?"

"Yes. They'll do whatever needs to be done. Buy a house. Set him up in business. They're that kind." She lifted the oars. "Think he'll want to live at Surry Crossing?"

"I don't know. Every now and then he talks about entering the pro football draft. I really don't know."

"Honey, I expect he'll do whatever you ask. Now, I'm not Bunny, but I can give you a bit of hard-won wisdom about men. Ask for the big stuff early while they are still head over heels in love with you, while they still need to prove themselves."

"Mom." Vic was surprised to hear this from her mother.

"It's just the way it is. As time goes by they take you for granted a little. They love you, yes, they do, if it's a good marriage, but they lose that urge to be the knight in shining armor."

"I guess." Vic leaned toward her mother. "Sometimes I think I don't know anything about men. But when I hear the word *marriage*, I hear a steel door shutting behind me."

"Well, that's natural, I guess."

"Did you?"

"Feel that way?" R. J. shook her head. "I was totally, completely in love with your father. I didn't hear a steel door, but certainly I had to wonder what I was getting myself into. What would the future bring? That sort of thing. We hadn't a sou. Mom and Dad could offer us a place to live, but they weren't doing too well in the money department, either."

"You didn't hear a steel door, though."

"No, I guess I didn't."

"Aunt Bunny always says it's just as easy to marry a rich man as a poor man," Vic quoted. "If a door is going to shut, I suppose it better be worth it," she mused. "What are you going to do about Dad?"

"Obviously, I can't let him sell any land. I've got to get him to put Surry Crossing in my name. I think he will. It's what it will do to him. Men are fragile."

This was something Vic did not understand. She'd heard this

sentiment expressed in a variety of ways from other women, all older than herself. Men appeared strong enough. Why couldn't they handle these blows? It didn't make sense. Were they truly fragile, or did women keep them that way so they could control them? She wasn't going to argue with her mother. She knew R. J. wasn't a manipulative woman. R. J. met everyone, man, woman, or child, straight on.

As R. J. rowed back to shore, Vic quietly said, "I've taken a lot for granted, Mom, and I forget to say thank you."

"Honey, you're twenty-two." R. J.'s lovely voice sounded happier. "I took things for granted then, too. But thank you."

"What is it that Grandma Catlett says, 'Life stuff.' " Vic drew out "'life" until it took up enough time for four syllables to be pronounced, a good imitation of the old biddy. "I'm learning about life stuff."

"Me, too."

After a day of September perfection, warm yet crystal clear, the three young women headed back to Williamsburg. Mignon missed them before they even passed the mailbox on the state road. R. J. draped her arm around her younger and gave her a driving lesson to cheer her up.

Back in town, Vic dropped off Jinx, who invited them to dinner Wednesday night. As the following weekend would be an away game, Vic was "off duty," as she put it. Jinx decided they'd all come back to Surry Crossing.

Vic laughed and thanked her for the invitation to her own home, and then drove Chris to her house. They pulled into the driveway.

"You could have parked at your place. I could walk over." Chris smiled as she opened the door. "Thank you. That was the most fun. I'm ready to turn around and go back."

"Next week. Jinx just invited us."

Chris leaned toward her, paused, and then slid out the door. "You know where I live, so come on over when you feel like it."

"You, too." Vic wanted to cut the motor and follow Chris upstairs, but she knew she'd better call on Charly.

She cruised down to his dorm. The football players, regardless of seniority, bunked together and ate together at the training table.

Charly hated it, but the coach felt it built camaraderie. It did and it didn't. A surfeit of red meat, vitamins, and the steroids illegally used by some of the players created a combustible mix of male hormones.

Vic parked, walked up to the front door, and knocked. Women were allowed in the lobby but not in the rooms. Coach thought segregating the boys would make it more difficult for them to get laid. He was right. He subscribed to the old theory that sex before a game robbed a man of his competitive drive. Of course, science had proved the exact opposite was true. Sex boosted testosterone levels. Perhaps it was just as well he subscribed to the old theory; otherwise a line of nubile young lovelies would have been enlisted as a training aid.

"Charly!" Tareq Nassar bellowed as he let Vic in the door.

Wiry and lean, Tareq, a cornerback, contrasted sharply with Orion Chalmers, the right guard, who was sprawled on a lobby chair. Orion looked as though he'd sucked on the air hose at the filling station and inflated himself.

Charly appeared. "Vic." He threw open his arms and gave her a bear hug. "Let's go for a walk. Away from these animals."

The men in the lobby howled, with a few wolf whistles added.

Once out in the twilight air, Vic noticed Charly's legs. He was wearing Bermuda shorts. "Jesus, you look like a Dalmatian."

"They hit hard." He reached for her right hand as they walked through the campus, the leaves on the trees swaying gently.

"Mom, Dad, Mignon, and Aunt Bunny send their regards. Oh, Aunt Bunny won the club championship again. She retired the trophy."

"Great." He leaned down to nuzzle her. "And you look great. I missed you."

"I missed you, too." She liked the scent of him, his aftershave, not too strong, added to his own clean smell.

People waved to them as they walked along, half leaning on one another, the picture of young love. He described the game and Coach's outbursts in the locker room, directed mostly at the defensive linemen. She told him about Mignon's pierced ears and Edward Wallace's butt full of ratshot. She didn't tell him about how bad it was with the money, nor did she mention the overpowering attraction she felt for Chris.

Seeing him was a relief to her, the familiarity of him soothed her. Apart from Jinx, Charly was her closest friend.

Yet the emotions Chris had ignited, the sheer feeling of lust, was something she'd never felt for Charly. She felt physical attraction, happiness, comfort, and trust with Charly. Walking with him, she felt as though she could breathe at last, as though she hadn't taken a deep breath since Friday afternoon. She also knew everything was the same but that she was somehow different. She made herself focus on what he was saying.

". . . it's only the middle of September!" His voice rose. "So she's going on about planning ahead and how Thanksgiving is so important to Uncle George since Nana died." He waved his hand in front of his face as though chasing away a bug. "Anyway, she went on and on. Compromise. I'll go home for Thanksgiving, do the family thing, but I'll come on over to your house that evening. Think of it as a dessert call."

"I'll think of you as a dessert call." She stopped walking and kissed him on the lips, his smooth lips.

"I like that idea." He hugged and then released her. "Hey, Vic, I'm starved."

"Did you eat—?"

He interrupted. "I did, but I'm starved. Maybe I've got tapeworm."

"Nah. You need to make up for all the torn muscle tissue, all those bruises. You really do look like a Dalmatian."

"I wonder if I'm a real shit. I love my mother, but she drives me crazy."

"Charly, she's" —Vic weighed her words— "a controlling woman."

"Yeah." He grabbed her hand again and then took two swinging steps to the right followed by two swinging steps to the left.

Charly delighted in Vic's presence. He felt he could say anything to her and she wouldn't judge him. He had never felt so free with another human being. She made him laugh. She made him want to be better than he was, to make her proud of him. He loved to listen to her stories of Surry County, to her sizing up of the people around him. He was often amazed at her insights, terse and on target. He was the talker of the two of them, and she used to tease him that he was perfect for politics. There were worse jobs than being governor, but he knew he wanted to make a lot of money. A man doesn't really make money in politics; he needs to go into it with money. Whatever the future held, he imagined Vic by his side. And even though he would inherit plenty, he wanted to make money on his own. He wanted Vic to be proud of him.

13

The *click, click, click* of her heels tapped against the gleaming black floor of the dealership, sending out an invitation. Hojo swayed slightly, enticingly, perched on those open-toed sling-backs with heels halfway between a flat and a stiletto.

The curving receptionist's desk reminded Hojo of the bridge of a battleship. She loved manning her station. As she sat higher than the floor, she could see over the salesmen, giggle to herself about their shiny bald spots. She felt above all of them.

She climbed up to her seat, picked up a mechanical pencil, and started scribbling sales figures. Being a receptionist had advantages, one being that there wasn't much pressure. But she wasn't stupid. She knew sales equaled money. Her salary might grow a little, but she'd never make a commission sitting on her butt overlooking the dealership. Quietly she was learning the business, learning the product. She wanted to be the first female car salesman at McKenna Dodge/Toyota.

The front door opened. She smiled broadly at Bunny and R. J. Like most women, she unthinkingly studied R. J., whose understated manner of dressing suited her perfectly. Hojo firmly believed more was more. She admired R. J., though, understanding that R. J. had found her style and stuck to it. Hojo considered herself still a work in progress, and at twenty-five, she believed she could and would progress.

"Good morning, Mrs. McKenna, Mrs. Savedge."

" 'Morning, Hojo." Bunny didn't smile but walked to the back of the receptionist's raised area and ascended the three steps that put her on the platform with Hojo.

Hojo reflexively covered her papers with her forearm. R. J. stood below her.

"Hojo, you pierced Mignon's ears, am I correct?" Bunny folded her arms across her chest.

"A needle and ice cubes. She didn't squeal a minute." Hojo smiled.

"Now why would you do a thing like that?" Bunny liked lording over the staff as much as they disliked her doing it.

"She asked me to." Hojo's amethyst earrings reflected the lights from the overhead tracks.

"She's fifteen," Bunny snapped.

"I didn't know that. She's a big girl." Hojo wasn't intimidated by Bunny.

"She is big," R. J. concurred. "She didn't say why she wanted you to do it? I mean, most girls will go to the mall to get their ears pierced with one of those, I don't know what you call them, guns. Of course, she'd have to show her ID there, which may explain why she came to you."

Hojo stood up and leaned over toward R. J. "Mrs. Savedge, she said she liked the way my earrings looked and she saw Courtney's ears at school, so she wanted me to do it."

Courtney, sixteen, was a class ahead of Mignon at school.

"It showed bad judgment." Bunny dropped her arms.

Hojo breathed in, counted to three, and then evenly replied, "I didn't know she was only fifteen and I didn't know Mrs. Savedge didn't want Mignon's ears pierced."

"Bunny, I'm satisfied." R. J. glanced out the window at the new trucks, which looked as bright as shiny jelly beans. "Hojo, the reason we're asking you these questions is just so I know whether Mignon told me the truth. She did."

"How are her ears?" Hojo asked, a touch too solicitously.

"Fine. Vic and her friend, Chris, bought her gold posts. Actually, she looks cute. I wanted her to wait until she turned sixteen, that's all. You didn't do anything wrong. Mignon can be very persuasive."

"She's a live wire." Hojo leaned farther down, her breasts touching the counter surface. "Vic is so quiet and Mignon's just bubbling over."

Bunny stepped back down. "Be back in a minute, R. J." She headed toward Don's office, which was filled with photographs of Bunny winning a variety of golf tournaments and of Don holding up sailfish and barracudas caught during his annual escapes to Florida each January.

"Mmm, mmm, mmm," Hojo half sang the sounds, three long notes indicating not disapproval but amusement.

R. J. pointed out a fire-engine-red Dodge half ton and smiled up at Hojo. "That's a beauty."

"We should take a picture and use it for an ad. You could be a model. You and Vic could do commercials, you know, like those mother-and-daughter commercials for soaps and stuff."

"Hojo, that's sweet of you to say."

Hojo trotted down the steps, joining R. J. to admire the truck. "She keeps that man on a short leash."

R. J., not about to criticize her sister with an employee, said, "She likes to stay involved in the business. She has a good mind for it."

"Mr. McKenna says Bunny will be the one that gets us the Mercedes dealership." Hojo lifted the edge of her skirt to wipe off a fingerprint on the plate-glass window, thereby exposing even more of her fit, feminine body. "He says Bunny wants to drive a Mercedes, but as long as we only carry Dodges and Toyotas, that's all she can drive."

"Bunny would look quite wonderful behind the wheel of a silver SL, top down."

"Wouldn't we all?" Hojo laughed. "Bet you two had fun as sisters."

"We still have fun."

"I mean in school and stuff."

"Yes. Bunny was always clever. She could figure out the angles. I more or less forged straight ahead. She's a lot smarter than I am," R. J. said appreciatively.

"But you're so beautiful—" Hojo stopped herself, quickly adding, "And smart. I've never heard anyone say you were anything but smart, Mrs. Savedge. People respect you and people know your life hasn't always been easy."

"It's not easy for anyone." R. J. smiled, wishing she could take a handkerchief and wipe some of the makeup off Hojo's face.

Bunny reappeared. "Let's rumble."

As if on cue a *boom, boom, boom* of thunder crashed, like the bumps of a moving caterpillar, one vibration following the other.

"Now, where did that come from?" Hojo ran to the door going outside.

The eastern sky, clear and blue, contrasted sharply to the western sky, dark blue-black with rolling clouds.

Bunny and R. J. walked outside to Bunny's car. "Oh, boy—we'll make it home just in time."

The rain was already pouring over Williamsburg, washing down clapboard houses in the historic center, sweeping the dust off the great wrought-iron gates to the House of Burgesses, drenching the cadmium-yellow and red marigolds, the mums of all colors, the tall zinnias.

Mary, Blessed Virgin Mother, appeared to be crying as the rain poured down her serene visage. Vic and Chris stood on the brick walkway, the lawn already soaked. They'd met after their last class of the day.

Chris, the rain sliding down her neck and along her back, was laughing. "Your tour of Williamsburg is original. You make these old buildings come to life."

"History is important. For instance, this statue of Mary will grant your wish if you make it during a thunderstorm." Vic grabbed Chris's hand, pulling her to the front door of St. Bede's, which was sheltered by an overhang.

A crack of thunder followed by pink light appeared. On the street they could hear the screams and laughter of folks running for their cars, for any doorway.

"That was close." Chris blinked, pressing next to Vic.

Vic put her arm around Chris's slick wet shoulders, drawing her next to her. She hunched over a bit. "The next one ought to be right above us." She released Chris for a second and tried the front door. It opened. They stepped, dripping, into the vestibule as a blinding bolt of lightning hit the lightning rod on the building next to the small well-kept lawn.

The temperature was dropping. They shivered together, the votive lights in small red chancels providing the only light as the power cut off. No one else was in the church.

"We're dripping all over the floor," Chris said, the water collecting in pools at her feet.

Another crack and they jumped closer together, laughing. "Glad the door was open." Vic put her arm around Chris again.

"Me, too."

"The sky was clear one minute and then the wind picked up." Vic loved watching the storms over the James. "Have you ever noticed how many different kinds of rain there are?"

"Hard rains, soft rains."

"There are rains with drops that fall here and there, big drops like wet polka dots. Then there are rains when the water falls like a beaded curtain, steady and silver. Sometimes rain falls soft, then hard, then soft again, as though it has an accelerator. I love watching it. I've seen rain come down sideways. Forty-five degrees to the ground. It's wild."

"I love the sound it makes."

"Especially on a tin roof."

The thunder rolled, still close but moving down toward the river.

"I don't know if I've ever heard that," Chris said.

"Sometime you'll be at the farm and a storm will come up. I'll take you to the tobacco shed. Sounds like BBs, or if the rain's hard, bullets, but you're standing on that hard-packed earth and all the curing smells rise up. God, it smells wonderful."

"I don't know if I would recognize a tobacco plant if I saw one."

Vic, who loved growing things, replied, "They're pretty amazing. They get big." A strong wind rattled the heavy door. Chris pressed her body into Vic's. "Are you frightened of storms?"

Chris said, "No . . . well sometimes." She looked up at Vic, holding her gaze. Chris's heart pounded as she shivered.

Vic fought back the impulse to kiss her. Instead she wrapped her other arm around her. "Once the lightning is gone we can run to the car. I wish I had some extra clothes in it."

"Take me to the coolest store. I'll buy us shorts and sweaters."

"You don't have to buy me anything."

"Hey, I spent a weekend at your house. Your mother stuffed me with food. The least I can do is buy you a sweater and a pair of Bermuda shorts before we both catch our death of cold."

"Does that mean we get naked?" Vic teased.

"Briefly." Chris stood on her toes, in anticipation of making a run for it. "Let's go." She wanted to stand in the vestibule, she wanted to strip right there and then wrap her arms around Vic's long body. She suspected the Catholic Church would not approve.

Chris opened the door. The rain, steady but not slashing, had filled the gutters, which spilled out everywhere.

They bolted for the Impala.

Vic pulled away from the curb, water tumbling along it. Leaves and small branches were scattered everywhere. "I'm glad St. Bede's door was open."

"Me, too." Chris pointed out an uprooted tree. "You know, we should have lit a candle for luck."

"I believe we make our own luck."

14

A soggy pile of clothes dampened the floor. Vic dried off in one changing booth, Chris in the other, separated by high partitions. The clerk, another student, gave them towels.

"I am so cold." Chris giggled.

"Put your clothes on. The coral sweater will help."

Chris yanked on the sweater, stepped into the jeans, and then tip-toed barefoot to Vic's booth. She put her hand on the doorknob, thought a minute, and returned to her booth.

"We forgot shoes. I'm not putting on those espadrilles. My feet are already a fetching shade of navy blue."

"Shoes are expensive."

"I said I was paying for all this."

"Chris, you can't do that."

"Sure I can. I can do anything. It's not like I'm on food stamps. Are you decent?"

"Yes."

Chris opened the door and walked out of the booth. Vic, hair pulled back, wore a soft-green sweater and a pair of Levi's.

"Green looks fabulous on you. Come on, shoes."

Vic looked out the store window, the name CASEY'S emblazoned in an arc on the glass. "What we need is duck boots."

"It's raining pretty steady." They started toward the shoe department. Chris found a pair of rubber boots, bright yellow. "I'll do yellow, you do green." She reached the stacks of socks, stuffing socks in each pair of boots.

"Chris, this will be a lot of money."

"I told you, just let me do it." Chris carried her pile to the counter.

With a slower step, Vic did the same. She had a keen sense of what things cost and how hard it was to earn money. And much as she liked Chris, she didn't want to owe her anything.

Chris motioned for her to move a little faster. "Here, while I do this, you can put our wet clothes in this plastic bag. You don't care if we take an extra bag, do you?"

The clerk, a redhead with an upturned nose, said, "No. Take two." The door opened and tourists, bedraggled, came in. "I'll be with you in a moment."

"Almost forgot." Chris threw in two bandannas. The clerk rang them up and they left the store, darting from awning to awning, over-hang to overhang.

"We're going to get soaked again." Vic laughed as the rain intensified.

"Never underestimate the purchasing power of a woman." Chris reached in her pocket, flashed her credit card, and opened the door to a luggage store that also carried multicolored umbrellas. She bought a green-and-yellow one.

Once outside she opened it. They squeezed under it together, tak-ing turns holding it.

"Sorry I had to park so far away. I should have dropped you off."

"This is fun. I have a lot of fun with you. In fact, I have more fun with you than anyone I've ever met."

"Uh-huh." Vic's tone sounded playful, disbelieving.

"I do."

They reached the car.

"Damn, I forgot to buy a towel!" Chris put her hand on her waist, her elbow sticking out in the rain. "Okay, where do we go to get towels?"

"I'll drive you—"

"No, we'll get wet."

"You didn't let me finish. You sit in the back."

"I'm not going to be seen in public with a woman who has a wet ass. Let's put our stuff in the trunk and we can buy a towel somewhere."

That took another twenty minutes. Finally, behind the wheel, Vic cranked the motor. She congratulated herself for putting a new white convertible roof on the car two summers ago. Not a drop of water worked its way inside the car.

"Where would you like to go?"

"I'm starved. Where can we go where there won't be a million people?" Chris pulled down the sun guard, reaching for the comb in her purse. "You know everyone."

"To say hello. That's about it. Hamburgers? Barbecue? Salads? Or fake food?"

"What?"

"Tofu, bean sprouts."

"Too bad we can't go to your house. Your mother is a fabulous cook. I'm not as good as she is, but I can cook. But I'm too hungry to buy the stuff and make it. Let's just eat somewhere, anywhere. I promise I'll cook for you soon. My mother, who could win the worry-of-the-week award, did actually teach me how to cook. This way even if stranded on an island, I could make a fire and survive."

Although Dukes was one of the most popular places in town, the rain kept most people at home or in the dorms. Vic and Chris shared the place with six other people.

By the time they'd finished their fried chicken, fries, and cole-slaw, they felt that glorious glow of contentment that attends a full stomach.

"Dessert?"

"Coffee. I'm too full for dessert," Vic answered. As they drank their coffee, Vic told her which were the best shops, restaurants, and bars. Then she asked Chris questions about herself.

"When I was a freshman at Vermont I partied every weekend. That got old by my sophomore year. Same old faces. Same old stories. I got tired of hearing myself talk." Chris stirred in more cream. "Luckily, I never partied so hard that my grades were in jeopardy. My dad would have killed me. Were you ever a partier?"

"No. Once there are more than eight people, I feel like I have a job to do. I have to speak to everyone, help the hostess. Hate it." She smiled. "Cotillion."

"Hey, we have it in York. We just call it dance school. I had to do it."

"Sports. I was always doing sports." Vic's long graceful fingers wrapped around the coffee mug. "That killed what vestige of socializing I might have had left."

"Golf?"

"No, I leave that up to Aunt Bunny. Baseball. I loved baseball, and then I reached the point where girls weren't allowed to play baseball. I mean, I could play with the boys in the summer but at school, only softball. So I took up tennis, and that was okay. Field hockey. Lacrosse. Track and field. Anything and everything. I liked track and field the best, but Mother and Aunt Bunny kept saying the long-term applications of running the one-hundred-meter dash were few."

"I thought you and Jinx played lacrosse for William and Mary?"

"We do. Jinx. I do it for Jinx. I'd be just as happy playing tennis for Mary not William." She laughed.

"Well, I used to swim backstroke. Being blonde and on the swim team isn't a good idea. Your hair turns green."

"How punk."

Soon they split the bill and ran for the car.

The rain on the windshield and the tempo of the wipers were the only sounds in the car. Through the rain, the blurred headlights of cars going in the opposite direction added to the sensation of privacy in the Impala.

"I see what you mean about each rain having its own character," Chris noted as Vic pulled into Chris's driveway. "Would you like to come up? Actually, we can wash our wet clothes. I can use the washer and dryer."

"You are so lucky." Vic had to take her clothes to the Laundromat.

They got out of the Impala and ran inside the house. Chris guided them to the washer, happily sorted their sopping clothes, and loaded the machine. Then they walked up the stairs to her apartment. She lit candles instead of clicking on the lights.

"John Coltrane, *A Love Supreme*? Bob James? David Sanborne? Or—?"

"The rain. I'd rather listen to the rain." Vic sat on the sofa.

"I'd better turn on the heat. I can't believe how raw it is."

"Late September. The changing seasons. You never know. I love it. When I was little I'd sometimes be out on the river; Aunt Bunny had a sailboat. We'd be out and within seconds the water would get a chop, the clouds would roll in. Magic."

"Where you live is magic." Chris sat down next to her. "The Savedges are magic." She leaned against the large curling arm of the sofa, kicked off her yellow rain boots, and put her feet on the sofa. "Take your shoes off. Get comfortable. You know, visiting you was—" Chris struggled to find the right words. "—a glimpse into another world. A happy world."

"We're all a little nuts, so take that into account."

"Your family is happy. Mine isn't." Chris stated this as a fact. "Mom and Dad go through the motions. Mom is real critical. Life has to be her way. She's a perfectionist, and she makes the rest of us miserable."

"But she loves you." Vic couldn't imagine having a mother who didn't love her.

"Mother wants a carbon copy of herself. She wants the table set exactly her way, the thermostat at seventy degrees, the clocks set at the correct time, not one minute fast or one minute slow. If I do all those things and agree with everything she says, she loves me." Chris smiled ruefully. "My mother is a control freak and not a very happy woman."

"What about your dad?"

"Works hard. Makes a lot of money. Puts up with her. Plays the role." She plumped up a sofa pillow. "Your family is happy. You all accept one another. In my family what you hear constantly is this is wrong, do this, do that. Your mom and dad might give you a chore but afterward they don't tell you what an awful job you did. Your parents love you. Being with your family, it's, I don't know, it's like being able to breathe."

Vic listened, not sure how to respond. "Well, you can come visit us anytime."

Chris tossed her head, her hair spinning out and then falling back into place. It was still a little wet. "Do you ever think about tomorrow? About who you'll be and what you'll do?"

"Sometimes. Mostly about what I'll do. You?"

Chris shrugged. "Off and on. Sometimes I'm off and sometimes I'm on. I get sick of everyone telling me my whole life is ahead of me. How do they know? No one knows. Especially me."

"I suppose it would take the fun out of it if we did know." Vic smiled.

"Or the terror."

"I'm not afraid."

"Really?" Chris, often tense inside, wondered how Vic could say that, feel it.

"Whatever is going to happen is going to happen. You'll drive yourself and everyone else crazy if you try to change it. I think you accept life. Accept yourself."

"It's probably the accepting yourself that's the hardest part. Accepting your limitations."

Vic watched Chris's mouth, well shaped with finely cut lips. "Maybe the accepting yourself is what makes life good. You only realize what you can do if you know what you can't do."

"I never thought of it that way." She lay back against the sofa arm. "People live their whole lives without knowing what they can do. They kind of drift along. I'd go mad."

Vic laughed at her. "It's not worth it. Nothing is worth going mad over."

"Do you really believe that?"

"Yes. Whole societies have been destroyed and people didn't go mad. Maybe some people did, but most didn't. Russia. France during the revolution. World War I swept away an entire world order. After World War II people in Europe and Japan lived in rubble. But they lived."

"See, that's the advantage of being a history major. English majors read the novels that come out of those wars. Of course, everyone is miserable or alienated or whatever. Maybe only unhappy people write."

"Nah. Chaucer. Shakespeare. I'm not an English major, but I think there are unhappy people and happy people. That's life. So you might as well spend time with the happy people. You can find them everywhere— even in bomb shelters in England during the Blitz."

"What makes you happy?"

"New clothes." Vic smiled. "The new clothes you bought me."

"That's easy."

"The river. Piper. My family. What about you?"

Chris noticed that Vic did not mention Charly. She didn't bring it up. "Beautiful things. Order. Beautiful people. You." She blushed.

A ripple almost like hunger startled Vic. She liked hearing that. She liked being in a candlelit room with Chris. She wanted to touch her. If Chris had been a man, she would have known what to do. She didn't want to offend her. But she trusted her instincts and her instincts told her that Chris wanted her as much as she wanted Chris.

Chris drew her legs up under her, shifting toward Vic. "I think the laundry is done." She paused. "And I don't care."

Chris slid over to Vic, rested against Vic's drawn-up knees and leaned over to kiss her on the mouth.

Although startled, Vic kissed her back. She put her hands on Chris's shoulders, dropped her knees, sliding her legs around Chris, pulling her up to her. They kissed for half an hour, kisses of liquid gold.

Chris bit Vic's neck and slid her hand under the new green sweater, feeling the hard stomach, the thin line between the abdominal muscles. She moved up to Vic's breasts.

Vic gasped. "You are driving me crazy."

"I thought you said nothing was worth going mad over." Chris bit Vic's lip lightly.

"I take it back." Vic pulled off Chris's sweater, kissing her breastbone and then her breasts.

"That feels good. That feels so good." Chris dropped her hand back for a moment, then she inclined it forward to bite Vic's neck again. She took the crew neck of Vic's sweater between her forefinger and thumb, pulling it over Vic's shoulder. She kissed her shoulder, then pulled the sweater back over it. She reached down with both hands, pulling Vic's sweater over her head. She pressed her body against Vic's, the cool flesh intoxicating, the air in the apartment still chilly.

Chris unzipped Vic's jeans, running her tongue alongside the zipper.

Vic reached around Chris, putting her hands down the back of Chris's jeans, feeling her smooth ass, pulling her tighter.

Chris exhaled. "I have never been so excited in my entire life."

"Me neither."

"Come on." Chris stood up, her breasts reflecting candlelight on smooth skin. She led Vic into the bedroom. She yanked Vic's jeans down to her ankles and stepped out of her own. She pulled back the covers on the bed, sliding underneath.

Vic slid in next to her. They lay on their sides kissing. Vic wrapped her arms around Chris's waist and then released her as Chris rolled onto her back, pulling Vic with her. She wrapped her legs around the tall woman. She kissed her hard. She ran her hands over Vic's muscled back, surprising Vic again with how strong she was.

Sweat trickled between Vic's breasts. The rain beat on the windowpane.

"Vic, Vic, I am so excited I can't stop."

"Don't." Vic inhaled traces of perfume on Chris's neck, a fragrance she couldn't identify.

Chris whispered in her ear, "I'm going to come all over you." Then she bit Vic's ear.

When Chris moaned, Vic followed, swept along. She had no control over her body. Like a dancer, she moved to the music, feeling for the first time the sonorous freedom of lust.

15

The world was sharper, more colorful, when Vic slipped down the stairs of Chris's apartment. She felt she could see every raindrop touch the pine needles, bouncing off into tiny fragments of water.

The white lintel over the doorway, the slight wave in the hand-blown glass windowpanes, the deep green of each grass blade, the world jumped out at her in its richness and beauty.

She'd left a note for Chris, sound asleep. Vic had an early morning class.

As she drove down to the campus, the texture of the brick buildings, dark persimmon, glistening in the rain, was exquisite to her eyes.

The faces of her classmates intrigued her. She couldn't concentrate on the French Revolution, but she sat there watching the rain, remembering Chris's breath on her neck, her hands, the sweet smell of her.

When class was over, she hurried down the stairs back out into the rain. There were two people she wanted to see, Jinx and Charly. Jinx because she could talk to her, Charly because she hoped she'd feel the pull toward him she felt for Chris. She hoped, somehow, that a sexual awakening meant she would awaken to him, too.

She stepped inside the science building. She usually picked him up after class. Then they'd go to the stadium and run steps.

"Beautiful!" He bounded toward her.

"Say it again." She hugged him, wanting to feel his body, needing him to banish the sneaking suspicion in her mind about herself. She needed his stability and his love.

He lifted his chemistry book over her head. "At least we'll be cool."

"I love the rain. I love every single drop."

He felt her happiness, a radiance enveloping him. "I love you."

"I hope so." She put her arm around his narrow waist. "I love you. I forget sometimes, I forget to tell you."

She parked at the gym. They changed in the locker room and met on the cinder track. They usually ran four laps on the track and then tackled the steps. Her energy surprised her, supercharged. She didn't feel the strain in her calves until the last set of steps.

Afterward they sat on the bottom step, both soaked. "If we could strip, we wouldn't need a shower." He tipped back his head, the water tickling his tongue. Then he kissed her, dribbling rainwater.

She laughed. "Rules. We should be able to take our clothes off and stand here in the rain. If we were home, we could."

"Let's go." He stood up, pulling her with him.

"For real?"

"Yeah, change your clothes. Let's go."

They were in her car in fifteen minutes and at Surry Crossing in another forty-five.

Piper barked in the kitchen as Vic pushed through the door. R. J.'s car wasn't there, so she must have been running errands.

"Come on." She stripped off her clothes, neatly arranging them on the kitchen chair. "I'll explain to Mom if she comes home soon." She grabbed two towels while Charly removed his T-shirt and jeans.

A thin line of blond hair ran across his pecs, the bottom of the line running down to a fluff of pubic hair surrounding an impressive penis.

They'd petted and played with one another for a year, but neither had ever seen the other naked.

"God, you are beautiful. You are so beautiful." He could barely breathe. A twinge in the small of his back told him that his dick would be standing at attention soon.

"I was thinking the same about you." She put the towels on the table, reached for his hand, and they ran down to the river.

Piper, bored with the rain, remained in the kitchen.

"I love it!" She laughed as they reached the dock. She dropped his hand, held out her arms, looked up at the sky. The James lapped the dock.

Charly copied her. Rivulets coursed over his body. He looked down at his stiff dick. "I can't always control this thing, you know."

She wrapped her arms around him. "Why should you? It means you're alive."

"I am when I'm with you." He kissed her. He thought if he died in that moment he'd die a happy man. Well, if he could enter her, then he'd die an ecstatic man.

Charly weighed 185 pounds, solid muscle. His bones were heavy, his jaw strong. Vic could feel the hair on his chest next to her breasts. Chris weighed maybe 135 pounds at five feet six or seven. The odor from her body was sweet.

Vic knew she didn't feel incinerating lust, but she felt a tug, a warmth. She liked feeling his penis against her stomach, the heat of it, the throb. She wanted to know what it was like to truly make love with him. If she liked it maybe she wasn't a lesbian. That seemed logical.

She reached for him, wrapping her hand around his satisfying thickness. His knees wobbled.

"Do you need to sit down?" She laughed.

"Vic, I can't breathe. I can't stand. I can't think."

"If we get into the water on the north side of the dock and Mom does come home, she won't see us before we know she's here."

"I'll do anything."

They slid into the water, which was warmer than the rain. The soft muck curled up through their toes. The rain, heavier now, tapped onto their skin. She moved her hand up and down, kissing him; then she slid over him but not onto him. He leaned back against the mossy dock timber, glad for the support. Even with the help of the water, his legs shook.

They drove one another crazy until she mounted him, a new sensation and not a bad one once she adjusted to his considerable girth.

Charly, sweating in the rain as though suffering from fever, whispered, "I don't know how long I can hold out."

She held the back of his neck with her right hand, her left hand in the small of his powerful back. "Don't—hold out."

He held her tightly, but was as gentle as he could be. He exploded in about sixty seconds.

Vic liked feeling him reach orgasm. She knew she could do it in another position. This one wasn't the easiest.

Charly had slept with two other women in his life. One was his high school girlfriend, sex snatched whenever and wherever they could get away with it. The other one was his first girlfriend at William and Mary when he was in his freshman year. He'd mastered the basics, but he knew there was a lot to learn and he couldn't wait to learn it all with Vic. But he was so respectful of her, so in awe of her, that he never pushed for it. Also, Charly possessed a wonderful sense of people. He knew without being told that Vic was not a woman who could be pushed into sex or anything else for that matter.

She hung on to him, kissing him, rubbing the small of his back until he slipped out.

"Think any of those little things are swimming in the James?" She kissed his cheek.

He sighed. "You feel so good." He paused a moment, the muscles in his back tensed. "Vic, I didn't think about—"

"Me neither. I'll bear the consequences should there be any." The unpleasant possibility of zero spontaneity in heterosexual sex had occurred to her.

There was no way in hell Vic would ever take birth control pills. Let other women screw up their hormone balance. She wasn't going to do it. This meant purchasing condoms—not in Surry County, obviously, where everybody talks to everybody else—or getting fitted with a diaphragm, which meant you had to plan sex or stop and put it in.

With Chris there wasn't a worry in the world.

"I'll marry you. I'll marry you anyway." He shivered a moment.

"You have to ask first."

"I do and I will." He kissed her.

Charly came from the same kind of background as Vic did. A man didn't just ask a woman to marry him. He first spoke to her father. If she had no father, he spoke to her mother or someone in authority.

The rules for correct behavior had lasted through centuries of up-heavals in Virginia. They weren't going to change. The man asked for a woman's hand, and if she accepted he'd better be able to provide for her. Fortunately, Charly could.

If two people just agreed to get married without the proper minuet it meant they were low rent, even if they were rich.

They walked out of the river and back up to the house, the hard rain washing off the river smell. Piper greeted them with a thump of her tail.

Vic wrapped a towel around Charly and one around herself. Then she rubbed him down, feeling him get hard again.

"Maybe we can get away with it."

They hurried up the steps, running into her bedroom and launch-ing themselves on her twin bed.

She wrapped her legs around him much as Chris had around her the night before. Coming was easy. The minute she did he did, and she was thankful that he had lasted that long.

He propped himself on his elbows. "To what do I owe this mo-mentous occasion?"

"I don't feel like waiting around anymore." She kissed him again. "Let's take a shower." As she stood up, his come ran out of her. "This stuff is amazing." She laughed.

A little was seeping out of the hole in his penis. He wiped it off with his finger. "Is there an etiquette for body fluids?"

"I think we either lick ourselves clean, wipe it up, or wash it off. They didn't tell me in cotillion. It's just a hunch."

They showered, ran back downstairs, and put their clothes on.

Vic had just opened the refrigerator when R. J. and Bunny walked in. After rapturous greetings, Bunny pulled a new pair of binoculars from a blue glossy shopping bag.

"Zeiss ten by fifty-six. I can see at night."

"That's great, Aunt Bunny."

"Don't ask what they cost." Bunny handed them to Charly. When no one did ask, she added, "A fortune."

"That's the truth." R. J. walked over to the refrigerator. "Hungry? Oh, what a silly question. You all sit here. I'll perform a culinary miracle."

"R. J., I'll eat every morsel you put in front of me." Bunny took the binoculars back after Vic inspected them too. "Aren't they the best? I'd tell you to look through them, but the rain—" Bunny stood up, putting her binoculars to her eyes. "Even in this weather I can see. Oh, this is just the best, best, best. Here, Charly."

He stood up to peer through the binoculars. "Wow, Mrs. McKenna, you could sign up for Special Forces with these."

While they were talking, R. J. was preparing their lunch. She adored feeding people. In no time she'd put cold roast beef on the table, a loaf of fresh whole wheat bread, potato salad, mayo, mustard, pickles, deviled eggs.

"Mom, you must have known we were coming."

"Actually, your sister had a pep club meeting here last night, officers only, and these are the leftovers. She's quite the organizer."

Bunny kept putting her fork down to pick up her new binoculars. She couldn't keep her hands off them. "Oh, I just love it. I'm not going to show Don the bill. I paid for these out of my own special account."

"Charly, we missed you last weekend, and I guess we'll miss you this weekend," R. J. said.

"It's always a pleasure to have you at the games, Mrs. Savedge."

"Maybe the weekend after that we'll all drive over for a game. Then you can come back with us and spend what's left of the weekend."

"That would be great." He smiled. He liked R. J., and Bunny, too. He'd gotten to know her a bit over the summer, playing golf with her and Frank Savedge.

"What were you two doing?" Bunny hoped she'd get a vague response, anything to fire her imagination, since Don wasn't firing it lately.

"We wanted to jump in the river in the rain," Charly said.

"Well, careful, you two—you never know what's swimming in there," Bunny warned.

"You're exactly right, Aunt Bunny," Vic agreed, smiling.

16

J esus, Vic, leave it to you not to do anything halfway." Jinx sat in her living room adorned with framed posters of Impressionist paintings.

Because of his curfew, Vic had dropped off Charly at his dorm. The minute she walked through Jinx's door she called Chris, telling her she'd had to run home, she was at Jinx's, and she'd see her tomorrow after class. Then she fell into a chair, like a shot duck, and spilled everything to Jinx.

"What do I do now?"

"Enjoy it." Jinx laughed. She'd made coffee and got up to pour it, returning with two large mugs. "Here, caffeine will clarify your muddled brain."

"I think it's always muddled."

Jinx sat opposite her dearest friend. "Neither one knows about the other?"

"No. Well, obviously, Chris knows about Charly. Doesn't know I slept with him."

Homosexuality would cost Vic; it did everyone. Jinx felt no repugnance for it, but she recognized that it was a complicated life.

"Do you love Charly?"

"What's not to love?"

"Do you love Chris?"

"That's just it, Jinx. I barely know the woman. But I can't be around her without wanting to tear her clothes off. Torrential sex."

Jinx put her feet up on the crate serving as a coffee table. "Before this—did you ever think you'd sleep with a woman?" Vic shook her head. Jinx continued, "I always thought Teeney Rendell had a crush on you."

Teeny Rendell, a pretty girl, a year younger, had followed Vic around like a puppy during high school.

"So?"

"Didn't give you a flicker?"

"Jinx, get real. Not in the program."

"She's hot—good-looking. Wish I had her legs."

"I never thought of it. Come on, you've known me forever, since we were born. If I were a lesbian, don't you think you'd know? Or sense it? Or something?"

Jinx shrugged. "How could I know if you didn't know?"

"People feel those things about other people."

"Only if it's in the computer." Jinx tapped her head. "Why would I look for it? But now that you've so spectacularly launched yourself onto the bosom of another woman, how was it?"

"You pig."

Jinx raised his eyebrows. "Like you wouldn't ask me the same thing if the shoe were on the other foot."

"I told you, torrential." Vic joggled the coffee mug, caught it before spilling, and placed it on the coffee table. "I don't know if I can explain it, but she touches me and I'm incinerated, fried. No brain waves."

"Sounds pretty fabulous to me, with the exception that it's a woman. I mean for me. I'm not passing judgment. You know I don't care." She leaned forward. "What about Charly? I thought you'd been sleeping with him and just not telling me."

"Oh, come on. I'd tell you. Jinx, I tell you everything. I can't believe you'd think that." Vic grew impassioned.

"Yeah, but one still has to be, shall we say, circumspect."

Vic sighed, looking out the window—still raining. "I like whatever makes him happy. Besides, seeing him get excited makes me excited."

"So?" Jinx voice rose.

"Oh, sex with Charly?" Vic folded her hands together. "It was okay."

"Just okay?"

Now Vic leaned toward her friend, reaching across the coffee table for her hand. "What do you want me to say? After Chris, I just had to find out. Maybe it wasn't smart or right or fair, but I found out. Sex with Charly is a pleasure, not a passion."

Jinx squeezed Vic's hand and then released it. "Ah, that does change things, doesn't it?"

"Maybe I need to sleep with them both more. A lot. As much as I can." Vic's face lightened. "Keep comparing notes."

"Do you think you could love Chris?"

"I kind of hope I can and I kind of hope I can't."

"Why not be in love with two people at the same time? Makes sense to me, although it may not make sense to them," Jinx said.

"I can hide the fire, but what about the smoke? I'm a bad liar, anyway."

Jinx held up her hands to stop the questions. "Don't tell either of them anything. Yet. You don't know enough. Really. You don't want to blow your relationship with Charly, forgive the pun. And if Chris really is the one, you don't want to run her off either."

"The funny thing is, I could tell Charly. The other funny thing is, I feel so close to him not because we made love, but because of what I feel for Chris. It's like I woke up. I see the world. I see him. He's beautiful to me."

"I'll take your word for it, but I don't understand it."

"I don't either." Vic lifted the mug, draining it. "I don't understand a blessed thing. But I feel everything."

A sly smile crossed Jinx's lips. "Oh, give me more details."

"Like what?"

"Tell me how they feel, since you're feeling everything and since I probably will never make love to a woman. I need a vicarious thrill."

"She smells different than he does, sweet, very sweet. He smells sharper, kind of, but maybe that's because men don't shave their armpits. Clean but sharper. Her skin is smoother. He's heavier, denser kind of, and in a way, more defenseless. I love that about Charly and maybe it's true of all men: They're strong but fragile at the same time. I mean he's physically strong, stronger than I am, and I'm no weakling."

"Brute. Your mother calls you a brute." Jinx's eyes sparked. She was loving the details.

"His shoulders are so broad I think he could carry the world."

"Vic, your shoulders are about as broad as Charly's."

"Nah. I love him, Jinx. I do. I love his mouth, his muscles—God, he has a beautiful body. I love his cock. I love his laugh. I love him. But I don't feel for him what I feel for her."

A cloud passed over Jinx's face, a recognition that things change in a split second, plans shatter, new paths emerge out of the rubble. She didn't know what any of it meant for her or for her friend. But she realized life happens, it just happens. Human attempts to control it would always be absurd.

"Vic, could you marry Charly?" She held up her right hand as Vic started to answer. "Don't interrupt me. Everyone, including Charly, expects you to marry. But could you marry him, have children, and forget what you feel with Chris? Could you live without that—torrential sex or torrid love or whatever you now know?"

Vic's hand flew to her face. She covered her eyes for a second as though shading them; then she dropped her hand. "Jinx, I don't think I could. I think sooner or later I'd find a woman or a woman would find me. Why?" She slapped her hands together. "This just fucks up everything. My parents will die. Aunt Bunny will shit a brick. We'll lose Surry Crossing."

"Hey, you can't live for them. They made their choices. And your parents won't die. I don't think they'll reward you for it. Yeah, I suppose marrying Charly could save Surry Crossing." She paused. "But you can save your home place without him. I don't know how, but there's got to be a way. This isn't about Surry Crossing. It's about you. Can you live a lie?"

"Loving Charly is hardly a lie." Vic raised her voice.

"You know what I mean."

"Maybe it's just about fucking."

"No."

Vic dropped back against the chair, a cozy wingback. "Guess not. Well, why can't I have both? Other people do it."

"Name one."

"I read about these things. Why can't I have two lovers for as long as I like?"

"Maybe you can and then again maybe you'll lose them both."

"Everything's a risk." She paused. "Why can't I take them both to bed, the three of us. Who's to know?"

Jinx sat straight up. "Now, there's an idea! Think you could talk them into it?"

Vic shrugged. "I was joking."

"I do wonder sometimes why it's two by two. Maybe it's hard enough to deal with one person plus the kids. Add another one, and it's impossible. Under the same roof, I mean. God knows people have affairs all the time. Maybe they have to do it, get the energy to go home. I feel like I'll never find out. I'm going to be single."

"Jinx, that's bullshit."

"Victoria, you are completely ravishing. You can have who you want when you want them. I am most emphatically not ravishing. And I need to lose ten pounds."

"You're beautiful to me. You're beautiful to anyone who takes the time to get to know you. If you want to lose the ten pounds, you will. I'm sick of hearing about the ten pounds."

" 'Get to know you' is the key phrase. Men don't want to get to know you. They make up their minds in one look whether or not they'll even bother. It's all about sex."

"No, it isn't. Some guys are smarter than that. Sure, they look and some women look better than others on the outside. But I know there are guys who can see you like I see you. And think of it this way: You've already weeded out the superficial jerks."

"Chris is great looking. Would you be as hot for her if she were, say, ten pounds overweight?"

"I don't know."

"See? You're as superficial as the guys," Jinx teased her.

"How would I know? I never looked at women before!"

"Now you will. You'll walk across that campus and think about who's fuckable and who's not. You will. You'll watch women's breasts sway, and then you'll look at the ones with the light round asses and—"

"Jinx, maybe you're the one who's gay."

"I really don't think I am, but I can imagine."

"Breasts are a good thing. Trust me. A really good thing." Vic grinned. "I think I'm demented. I've turned into a sex maniac. Overnight. I can't stop thinking about it."

"I'm not even getting any, and I can't stop thinking about it."

"It's kind of exhausting."

"Vic, are you going to spend all your time with Chris?"

"Huh?" Vic was still thinking about being exhausted.

"Is a female lover, wait, let me rephrase that, is Chris your new best friend?"

"No. Why are you asking me that?"

"Because—" Jinx's voice trailed off.

"You're my best friend. You'll always be my best friend."

17

Vic couldn't blame Jinx for it, but she did look at every woman she passed. She noticed their breasts, their waists, whether they were fit or flabby, the way their hair complemented their faces or didn't.

She had called Chris when she woke up in the morning. She remembered that Chris had an eight-o'clock class. She told her she'd see her after classes.

Then she called Charly. He told her he loved her and couldn't live without her, and could he see her after class? With a pang, she said she couldn't today but she'd see him tomorrow after training table.

Nothing said in her classes penetrated her skull. She bought sandwiches and a bunch of asters in a blue vase on the way home. She still had no furniture except a kitchen table, four chairs, and a bed, but the flowers decorated the center of the table. She set two places, and time crawled until she heard Chris's footsteps in the stairwell.

Carrying a huge bouquet of roses, Chris handed them to Vic. "A rose by any other name." She kissed her on the cheek.

"These are beautiful. We had the same idea, only yours was better." Vic didn't have another vase, but she did have a coffee can. She put the grounds in a Ziploc bag, washed the can and added water, and put the roses in it.

"They'll tip over." Chris laughed. "Either let me go home and get a vase or let me trim off the ends."

"No, don't go." Vic reached for her wrist.

"All right. Give me a pair of scissors," Chris requested.

Vic rooted around the catch-all drawer, filled with string, rubber bands, pencils, and coupons. "Here."

Vic watched Chris, the motion of her hands as she clipped off the end of each stem, cutting on an angle under running water.

"Are you hungry?"

Chris shook her head. "Not very."

"When you are, I have sandwiches in the fridge. Give me credit. I actually thought about food."

"What'd you do yesterday? I missed you." Chris caught her breath, a quick intake. "Thank you for calling me. I was afraid it was a wham, bam, thank you, ma'am."

Vic put her hands on Chris's waist as Chris stood over the sink. She kissed the nape of her neck. "No way, ma'am."

"That gives me chills." Chris hunched her shoulders.

"Me, too." Vic nuzzled her.

"Yesterday?"

"Drove home. Aunt Bunny bought serious new binoculars. Mom says hello. I left before Mignon came home from school."

"It's great that you love your family so much."

"Oh, sometimes they get on my nerves, but I do love them." She released Chris's waist, leaning against the counter, her elbows behind her so she could see Chris's face. "Actually, I wanted to talk to Mom again about my leaving school, but Aunt Bunny was there."

"Leaving school?" Chris face whitened.

"I wouldn't be far."

"You can't leave me. I just found you."

"I wouldn't be leaving you. I'd be leaving school. I need a job. Money."

"Is it that bad?"

"It's not good." Vic smiled faintly.

"It never hurts to have a degree," Chris said sensibly.

"I guess." Vic smelled the fragrance of the roses, an electric pink.

"And I really do love William and Mary. I wouldn't mind a framed diploma from the same college that educated Thomas Jefferson."

Chris put the roses on the table. "Why don't I take these asters back to the bedroom?"

"Sure." Vic followed her.

Chris placed the asters in the blue vase in the middle of the dresser. When she turned, Vic put her hands on her shoulders, leaned down, and kissed her.

Chris wrapped her arms around Vic's waist. Within minutes they were out of their clothes and in bed. They couldn't get enough of each other. By twilight, hunger took over and they walked out to the kitchen for sandwiches. Chris wore Vic's robe. Vic wore a towel around her waist.

After they ate they went back to bed, leaning against the pillows, against one another, watching the stars emerge as the last of the long September twilight faded.

"Chris, have you made love to women before?"

"Would it make any difference?"

"Meaning, would I be jealous or feel like a number? I don't think so, but I just wondered."

"In high school. I had a girlfriend, and we fooled around. But we fooled around with our boyfriends, too. I didn't exactly think of it like being gay, you know?" Chris leaned her head on Vic's breasts, as she lay with her back between Vic's legs. "Have you?"

"No. I never even thought of it."

"Funny."

"Why?"

"Because when I met you I thought you were gay. I thought you were the most beautiful woman I'd ever seen and I was thrilled you were gay."

"Is that supposed to be a compliment?"

Chris's laughter was light and rolling. "I don't mean you were like some dyke, but, you know, you're all muscle and you're tall and, I don't know, so independent or something. This is probably the wrong time to say this, but I fell in love at first sight."

Vic blurted out, "I did, too."

As they lay in silence, a cat meowed nearby.

Chris said, "I'm surprised you don't have a cat or dog."

"Piper. I want a cat, but not until I'm out of school. I hate making an animal stay at home alone." She put her hands under Chris's shoulders, lifting her up. "One sec." She wriggled out from under her and then sat facing her. "I missed your face. If I worked and lived at home for a while to save money, that cat wouldn't be lonesome."

"Could you live at Surry Crossing?"

"I was thinking maybe Mom and Dad could deed me a little land. Eventually I could build a small house. But I know what Mother would say: 'That's silly. I rattle around in this gargantuan house. In the old days, fourteen and twenty people would live in a house like this, plus the servants.' " Vic expertly imitated her mother.

"Your mother is the second most beautiful woman I have ever seen."

"Will I ever meet your mother?"

"Vic, I suppose you will but—" Chris paused. "I can't keep my hands off you. The sight of you makes my stomach drop to my toes. I feel like every bad love song I've ever heard. If I took you home, my mother would know about us in a minute. She would not be pleased."

"You're expected to marry well?"

"Isn't every woman?"

Vic, silent a moment, finally asked, "Do you know what you want to do with your life?"

Chris draped her leg over Vic's. "In a way, I do and in a way, I don't. I don't want to be poor. My parents spoiled me that way, I guess, but I want money. Enough to do what I want. I don't have to be the richest person, but I want to fly to London, then—" She made a flying motion with her hands. "I don't mind working. In fact, I like being occupied. I don't think I could marry a rich man and be a volunteer lady. If I teach, I get my summers off. I like that idea. That's about as much of a plan as I have."

"Well, you've got more of a plan than I do."

"I wouldn't mind teaching at the college level. I don't have an aptitude for business or science. That doesn't leave much. But I do not want to be bored!" Chris said emphatically.

"I don't either, but if I have to be a little bored to learn what I need to know, I suppose it's not so bad. Like working for Uncle Don this summer. I did everything. I washed and waxed cars. I changed tires. I manned the reception console, as he calls it, when Hojo was off doing whatever. I worked on the roof when flashing had to be replaced. I liked that every day wasn't alike, and I especially liked that I could be outside. At first Uncle Don was going to stick me with girl stuff. I pitched a fit—a nice fit. So he called me his rover. I learned a lot."

"Like what?"

"The public is demanding. You smile at the assholes same as at the nice people. It's their money. If they spend it in your place, they have a right to expect a good product and good service. Uncle Don taught me that. Aunt Bunny, who is smart, taught me to think ahead and to scope the competition. So I'd cruise around other car lots. How did they display their cars? What were their service hours? It sounds dumb, but I really liked it. Mostly, I liked being outside."

"I don't think farmers make money," Chris teased her.

"Yeah, I've even thought about working for the government in the forestry service or something." She smiled. "I could be a fishing guide. I know the river." Vic sat upright. "You don't know. Stranger things have happened." Then she lapsed back on the pillow.

"Marriage?"

"They all expect me to marry Charly."

"And?"

"I expected to marry Charly—until now."

Chris, more tense than she realized, relaxed. "Oh."

"What about you?"

Chris shook her head. "No. I don't think I could do it. On the other hand, I don't want to get the shit kicked out of me for being queer."

Vic fell silent and then spoke again, "Are we lesbians?"

Chris laughed. "We sure are when we're together." She leaned forward on her hands and knees and kissed Vic. She kissed her breasts, running her tongue around the circumference. Then she moved down her stomach.

"What you do to me." Vic ran her fingers through Chris's blonde hair.

"Lie there and let me worship you."

Vic had an orgasm, wondering if a person could die coming.

Then Chris slid back up, resting her head under Vic's chin. "Proof."

"What?"

"Lesbian proof."

Vic kissed her hair as Chris settled into a more comfortable position. "Maybe I'm not gay. It's just—you. What you do to me."

"Does it matter?"

"No." Vic breathed in deeply. "I don't think I'll be one of those people who can live in a closet."

"Don't worry about that right this minute. We can worry about that later."

A brilliant sliver of crescent moon climbed in the sky.

Vic watched the pines sway. "I'm not worried, exactly. I just don't want to blurt it out. I guess I'll have to weigh my words for a while."

"Me, too." Chris closed her eyes and then opened them, abruptly changing the subject. "Did you hear about what happened at Alpha Tau?"

"No."

"They were hazing pledges, and one guy drank so much he fell out of a second-story window. Broke his legs, broke his ribs, broke things I don't remember. It wasn't in today's paper, but you know it will get in soon enough. The administration won't be able to keep a lid on it."

"That's pretty awful. I hadn't heard about it."

"Can you imagine getting that shitfaced?" Chris wondered.

"No," Vic replied, hearing a bird twitter outside.

"There will be the usual denouncements when it gets in the news, you know, the young are a disgrace," Chris said.

"Mmm."

"I think old people are angry at us because they're old and we're not. It's not our fault."

"I never thought about it."

Chris snuggled against Vic. "Let's live forever."

"It's a deal." Vic kissed her.

At six-thirty Vic and Chris drank coffee while the pale early-morning light flooded through Vic's windows. The major decision of the moment was whether to make waffles or eggs. After rummaging through Vic's sparse pantry, Chris swore she could do either. Vic's robe, tied loosely around Chris's slender waist, hung open to reveal her breasts. Vic wore jeans and an undershirt, which made her even more tantalizing to Chris as the opaque white of the T-shirt both revealed and concealed her body.

Footsteps and a knock on the door surprised them both.

"Who's there?" Vic called.

"Prince Charming," Charly answered.

Vic opened the door and he stepped in, picking her up and kissing her. Then he saw Chris. He put Vic down.

"Chris Carter, Charly Harrison. Charly, Chris."

He walked over and shook her hand. "Pleased to meet you."

"Coffee?" Vic offered.

"No, thanks, I can't stay. Could I borrow your car? I promise if anything happens to it, I will fix it. I need to see Dad."

"Sure. Excuse me a second, and I'll grab the keys." She walked back into the bedroom thinking to herself, Thank God I had clothes on.

"Vic's starting a new trend in interior design, the barracks look," Charly joked with Chris. It didn't dawn on him that Chris was in Vic's robe since he'd never seen the robe. But even if he had, he would have assumed they were girlfriends sharing clothes. Women were close in a way that men were not.

Vic returned and handed him the keys. "Take care of my baby."

He kissed her on the cheek. "Hey, you're my baby." He winked at Chris and sailed out the door. "Bye. Nice to meet you."

"Bye," Vic called after him. "He cracks me up," she said as she closed the door.

"God, Vic, he's gorgeous. To-die-for gorgeous." Chris wished she hadn't met him.

"And he is the best guy. The more you know him, the more you'll love him."

"I'm not sure I want to know him." Chris had suddenly lost her appetite.

"Don't worry about him. You'll like him."

"I feel like the world will push you into his arms."

"Don't underestimate me." Vic's jaw set and then relaxed. "Okay, it's a little awkward. I mean, I've been dating him for a year and I love him, I love him for the person he is, but it's not the same. My life would probably be easier if it were, but it's not. If I hadn't met you, I would have never known. But I'm glad I met you now and not ten years later."

Chris smiled, lowering her eyes and then raising them. "I thought it would be simple. Guess not."

"Don't worry."

"It's all happened so fast. It scares me."

"Why?"

"Well, what if this doesn't work? What if we blow up or you decide you will stick with Charly or people find out and you hate me?"

Vic took a deep breath. "I could never hate you. And no, I don't know if you and I are going to, well, whatever women do—ride off into the sunset together. I don't know anything. But I know I am alive and I'm strong. And maybe whatever happens is supposed to happen. I'll learn from it. I'll be a better person for it. Fear isn't an option."

As Charly drove to Richmond, he envied how close women's friendships were. He didn't think he'd ever be as close to a man as Vic was with Jinx or this new friend. It seemed they could tell one another anything.

He wasn't really looking forward to seeing his father. Thomas Harrison ran a large brokerage firm in Richmond. Sometimes he'd drive home for a night, but usually he only came home on weekends. The arrangement suited both his parents.

Charly respected his father and he supposed he loved him. One had to love one's father. But he felt no special closeness to Thomas. Demanding, critical but fair, the older Harrison pushed his brood to be better, to be good sports, but to play to win. He'd say, "Who remembers the runner-up in the Kentucky Derby in 1960?"

One way of winning was to make more money than the other guy. As a young man Charly understood that money meant winning; it was important, and a man without resources wasn't much of a man by American standards. Even if he thought it was emotionally and spiritually stupid, money mattered. You couldn't support a family on love alone. A clean conscience wasn't going to pay the bills. Money mattered.

He'd thought about a career in pro ball. He knew his stats were good, even though William and Mary was not a hot spot on any team's recruit list. But he averaged 4.9 yards a carry last season and could run the forty-yard dash in 4.3 seconds. And not only could he run, he could block, too. There was a slim chance for him. But he'd destroy his knees—a running back's lifespan was slightly longer than the mayfly in professional football. Even if he did get drafted, he wanted a profession when that career was over.

Externally affable and good-natured, Charly possessed a keen mind. He'd turn problems over in his mind, speaking to no one about them, not even to Vic, although he felt he could tell her anything. He didn't like talking about something until he had figured out a solution.

By the time he pulled into the parking lot of Bishop and Harrison, confidence surged through him. He felt he knew how to approach his father.

His appointment was at nine-thirty. Thomas didn't like to be surprised, so Charly couldn't drop in. He had made the appointment with his dad's secretary yesterday but then forgot to ask Vic for her car.

One of the strings attached to having his college education paid for by his father, was that Charly couldn't own a car while in school. Thomas believed students without cars made better grades than students with cars. He was probably right.

Since he was early, Charly walked around downtown for a half hour. The temperature would climb so that it still felt like summer, but the light told another story. Fall was on the way. Charly knew one morning soon he'd awaken to smell the leaves and the odor of the earth. The ensuing weeks would bring crystal-clear days and nights, extraordinary color, and a quickening of pace.

Charly strode into his father's office at precisely nine-thirty. Thomas admired punctuality.

"Son." The tall man shook hands with his boy. "Sit down. Can I get you anything to drink? Are you hungry?"

"No, Dad. Thank you."

"How's school?"

"Fine."

"Grades?"

"So far so good. I ought to graduate with a three-point-six at the lowest."

"Good. You don't know any of those Alpha Tau boys involved in this pledge hazing, do you?"

"Well, I know who they are, but I don't really know them."

"Binkie Marshall is on the board of trustees. He called me last night and said the administration is going to crack down on this kind of foolishness. It's in today's papers."

"I haven't read the papers."

"Even in the *Richmond Times-Dispatch*. Well, public relations will take a nose dive. I don't know what people expect. Young men often lack judgment. What is the old saying? 'Good judgment comes from experience and experience comes from bad judgment.'" The corner of his mouth turned up slightly. "Binkie was taking my temperature, of course. I'll still be making my contribution as an alumnus." Thomas smiled, the light overhead catching the silver beginning to weave throughout his own blond hair. "Well, Charles, what can I do for you?"

"Dad, do you remember how you felt when you graduated from college?"

Thomas, a wild man during his own days at William and Mary smirked. "Sick as a dog, that's how I felt."

"Besides that."

"Naturally I told myself I'd conquer the world. And I knew I was lucky. I just missed the Big One. Korea, too. But I knew I'd have to compete against those men. I don't recall anything else. Why?"

"I thought if I knew how you felt, it might give me perspective on how I feel."

"Which is?" Thomas linked his fingers together, placing his hands behind his head.

"Excitement. I can't wait, Dad. I feel like anything is possible unless something beyond our control happens, you know, like war with the Russians."

"Mideast, more likely," Thomas tersely responded.

"Right. But if there aren't those—eruptions, I think we're poised, my generation and all of us, really, on the brink of incredible financial opportunities. I want to be part of it. If I don't try for pro ball, I want to go straight into business, your business." He knew he had his father's total interest. "I don't want to work for your firm, though. I want to get a job with Merrill Lynch or Dean Witter. I want to work my way up."

Thomas brought his hands down to his desk. What father doesn't want a son in the business? "And how did you arrive at this decision?"

"A lawyer has a ceiling on earnings. Even the best. Same with a doctor. I want unlimited opportunities to create wealth—for myself and my clients. I want the challenge of it. I think if you've seen one gallbladder, you've seen them all." He paused while his father listened. "And the same with law. The repetition of it isn't appealing. And no criminal law, either. I'm not representing pimps, drug dealers, and rapists."

Intensely pleased, Thomas said quietly, "Have you spoken to your mother about this?"

"No, sir. I needed to talk to you first. I think Mother will be okay. Don't you?"

"Yes. Her only concern is that you be happy."

"Do you understand why I can't work for you?"

"I do. But that doesn't mean I can't hire you, say, six or seven years from now when you're making your mark." Thomas smiled broadly.

"One other thing." He paused and then spoke deliberately. "I want to marry Vic after graduation."

"I see." Thomas liked Vic, as did his wife. She was well bred and would fit into the world they envisioned for their son. A pity about her father's lack of financial acumen, but that was no reflection on the girl.

"I love her."

"The early years of establishing yourself can be punishing. You won't have much time for a home life . . . not if you want to be the best. And what about relocating? There may be a point in your career trajectory when you'll need to work in New York or London. Can she adjust to this?" He turned his hands upward. "I'm not criticizing, son. I think she's a lovely girl, a beautiful girl, and I think she will make a great life partner. But you're both very young, and she's never been out of Virginia in any significant fashion."

"She's flexible. She'll do it."

"You also have to be clear with her about her wishes. Does she want a career? You know this has altered your mother's and my relationship. She gave up her ballet career to marry me. At first she seemed comfortable, but over the years, especially when she approached middle age, she became very resentful of me. I wouldn't want that to happen to you."

"Yes, sir, I understand. I will be clear, I'll talk to her. She won't say something just because I want to hear it. She's a very honest person."

"That she is. Understand, I'm not throwing cold water on your plan. I was young once." He smiled wanly. "I'm thinking ahead, that's all. Divorce ruins careers. Once married, stay married, no matter what. In the best of all possible worlds, you'll stay in love, you'll remain faithful, but should you" —he cleared his throat— "stray off the reservation, the bond must be strong enough to endure. Believe me, son, divorce derails careers, especially in our profession. You must be above reproach, which means if you can't fulfill your marriage vows to the letter, you must be discreet."

Charly hadn't expected this advice. "With a wife like Victoria, why would I even look at another woman?"

Thomas laughed. "You've got a point there, son."

"One other thing. What if she strays off the reservation?"

A cloud, a fleeting shift, passed over the older man's rugged features. "What's good for the goose is good for the gander? I don't think women . . . well . . . I don't know. I was going to say they don't fall victim to such behavior as often as men, but perhaps they don't have as many opportunities. It's not for me to say."

"I intend to speak to Mr. Savedge before Christmas. I still have things I want to sort out, and you've given me a lot to think over. I do want to talk to Vic."

"Have you asked her to marry you?"

"No. I had to speak to you first, Dad. And I need to speak to her father. I hope she'll say yes when I do ask her. I don't know what I'd do if she said no."

Thomas waved his hand, batting away the notion of a refusal. "Charly, I don't think you will meet too many women who would say no to you. You know, sex will get you together but won't keep you together. Marriage is a partnership. And when the children come, you are truly bound for life. Your blood and hers. Don't misunderstand me. I'm not hurrying you along to have children, but a man isn't a man until he's a father. You children have brought me the greatest happiness of my life."

Stunned, for his father so rarely opened his heart, Charly stammered, "Dad, I'll try to live up to your example."

Thomas, recovering from his outburst, laughed. "Might have to live some things down, too." He glanced over his son's blond head at the huge wall clock opposite his office. "I hate to cut this short, but Howard Nantes has an appointment with me. I should have scheduled more time."

Charly stood up, as did his father, who walked around from behind his desk, clasping his son by the shoulders. "Your mother and I are driving to the game. We'll take Victoria if you like."

"Thanks, Dad. She's going home. She's trying to help her mother out because Mr. Savedge has lost all their money again."

"I see." Thomas shook his head. "Well, I am sorry. R. J. is a wonderful, wonderful woman, and she doesn't deserve such problems." He quickly added, "No disrespect to Frank. He's a brave man. He just doesn't have the tools for business."

"Yes, sir."

Euphoric, Charly sang along with the radio the whole way back to Williamsburg. Vic had returned from her last class, and she and Chris were sunbathing in the backyard.

"Hey!" He bounded over to them. "I am taking you two to dinner."

"What about the training table? Coach will have a fit."

"I'll be there right on time, if we go now."

The three of them drove out to The Roadhouse and ate clams and corn chowder until they couldn't eat any more.

By the time Vic dropped him off at the jock dorm, he was giddy with happiness.

Chris realized Vic was right. She couldn't help but like Charly Harrison.

19

"More money than God, and what good does it do him?" demanded Sissy Wallace, her voluminous shell-encrusted purse on her right arm, hands on her hips.

"Uh-huh." Hojo filed her nails.

Georgia, standing next to Sissy, pointed her finger at Hojo, who was secure in command central high above them. "Girl, you don't do a lick of work. Or then again, maybe you do." Her eyes narrowed, her mauve eye shadow sticking in the creases of her eyelids.

Hojo slammed down her nail file. "What's that supposed to mean?"

"That you're no better than you should be." Georgia smiled falsely.

"Oh, Georgia, you got a mean mouth on you today. Mean reds." Sissy loved it, of course. "You're jealous of Yolanda. Ha. Jealous of a cow, and you're taking it out on Hojo."

"I don't have to take that kind of talk."

Before Georgia could embellish her retort, Bunny, followed by R. J., Vic, Chris, and Jinx, pushed through the door.

Georgia turned her back to Hojo. "Bunny, if you hire trash, you'll take out trash."

"I beg your pardon?" Bunny steeled herself for a Wallace Moment, as she called such events.

"Sissy and I walked in here to see Don, and this made-up cow

won't buzz him. Says he's in a meeting. She doesn't know her place."
Georgia pulled out from her cleavage a linen hanky with a G embroidered on it. She wore an orange halter top, in a small fit of rebellion as
well as a concession to the heat. It was not a good idea.

"Georgia's being fussy. Aren't we surprised? Hojo was perfectly polite," Sissy said, folding her arms over her chest.

R. J. nudged Vic, who tiptoed around the back of the reception
desk, heading toward the meeting room.

Bunny spoke sharply to Hojo, who still held a nail file in her right
hand. "This is a place of business, not a beauty parlor." Then she focused on Georgia and Sissy while Hojo fumed and Jinx and Chris
watched in fascination. "It's not unusual for Don to meet with people
on Friday afternoons. I know that Hojo would never keep you all from
my husband. Even though I am not happy about this filing of the nails
business, he really is in a meeting."

Vic reappeared. "He is."

"Perhaps I can help you all." Bunny smiled.

"We want Donny to get a Cadillac dealership," Sissy sweetly
pleaded. "Then we can drag Poppy down here and make him buy us
both Cadillacs. He won't let either of us drive his white Caddy. We
can't wait any longer. I have been waiting for a Cadillac since I was
twenty-five."

"Fourteen years." R. J. smiled sweetly at Sissy.

"Oh, R. J., you're such a card." Sissy playfully slapped R. J.'s bronzed
forearm.

"Getting a dealership, mmm, that takes some doing. Negotiations.
But I know how much you want your Cadillacs, and beautiful women
deserve Cadillacs. In fact, I think I should get one, too." The sisters
tittered, and Bunny put an arm around each sister's shoulder, gliding
toward the front door. "I will talk to Don about getting two Cadillacs
at a discount. I don't know if he can work it because the Williamsburg
dealer will want something in return, but I will make this my personal
mission."

"We knew we could count on you, Bunny," Sissy cooed as Bunny
artfully shoved them out the door, propelling them toward Georgia's
tank of a car.

R. J. checked her watch. "We'll just make it."

Bunny left her car, took a set of keys off Don's sales board, and pushed everyone into a used Jeep Grand Wagoneer that had just been traded in.

Mignon, standing with a group of friends in front of her school, didn't recognize her aunt or mother when the red Jeep pulled up to the curb. She coolly walked toward her mother, not wishing to appear too happy to see her until Vic rolled down her window in the backseat.

"Creep."

"Vic!" Mignon skipped over, opened the door, sprawling on her big sister's lap.

"Oh, God," Vic complained loudly. "My legs will be crushed."

"Oh, we are so funny today. I mean I could just die laughing. Hey, Chris. I'm glad you came back to see us. You could have left the Weirdo at school. Hi, Jinx."

"Hi, Mignon. Wasn't that Marjorie Solomon you were talking to? I thought you hated her?"

Mignon slid off Vic, squeezing herself between Chris and her sister as Bunny pulled out into the road. "It was, and you'll never guess what she did."

"Manners," R. J. said dryly.

Mignon leaned forward and kissed her mother on the cheek. "Hi, Mom." She kissed Bunny. "Hi, Aunt Bun. Cool wheels. I'll be sixteen in December."

"Don't start," R. J. warned as Bunny headed back to Surry Crossing.

"I could take everyone on field trips if I had this car."

"That's what worries me." Bunny winked as she looked back in the rearview mirror.

"Okay. I won't drive anyone under pain of death." She stopped midstream. "Hey, there's Walter Rendell. Slow down, Aunt Bunny. I want him to see me in the Wagoneer."

"For God's sake." Bunny did, however, slow down.

Mignon waved and then flopped back to the seat. "You'll never guess what Marjorie Solomon did."

"I can't wait, Mignon. I am sick with excitement," Vic said in falsetto.

"You are such a twit." Mignon turned her back on Vic, giving Chris and Jinx her full attention. "Marjorie flashed Buzz Schonfeld."

The name Schonfeld captured Bunny's attention, although she said nothing.

"What do you mean 'flashed'?" Vic reached for the Jesus strap as Bunny ran over a pothole.

Mignon unbuttoned her blouse, reaching in.

Vic reached around, grabbing her sister's wrists. "Stop. You'll create nausea."

"I wasn't really going to do it, but she did. She reached right in there, pulled out that puppy, and shook it at Buzz and Teddy."

"My little brother." Jinx's eyes widened.

"He didn't do anything. He just happened to be leaving the gym with Buzz. And Marjorie's got a set of bazookas!"

"Dear, what constitutes a bazooka?" R. J.'s silvery tone floated to the backseat.

"Mom, like so big if she jumped off a rock, she'd give herself a black eye. Like so big she can hold pencils underneath them. Like so big if she was as tall as Vic and ran into you, you'd be blind. Blinded by an erect nipple."

"Mignon, that's quite enough." R. J. put her hand to her eyes.

Bunny started laughing. "Now, Mignon, honey, tell me more about erect nipples."

"Bunny, don't encourage her." R. J. was laughing, too.

"She twists her nipples to make them stand up. No lie! She does it and then walks past the boys. And she has the top of her blouse unbuttoned. Poor Buzz."

"Poor Buzz?" Bunny fed her.

"Boner."

"Mignon!" R. J. was laughing and appalled at the same time.

"In his gym shorts. Grossed me out." Mignon made a face.

"Oh, sure," Vic teased her. "You probably ran for a camera." She squeezed Mignon's biceps.

Mignon turned around, sitting back properly on the seat. "Oh, yeah, you spent the summer sucking face with Charly Harrison. The summer of your erection."

"Actually, it would be the summer of *his* erection," Bunny said dryly.

"Mignon, you are vile." Vic crossed her arms over her chest.

"I may be vile, but at least I'm not exposing my breasts. And Coach had his back turned to Marjorie. I think she needs a breast reduction."

"The breast expert." Vic sighed, but she was laughing, too.

"Yours are perfect." Mignon pursed her lips. "She should copy yours. Of course, Jinx's are good, and Chris, I haven't seen you naked yet, but—"

"Mignon, you are quite out of line." R. J. stared at her in the rearview mirror.

"Oh, Mom, it's not like nobody knows what everybody has. We're all naked in gym class, and some of those poor girls need help. I am going to become a plastic surgeon and get rich, rich, rich."

"My sister, the boob doctor."

"I could do worse." Mignon basked in the attention. "Proctology."

By now they were all laughing so hard Bunny struggled to stay on the road.

"I was unaware that you paid so much attention to breasts. Mother, maybe we need to rethink Mignon's direction in life," Vic said.

"Ha ha." She closed her eyes then opened them. "But the best part was watching Buzz try to hide his you-know and walk at the same time."

R. J. turned to Bunny. "I don't remember having these conversations when we were her age."

"We didn't, sweetie. You were much too repressed. In fact, I'm flat-out amazed that you produced those two fine specimens in the backseat. I assume you only did it twice."

Mignon lurched forward, one hand on Bunny's seat, one on R. J.'s. "Aunt Bunny, was Mom really repressed? Like Episcopalians?"

"We are Episcopalians." R. J. shook her head.

"Your mother has remained a proper lady."

"Gee, we'll have to make up for it." Mignon pinched her mother's earlobes.

"Chris, I apologize for my unruly child."

"Mrs. Savedge, she's a one-woman show." Chris smiled.

"*The Gong Show*," Vic stated.

"*Laverne and Shirley*," Jinx added. "Mignon, if you're on boob patrol, I wonder what Lisa's up to. And for God's sake, don't tell my mother."

"Lisa's no flasher." Mignon liked Lisa, but knew she had a rebellious streak.

Bunny turned into the drive, slowed to miss Piper, and then parked the car. Mignon climbed over Vic and ran to embrace the dog.

"I will never have children. I live in fear of my genes," Vic said. She closed the door after Chris emerged, lightly brushing against her. A delicious chill ran across Vic's stomach.

"You'll have a house full of them," Bunny predicted. Mignon walked back to them, her arms raised at shoulder level, shaking her bosoms like a stripper, as she sang the stripper's song from the musical *Gypsy*.

Jinx called to R. J., "That's it, Mrs. Savedge. Put her on the stage. She can be a stripper."

"Porno movies," Vic said.

R. J., walking to the back door, asked, "Victoria, have you seen porno movies?"

"Yes, Mother." Vic blushed.

"I can't believe it." R. J. blushed.

As soon as they entered the house, Mignon zoomed straight for the refrigerator.

"Well, actually, Mrs. Savedge, a bunch of us rented one. It wasn't just Vic. Kind of a girls' stag party," Jinx explained.

"I have never seen such a thing." R. J. seemed genuinely surprised.

"Oh, I have," Bunny airily admitted. "They lack imagination, but, on the other hand, it does beat playing bridge with the girls."

"Mignon?" R. J. closed the refrigerator door.

"I haven't seen one."

"What a relief. Offer our guests refreshments before you partake of them yourself."

"Oh, yeah. Sorry, Mom." Mignon asked who wanted Cokes or drinks and filled the orders. Every time her mother's back was turned she'd perform the stripper shake.

Vic whispered to Chris, "If you did that, I'd tear your clothes off right here in the kitchen."

"You can do it later," Chris whispered back.

"You're talking about me!" Mignon handed Jinx a tall glass of soda water with a slice of lime.

"You wish." Chris laughed at her.

"But you were talking about breasts. My sister is" —Mignon lowered her voice— "the only six-foot-one-inch girl in Surry County. Some of those inches are her boobs."

"You are so out of control." Vic was ready to swat her.

"Mignon, since you have so much energy, I'm going to put it to good use." R. J. handed her a pair of gardening gloves. "Weed."

"Mom, I'm supposed to go to the game tonight."

R. J. checked the wall clock, a plastic cat whose eyes and tail moved. "One hour of weeding, a shower, then I'll drop you off back at school."

"I'll help you," Chris volunteered.

"Now, Chris, you sit here and enjoy yourself." R. J. pulled out a chair at the kitchen table.

"Thank you, Mrs. Savedge, but I would enjoy weeding the garden. I miss gardening."

Vic, Chris, and Mignon weeded while Jinx turned over soil with a little claw. She then put down a layer of rich, seal-brown mulch.

"Your ears look better," Jinx observed.

"Thanks," Mignon said. "I twist my posts about a thousand times a day. Thanks again for helping me buy them. You, too, Vic, even if you are hateful mean."

"So, Mignon, how did you get Hojo to pierce your ears?" Jinx figured there was more to the story than Mignon was telling.

"Asked her."

"Short answer from a usually long-winded twerp," Jinx observed.

"Hojo thinks she is the last word on fashion. Like, you should see the cropped fringe top she wears with painted-on jeans, cowboy boots, and a hat the color of her boots. Paints her fingernails to match. She doesn't always wear a bra either. Wowee."

"You are obsessed with breasts today." Vic laughed.

"It's hard not to notice when they're sticking right out at you, you know. I mean, where can you look? Hojo's got a good body, and she knows it."

"You just walked up to the reception desk and said, 'Pierce my ears'?" Jinx thought sooner or later she'd wheedle the truth out of her.

"Kind of. I told her I was a social outcast. Every girl in my class has pierced ears and Mom and Dad live in the Dark Ages, like, right after the fall of Rome. It took me a couple of visits because she knew Mom would be less than thrilled, like frosted Antarctica. But I told her it wouldn't last long. Mom is a very forgiving woman, and did she want me to be warped for life by my high-school experiences? Low self-esteem. Forever. Bad men." Mignon shuddered.

"Since when have you lacked in the self-esteem department?" Vic asked as she battled chickweed.

"Look who's talking."

Vic ignored her. Chris stood up, grabbed the wheelbarrow, and rolled it closer as they'd moved away from it, leaving piles of weeds in their wake.

Jinx listened as a boat under power tooted to one under sail. A vessel under sail always has the right of way.

"So what do you do when someone flashes you?" Mignon lagged behind the others in weeding.

"No one has ever flashed me," Vic said. "Come on, Mignon, work harder. You are a lazy ass as well as keeping us *abreast* of the times."

"We are so funny." Mignon minced about. "I know Marjorie Solomon is going to do it again."

"Don't look," said Jinx, offering sensible advice.

"Wear sunglasses," suggested Chris, gathering weed piles and tossing them in the wheelbarrow.

"Yeah. Great idea. I can see everyone, but they don't know I'm looking. That is so cool."

"Ray-Bans," Jinx said. "Sleek."

"I'll wear them in the shower in gym class, too. Surrounded by boobs. The really big ones are the worst, and Itsi Giorgianis has hair around her nipples. Can you stand it? I would die! I would shave every night. I would risk cutting off my own nipples."

"Puh-lease!" Vic threw weeds at her sister.

"It's just personal hygiene. Aunt Bunny had her upper lip waxed and a bikini wax—oh, ouch—so why can't Itsi get her tits waxed?"

"Because she knows you want to look at her," Jinx said, laughing.

"I do not." Mignon let out a small scream of disgust.

"It's okay, Mignon. You're my little sister. I love you no matter what." Vic feigned sincerity.

"Me, too. I have lots of gay friends. You can be my newest gay friend." Jinx reached the end of the rose bed.

"I would die!" Mignon's voice approached her upper limits.

"Bet you wouldn't," Chris teased her.

"I know you give Charly blow jobs, Vic."

Vic advanced on Mignon, who threw up her hands. She was no match for her taller, powerful sister. "I do not."

"I saw you this summer. He had his hands all over you."

"That doesn't constitute a hummer, Mignon." Jinx sank the spade into the mulch pile.

"If she jerks him off, she sucks him off."

"First off, you little asshole, I don't. But this is no way to talk in front of Chris. It's wearing thin, you know."

Mournfully, Mignon asked, "Hasn't anyone here even given a guy a blow job? I want to know all about it."

"Ask Hojo," Vic fired back.

"If she pierced your ears, she'll show you how to do it," Jinx added. "No teeth."

"Grooooss!"

"You're the one who wants to know about blow jobs," Chris reminded her, cleaning up the debris to her satisfaction.

"I do. I'm left out. Marjorie has great tits, and everyone knows it. She can get any boy she wants. Lisa has boys all over her. I'm like the slug of the tenth grade."

"Hey, I'm twenty-two, and I'm not doing anything. Besides, doing it just to do it is really uncool." Jinx was sympathetic.

"Yeah," Mignon agreed, but with little conviction. "If you did it, though, you'd tell me, wouldn't you?"

"Sure." Jinx laughed.

"Not me. You can't keep a secret," Vic taunted her.

"I can. I'm already keeping secrets."

Later the three college girls drove Mignon down to the high-school football game; then they trolled around town in the Impala, top down. With the three of them in the front seat, Vic could drive with her right arm around Chris. Jinx put her left arm around Chris so it looked okay.

By the time the game was over, Mignon back in the car, Vic's heart was blasting away. She could feel the pounding all over, especially in her crotch. She wondered how men functioned with a hard-on because the sensation she was feeling was pleasurable and painful.

While Mignon chattered away, Jinx, now in the backseat, rested her head back to stare at the stars. She envied Vic and Chris. She didn't envy them being women together, but she envied that physical connection, that excitement. She worried that she would never find it.

20

Once everyone finally crawled into bed, Vic waited for fifteen minutes and then bade Jinx good night.

She opened the door quietly to the guest room, whispering, "I thought I'd die. I thought they'd never go to bed." She closed the door behind her, locking it.

Just then a note slipped under the door between the guest room and Mignon's room. Vic retrieved it. Chris whispered, "She's relentless."

Vic scribbled, "Get lost!" on the note.

Chris said, "You can't do that. She'll know you're in here."

"Forgot." Vic's eyebrows shot upward.

"This ought to do it." Chris wrote, on a new sheet of paper, "Going to sleep. See you in the morning."

Vic shoved it under the door. To be sure, she carefully picked up the chair from behind the small desk and wedged it under the doorknob of the shared door. She switched off the small lamp by the bed and pulled up the covers, feeling the cool, clean sheets.

"Come here." Chris reached for her, pulling Vic onto her. She wrapped her arms around her neck, kissing her.

Try as they might, a few muffled moans escaped their lips. Enough to alert Mignon, who put her eye to the keyhole but couldn't see anything because of the dark. She listened intently. Someone was in there with Chris. She opened the door to the hall, tiptoed to the guest-room door, peered in the keyhole. There wasn't any more light from that angle.

Then she walked down the hall, careful not to step on the floor-boards that creaked, and opened the door to Vic's bedroom. Jinx was sound asleep. Vic's bed was empty.

Mignon, at first, was shocked that her sister was in Chris's room. Clearly, they weren't playing bridge. The shock quickly passed, curi-osity taking its place. Mignon now had another secret to keep.

21

The distinctive tang of fall filled the air, a rich perfume of river, leaves, and soil. Heavy with mist, opaque sunrise filtering through silver, it was a late September morning according to the calendar, but fall had arrived overnight. Nature's tempo changed, creatures moved faster, birds' eyes glittered more brightly, crickets sang louder. Even the river shrugged off its massive lethargy, flowing with a quickened pace.

Jinx, usually loath to rise early, surprised herself by waking at six. Vic, already dressed, smacked her bottom.

"Bacon." Jinx sniffed.

"Fall," Vic replied.

"Mmm." Jinx's feet hit the floor. "When did you get back in?"

"Uh, fourish."

"Must be good."

"Better than good. Rhapsody."

Jinx, now in the bathroom, toothbrush smeared with paste, said, "Rhapsody. I'll remember that."

Frank chattered at breakfast, a brief burst of happiness before retiring to his home office. Mignon scrutinized her sister as though seeing her for the first time, but she yakked like her old self.

Lisa Baptista tore down the drive at eight o'clock, honking all the way.

"Wow!" Mignon, who had been helping her mother spread fertilizer, let go of the handle and didn't notice as the spreader rolled down the undulating lawn.

Vic ran after it, catching it while her mother shouted how expensive fertilizer was.

Chris and Jinx were plucking apples off the two trees since that was the task R. J. had assigned them.

"Mignon!" R. J. yelled.

Mignon, squealing with excitement as she stood with Lisa admiring her "new" ancient Volvo, called, "I'm sorry, Mom. I'll be there in a minute." She clapped her hands at Lisa, unable to contain her enthusiasm. "This is so cool. Ultimate cool. Beyond cool. Frigid. December!"

"Well, the test was easy except for parallel parking. I had to do it twice—I was so nervous—but Mr. Trasker was real nice. Glad I got him for my test and not Miss Pyle. She'd have flunked me. She flunks everyone. I mean, like, she can't stand the thought of anyone getting their license on their birthday."

Jinx climbed down the ladder, walking over to her younger sister. "Wheels."

"Daddy bought them for me. Can you stand it!" Lisa jumped up and down as though on a pogo stick.

"Pretty cool." Jinx smiled. "You are so spoiled rotten, Lisa. I didn't get a car on my sixteenth birthday."

Vic joined them, Chris coming up behind her. "Jinx, your dad's making more money now."

"I have to pay for my insurance and the gas. Daddy says I have to learn the value of money." She pointed to her gold earrings. "He says I won't have any left for stuff like this, but I don't care. Wheels!"

"I'll bet Mom is thrilled," Jinx commented dryly.

"Yeah, she doesn't have to drive me anymore. She really is thrilled. But you'd better come home. Even for ten minutes. Just come say hi and don't have a fight. Then she'll be happy. And, well, I can't help it if Daddy didn't buy you a car. But come home. Really. It will shut Mom up."

"Mother will never be happy with me." A note of sourness crept into Jinx's voice.

"Just agree with her." Lisa, exasperated and with a tendency to dramatize, threw up her hands. "Mom is great if you agree with her. Doesn't matter if you really believe it or not. Lie."

"You'll make a wonderful politician," R. J. said as she joined them. "Happy birthday."

"Oh, thank you, Mrs. Savedge. May I take Mignon for a ride?"

"Of course." R. J. smiled. "Mignon, you will finish your job when you return. Right?"

"Yes, ma'am."

The two girls hopped in the sturdy faded-blue vehicle and backed around. As Lisa nosed down the driveway, a car careened in front of her. She drove off the crushed oyster shells and onto the grass.

Mignon, nonplussed, said, "Georgia might be right behind her, so be ready to get off the road again. If I were you, I'd get the hell out of here."

Lisa stepped on it once back on the driveway, sending shell bits scattering behind her.

Sissy slammed the door of her Plymouth, leaving the motor running. "Where's Frank?" she yelled to R. J., who was walking back down the lawn.

"In the house."

Vic trotted over and turned off Sissy's motor just as Georgia appeared in the driveway. Georgia had the presence of mind to turn off her motor.

Piper barked nonstop.

"Where is the slut?" Georgia's eyes bulged.

Chris, without thinking, shrank behind Vic.

"I beg your pardon?" Vic played for time.

"Sissy, my slut sister, and don't look surprised when I say that. Oh, hello, Chris, hello, Jinx." She waved at R. J., who rubbed her temples for a moment and then strode back up the lawn.

"Well, Miss Wallace, I'm sure you have your reasons." Vic kept an even tone.

"Reasons. Here's a reason." She held out her two hands indicating the length of a penis, in this case about seven inches. "I caught her. Oh, yes, I did—and I will kill her. I don't care if I spend the rest of my life in jail. It will be worth it!"

"Georgia, we couldn't have that." R. J.'s voice soothed, silky smooth. "Now, could we, girls? We just couldn't get by without seeing you out and about. Sissy's not worth killing."

This pleased Georgia, somewhat diverting her righteous anger. "That's nice of you to say." She lowered her tone. "I know, I have always known" —she dropped half an octave on "known"— "that Sissy has her weaknesses. No self-control. The smoking. The eating. The drinking. Adding fornicating to that list is not exactly a major surprise. Not that I spoke of it." She held up her hand as if asking for silence. "A woman is entitled to a little pleasure, but this really is, well, this is too much."

"Could I fetch you a drink?" Vic asked pleasantly.

"Oh, honey, the sun's not over the yardarm." Georgia shook her head. "But I could recover myself with some fortified orange juice. Yes, that would be most refreshing."

Vic understood that the word "fortify" meant load the goddamned orange juice with vodka. Since Georgia didn't wish to be seen guzzling a vodka martini at quarter past eight in the morning, she'd make do with laced orange juice.

Vic hurried into the kitchen, grabbed the OJ, and told Chris to get the vodka from the bar. Then she filled the glass half with vodka, half with orange juice.

"You'll flatten her," Chris observed.

"Are you kidding? Mother's milk to Georgia. This will kick-start her day." She kissed Chris on the lips, lightly, and then sailed out the back door, glass in hand, napkin underneath.

"Oh, thank you, dear." Georgia knocked the contents back in three huge gulps.

"Another?" Vic smiled.

"Wouldn't hurt me to get my vitamin C, now, would it?"

Vic returned shortly with another, although Georgia sipped this one, as R. J. maneuvered her into a seat, hoping that Frank had shut the door to his small office just off the house in what used to be the old summer kitchen. If they could humor Georgia, maybe they could avoid another catastrophe. Something usually got broken, and R. J. preferred it not be anything in her house.

The three young women stood in a semicircle around R. J. and Georgia, who were seated on the lawn furniture.

"Would you like toast?"

"I'd like to turn that immature vulgarian into toast. I'd like to toss her in a crocker sack in the James. Oh, R. J., you don't know what I put up with and all these years keeping her—depredations from Daddy. It would kill him—indeed, it would."

Jinx winked to Vic. Vic reached over, running her forefinger over the back of Chris's hand.

"I know how you protect Sissy. We all do." R. J. wondered how long this was going to take.

Georgia rolled her eyes. "Started when she was in tenth grade. Kissing and cuddling. Oh, my—my little sister was popular. Indeed. For all the wrong reasons, and it didn't take long for the kissing and cuddling to progress to more, uh, athletic forms of contact with the opposite sex. My sister is fairly fascinated with the hydraulics of the male member." Georgia closed her eyes, sipping for the strength to continue. She pointed at the three women, using her glass. "Girls, I remember what it was to be young. Someone comes along, someone like your Charly, and you can't sit still. The entire world revolves around him. I know. But with Sissy, the entire world revolves around whoever is around. And I don't think Daddy has a clue."

"You've done a good job keeping such upsetting information from Edward. He is not the most liberal of men." R. J. kept pumping her up.

"That's putting it mildly. Daddy puts women on a pedestal, and he expects them to stay there. Oh, yes." Another sip. "Well, I knew by the time I was at Mary Baldwin that Sissy was going to have a very different personal history than myself. Very different. Mmm-huh. And she never got pregnant. Not once. Her ovaries must be tilted. I know her mind is."

"Miss Wallace, are you sure I can't bring you something to eat? We have some biscuits left from breakfast. You know how good they are." Vic watched the orange juice go down.

"Oh, if it will make you happy. And I'd like some more orange juice, too. Vic, honey, you have the best orange juice."

As Chris and Vic disappeared to fill the order, Jinx put a stool under Georgia's feet. If Sissy did emerge before her sister was plotzed, this might impede Georgia's lurching up to assault her. "There you are, Miss Wallace."

"Thank you, Jinx, you have always been the most thoughtful child. You know I was watching those two go into the kitchen—salt and pepper, aren't they? One just as blond and the other jet-black hair. Such beautiful girls. Oh, well, where was I? Oh, thank you." She smiled broadly as Vic and Chris brought her biscuits, jam, butter on a tray, and another glass of orange juice. Vic had taken the precaution of also putting a cup of hot coffee on the tray. "She's been going down there to Don and Bunny's car lot. That's all right" —she waved her hand as though dismissing the visitation— "I go there, too, but she's fallen in with that Hojo. Thirty years difference between them if there's a day, but Sissy says they're 'girl pals.' Well, let me tell you, Hojo is not going to be a Sunday-school teacher. No, ma'am. And she tells my sister, 'You only live once. Do it now.' You get the idea."

R. J. crossed her long, lean legs. "Georgia, dear, exactly what did she do?"

"Hojo? I don't know what she's up to, and Sissy won't tell. Not that I'm interested." She popped a biscuit slathered in butter and jam into her mouth. "Marry young. That's my advice. What did Sissy do? I caught her giving Buzz Schonfeld a—I can't put it delicately. She had her mouth on his instrument, and the only reason I found her was because I went down to Don's to see a new truck. Just pricing."

"She did this at Uncle Don's?" Vic's mouth fell open.

"Not out on the parking lot." Georgia's voice rose. "No, she was back in the ladies' room, and Hojo was guarding it—trying not to be obvious. I knew perfectly well my sister was in there doing something. I thought burning one." She held up her hand. "Oh, yes—smokes dope. Grows it, too. Pin money. So I pulled my way right by Hojo, who grabbed my belt, and there she was. I was appalled!"

"Is it statutory rape if a woman engages in oral sex with a minor?" Jinx wondered.

"I don't know, but it's certainly bad manners. But then the Schonfelds are very interested in sex, mmm-huh. And I know Bunny put a stop to that. Damned straight." Georgia raised her forefinger.

R. J., processing this unsavory but ludicrous news, exhaled through her nostrils two streams of blue Lucky Strike smoke. She put her cigarette on the ashtray. "Georgia, I think none of us should speak of this."

"Of course, you know she carried on with Boonie Ashley." She paused while she waited for the name to have an effect, which it did. Boonie, proprietor of the local convenience store, was married. "I told myself then that they were both white and over twenty-one, if you'll pardon the expression. I like black people, I do, but I grew up with these expressions and I don't see a thing wrong with them. But a high-school boy—now that's trouble."

"Yes, it is. I expect, Sissy is seeking Frank's advice." R. J. couldn't get the picture of Sissy sucking off Buzz out of her mind.

"Hojo won't tell." Vic thought she had a bead on Hojo's character, smart with a wild streak.

"If Buzz has a grain of sense, he won't either." R. J. picked up her cigarette.

Georgia's hand flew to her bosom. "I'm certainly not going to put my sister in jail, ruin the family name, but I am deserving of some recompense for my watchful duties over Sissy. Really, you all have no idea."

"When things have cooled down, perhaps you, Sissy, and Frank should broach this subject without Edward, initially." R. J. reached for a biscuit.

"Yes." Georgia drained the coffee cup and then reached for the orange juice. "I am so thirsty and hungry, the change of seasons."

Frank, Sissy on his arm, walked around the house, Piper behind them. "Why, hello. Georgia, how good to see you."

Sissy's eyes, red and puffy, attested to her tears. "Don't you hit me."

"I'm not going to hit you. I just don't understand how you could do something like that at eight-thirty in the morning. I knew when you pulled out of the driveway you were up to something. So I followed you. How could you? In the ladies' room!"

"Well—" Sissy had no defense.

"Aren't you the lucky duck that everyone who works there is a man and uses the men's room?" Georgia, now feeling mellow, said to Frank, "This has got to stop."

"I believe it will. No reason to discuss it." He blushed slightly.

"We'll call on you later in the week." Georgia, with assistance from Vic, stood up.

"We will." Sissy was surprised.

"Yes. I'll talk to you about it later." Then to no one in particular Georgia said, "Heterosexual overdrive. Hotter than forty balled tomcats. That's the trouble."

"I can't believe you said that!" Sissy affected a pose of shock tinged with moral superiority.

"You just shut your mouth, girlie." Georgia, steady as a rock, pounded the bricks to her car.

Sissy, after a squeeze on her shoulder from Frank, daintily walked to her Plymouth.

As they both drove out, Chris said, "Girls just got to have fun."

Everybody looked at her and then laughed.

"Dad, could Sissy wind up in jail?" Vic asked once she recovered.

"Only if Nora presses charges, and she doesn't know. I doubt Buzz is going to enlighten her. It's all so embarrassing."

"But it is funny, Frank, you have to admit." R. J. laughed.

"Well, I guess sex is funny when it happens to someone else." He blushed again.

Juggling two lovers tested Vic's creativity. Charly, blessed with male myopia when it came to women as lovers, never had a clue. Chris, far more insightful, suspected Vic was sleeping with Charly, but she was terrified to ask. She knew Vic would tell her the truth.

Since Charly had a curfew, Vic would invite him over when Chris had classes and Charly didn't. This turned out to be only on Wednesday afternoons but he didn't complain, he was so thrilled they were sleeping together. Every night Vic slept at Chris's or vice versa. They couldn't stay away from one another. Since they were in different departments at school, they were rarely seen together on campus. Off campus they were inseparable.

Vic dutifully attended the next few home football games, taking Jinx and Chris with her. On weekends of away games, she drove home. She worried about money, and used that worry to keep her mind off her confusion over Chris and Charly. Mignon, in a growth spurt, shot up one full inch. She said her bones hurt from growing pains. As October unfolded with crystal-clear skies and the beginnings of color, Mignon moved into more maturity. The family breathed a collective sigh of relief. The Wallaces bickered, but no shingles were dropped from the roof, no ratshot was fired. Hojo transformed her red hair to brittle blonde. Bunny researched the nursery business with her usual thoroughness. R. J. told Frank he had to sign everything over to her. He did so and promptly sank into a genteel depression. The sisters began staking out where they were going to plant trees and shrubs for their nursery.

The days stayed toasty, the nights were crisp, and with each passing day the light softened. High color usually occurred in Surry County the last week of October and the first week of November, and this early November proved especially brilliant.

Williamsburg, across the James, was jammed with tourists. The campus of William and Mary glowed in the buttery light, the bricks warming to a paprika shade, the white window frames and doorjambs appearing even more white in contrast. Young people tagging along with parents often fell in love with William and Mary on such visits. They would return as students in a few years. The current students trotted across the quad and lawns. Blow-out exams were safely in the future. Like ships anchored offshore, they wouldn't come to port for some time. Late October and early November just made people happy, even giddy with happiness, and many declared it the most beautiful time of the year. They said the same thing during high spring, too. But fall's tapestry had a few melancholy threads woven alongside the brilliant reds, blazing oranges, and rich cadmium yellows. This knowledge of the coming winter sweetened the season.

Thoughtful people, or those old enough to remember, have reflected on how people party with a frenzy, couple with abandon, swim in champagne on the eve of disaster. Diaries and letters attest to the fact that the best parties ever in Virginia were held from 1859 to 1863. Somehow it made sense, like having Mardi Gras before Lent makes sense. Fall carried that sense of ending, of fleeting beauty.

Vic celebrated not at parties but with every breath. She loved the scent of fall. She loved the turning leaves. She loved the soft squish of the grass underfoot when she walked. She loved going home, rowing on the river, the water shining off her oars. She loved William and Mary with the fierceness of one who must soon say good-bye. The fact that she was a senior finally hit her. She loved her mother, father, and sister. She loved Piper. She loved the creamy, majestic cumulus clouds hovering over the tidy, sensible layout of the oldest part of the campus. She loved the zinnias in the garden, the late blooming roses. She loved the rose between Chris's legs. She loved Jinx's laugh. She loved the soft hair on Charly's chest. She loved her own body, the speed and strength of it. She loved hearing the screech of a seagull, the sound of ropes slapping against a mast. Life's fragmented beauty finally revealed itself, the pattern of the mosaic becoming clear: celebrate, dance, laugh, love.

Sex initiated her enlightenment, but it spread far beyond that activity. She understood that her mother loved life in a way Bunny did not. She thought Charly might surrender to the world's beauty in time. She wondered if it took men longer or if other men kept them from this wild, ferocious tide of emotion. Duty hung about their necks, a heavy wooden yoke much different from the yoke around female necks and, to her way of thinking, much worse. She began to see men differently; she began to see their suffering, and her heart opened to them as never before. Loving Chris made her sensitive to men. Loving Charly made her sensitive to women.

Life was older than reason. She now knew it, and she was astonished at how many people did not. They believed in false prophets when the smallest butterfly was proof of life's holiness.

She hoped Chris would follow her into this uncharted territory of feeling, of vision, of sensing. She knew Chris loved her, and she began to know that Chris, constrained by inner fears, carried more baggage than she herself did. Vic also began to understand that loving Chris would be a piercing social burden even as it was the springboard to her own spiritual awakening, to emotional fullness.

She loved Charly and Chris. She loved them differently and curiously, she wanted them to love one another. Why choose? Why accept the world's limiting structures? It was easy to love more than one person at a time. The world made it hard, the heart made it easy.

Thank God for Jinx. Vic could tell her what she felt and Jinx listened intently. Occasionally, she felt a flash of jealousy from Jinx over the time she spent with Chris, but it quickly subsided. Friendship was the truest love.

Charly, bursting with joy, dreamed of a future with Vic, one with a house and two cars and eventually children. Intelligent as he was, he didn't look beneath the surface, he didn't ask the difficult questions. Why? The world was made for Charly. He had a good heart. He would make it a better world. Loving gave him more compassion, but he didn't question the unwritten laws.

Chris questioned them silently. She feared the future. Love made her both happy and wretched, for she feared losing Vic. Why would a woman like Vic give up the privileges of eventually marrying Charly for the sake of loving her? It seemed incomprehensible to Chris that anyone would truly follow their heart, for childhood had taught her that social position and things were more important than people. She could see that the Savedges weren't that way, but could she let that old belief go? And why shouldn't Vic marry Charly? The more Chris was around him, the more she understood he was a lovable man. She evidenced little sexual feeling for men, but she could see his particular beauty. The more one loves, the more one has to lose. She tried to govern her love for Vic, but she couldn't. The force of the emotion blew away all restraint. She experienced moments when the fear evaporated, when tight in Vic's arms, she felt safe, light, silly even. She lived for those moments, and for the laughter. She had never laughed as much as she did around the Savedges, Jinx, and Charly. Even Piper made her laugh, and she fell in love with golden retrievers.

The laughter reached a crescendo the week before Thanksgiving vacation. No one could concentrate on their studies, as every student was thinking about going home or to a friend's for the holiday. Even professors, valiantly trying to cram facts, theories, and themes into young heads, struggled to concentrate.

Thursday at seven o'clock, it was already velvety dark. Vic and Chris picked up Charly from his forced feeding at the training table. He insisted on taking the women to dinner, where he sipped a Coke, watching them eat.

"We need to do something to remember this year. Something outrageous. Something that will become a legend at William and Mary," Vic said.

"What kind of a legend?" Chris munched on a French fry.

"If I were the drum major, the last time I'd take the home field, at the fading away of the drumbeat on the last song, I'd have the whole band turn its back to the opposing side and drop trou. That kind of legend."

"Wouldn't it be more exciting if they showed their front, too?" Chris giggled.

"I could catch a pass, make the touchdown, of course, and then keep running, just keep running," Charly offered.

"Poetic." Chris smiled.

"Come on, we've got to do something," Vic persisted. "We've got to let people know we were here. Provoke them to top us."

"What about locking all the doors to the administrative offices? You know, taking a soldering iron and sealing the locks shut," Charly suggested.

"Good," Chris said appreciatively.

"We could paint the grass on the quad," Charly suggested.

"Paint what?" Chris asked.

"A naked lady," Charly said.

"Only excite half the students. Have to paint a naked man, too," Chris added.

"I don't know," Vic said. "Everybody likes a naked lady." She didn't care what she said, she felt so free.

"What about all those teeny weenies dragged through campus by Mommy and Daddy?" Chris imagined the outrage. Plus the administration was still trying to live down the Alpha Tau incident.

"Well, let's do something." Chris finished the last of her fries. She would have hated to leave any.

"Follow me." Vic stood up.

23

The elderly monsignor of St. Bede's parish lived in a tidy house directly across from the church. A faithful laborer under the sign of the cross, his was an obedient nature. Monsignor Geoffrey Whitby believed in the sacraments, kept his questions about the infallibility of the pope to himself, and exhibited little or no sense of humor. Nothing about Christianity was funny to him. He couldn't imagine a waiter at the Last Supper calling out "Fettucini for Jesus." Or Mary Magdalene wearing a lift-and-separate bra. No. Christianity had to be solemn, serious, even censorious. If the God of the Old Testament only laughed two times, then so it would be for Monsignor Whitby. Therefore when he glanced out his upstairs window on that velvety night and beheld the Blessed Virgin Mother being transformed, he was not amused.

The Blessed Virgin Mother looked fetching in an apron, a chef's hat on her head, a hibachi in front of her. In her upraised hand, the one giving the blessing, Vic had taped a long fork with a blue handle. Rubber chickens laid on the hibachi. A blackboard announced in colored chalk, MARY'S BAR-B-QUE.

Vic and Charly had worked to transform the Mother of Jesus into a more contemporary mother while Chris, after writing the sign on the blackboard, had watched out for intruders.

When Monsignor Whitby, still wearing bedroom slippers, barreled out the front door of the house, Chris was amazed that an old man could move so quickly.

"Blasphemers!" He shook his fist.

"I've never seen a face exactly that color of purple," Vic gasped as Chris turned and broke into a dead run.

Charly replied, "I think that's the normal color of his nose. You ready to leave this party?"

They both ran out the back way, soon overtaking Chris. They flew down Richmond Road. Chris, not the athlete the other two were, begged for mercy.

Vic and Charly skidded to a stop and then turned back. Each one grabbed an arm and picked her up off her feet. They shuffled a few steps with her then got to laughing so hard they nearly dropped her.

"Oh, my God, the monsignor," Chris gasped. "He's going to die of heart failure."

Charly hummed a few bars of "Nearer My God to Thee," which set them off again.

"Mary looked great. She looked happy. She looked young. If the monsignor loved her he'd buy her an entire wardrobe. That would make any woman happy." Vic wiped her eyes.

In the distance they heard a siren. At first they paid no attention to the whining sound, but it kept getting closer and then cut off near where the church stood.

Charly frowned. "I bet the monsignor called the cops."

"Because of Our Lady of the Barbecue? We didn't harm anything." Chris suddenly had a vision of herself calling her father from the police station. This was not one of those reassuring visions where the Blessed Mother appeared to bestow her grace. She could imagine her father yanking her right out of school. He complained enough as it was about paying out-of-state tuition.

Vic checked her watch. "Charly, you'll never make it back on time."

"One thing at a time. Let's split up. I think I can get back in the dorm. Anyway, that's my problem. I'd rather not face the monsignor."

"Good idea," Vic agreed. "Chris, I'll take the longest route home by the east side of campus."

"Okay."

Charly loped to the corner, waved, and crossed the road as the two women quickly walked in opposite directions.

The police cruiser slowly drove by. Vic had the presence of mind to duck into a convenience store, where she bought a magazine. She watched the cop from inside. The monsignor might be old, but he wasn't blind, so she hoped he didn't get that good a look at them. She'd be easy to describe. How many six-feet-one-inch women with jet-black hair were there? Not that he would get her height exactly right.

Once the coast was again clear, Vic meandered homeward. A light shone in Chris's window. She tossed a small stone. Bull's-eye.

Chris opened the bedroom window, the cool November air rushing in. "Come on up."

Vic opened the back door, bounding up the steps, taking them in twos and even threes. The door to the apartment was open.

"I'm in the bedroom."

Vic closed the door behind her and dashed into the bedroom. Chris, wearing only her jeans, smiled. Vic wrapped her arms around Chris's small waist. She kissed her lips and then ran her tongue from her breasts down to the top of her jeans. Chris put her hand behind Vic's neck, leaning back.

"I have to have you." She picked Chris up, gently placing her on the bed. She covered her, kissing her, biting her, her head pounding.

"Take your clothes off," Chris gasped.

Vic rolled off, pulled her shirt over her head, unbuttoned her 501s with one swift motion of her hand, and untied her sneakers as Chris pulled off her own jeans.

The house was cool, a counterpoint to the heat of their bodies. Chris drew back the covers as Vic grabbed her from behind and bent her over the side of the bed.

"I love your ass." Vic's breasts touched Chris's back as she entered her with her fingers.

Chris crashed through the biggest orgasm she'd ever had, amazed at what Vic could do to her, amazed at her own body.

Chris, facing her, stomach flat against Vic's, rested her forehead on Vic's shoulder. "We don't even know what we can do."

A knock on the door brought their heads up.

"Chris," Charly called from the other side of the door.

"Oh, shit," Chris whispered.

Vic hopped out of bed, grabbed Chris's robe. "He couldn't get in the dorm. I have to let him in."

"Wait. I'll put on my robe and answer the door. You put on your clothes."

"Right." Flustered, Vic ripped off the robe, threw it at Chris while reaching for her jeans.

Chris ran her fingers through her hair, shook it, and then hurried for the door. "Be right there."

She opened the door and a grateful Charly stepped in. The temperature outside had dropped into the high forties, and he was wearing only a shirt, no jacket.

"I'm sorry to bother you—I'm stuck." He grinned. "Vic's not home, so I thought she might be here. I'm locked out."

"I'm here." Vic, hair combed, clothes back on—although she was in her bare feet—walked into the small living room. "God, Charly, you must be cold."

Had Charly not been raised as a Virginia gentleman, he would have said, You can warm me up. But he didn't. "Never compromise a lady good enough to share her body with you" was a rule drummed into his head. "A little." He smiled.

"Sit down." Chris breathed deeply. Maybe they'd wiggle out of this. "Let me get you coffee or something to warm you up."

"Thanks, but it'll keep me awake."

"Hot chocolate?"

"Uh—thank you."

Chris went into the kitchen, and Vic sat next to him on the sofa. He could smell her sweet odor, he could smell the sex, but thought it was his desire.

"Let's hope Todkill doesn't check your room." He was the graduate student in charge of keeping the football players in line during season.

"You've got one last game to play. It'd be awful to miss it." She paused and then smiled. " 'Course, they haven't a prayer without you."

"I haven't missed a curfew in four years." He dropped back on the sofa and put his hand on his knee. "If Coach finds out and benches me, well, I'll be bummed, but it's the only time I've screwed up."

Chris returned with hot chocolate, one for each of them. She needed chocolate. She sat across from the sofa in the comfortable Queen Anne chair.

"Come on, sit on the other side of Charly. He's cold." Vic smiled.

Chris rose, left the room, returning with a red blanket she draped over his shoulders. But she did sit next to him.

"Body heat." Vic felt incredibly excited. She wasn't sure why.

Chris looked over at Vic, picking up on her energy. She thought Vic was the most beautiful woman she had ever seen and Charly was quite handsome. It made sense that they would marry, but the thought of it tore her heart out. She wanted to marry Vic.

"Men would kill to be in my position." He laughed. "Being a little cold—hey, it's worth it."

"Flatterer," Chris replied, the shawl collar of her robe gaping just enough to reveal the outline of a lovely breast.

Charly noticed, his face reddening.

Vic noticed, a surge of lust flaming through her. Then she realized Charly had also noticed.

He turned to Vic, his face flushed, saw that hers was, too. Charly was not an unintelligent human. Chris was in her robe. Vic in her bare feet. It had taken Chris a little while to reach the door; Vic had emerged from the bedroom. He got it. His first reaction was shock. Not that the two women were sleeping together, but that Vic, his woman, was sleeping with Chris. Fear rapidly swept in where shock had been. Mingled with the fear was desire. His dick began to stiffen. It was confusing. He didn't want them to know he knew. He placed his mug on the coffee table, folding his hands in his lap, but it was too late.

Vic winked at Chris, "Honey, I think you're causing distress." She patted her own breast.

"Uh." Chris looked down then pulled her robe tighter. "Sorry."

"Don't be sorry." Vic laughed. "You've given us both pleasure." She turned her body to face Charly; she knew him well. She removed his hands from his crotch. "She's hot, isn't she?"

He blushed. "She is." Then he turned to Chris, "I hope I haven't offended you."

Chris glanced down at the considerable bulge in his pants. "I'll take it as a compliment."

He breathed in. "You know I was going to stay with you, Vic, but I can call Tom McBride. I can bunk in with him."

A flash of concern crossed Vic's features. She didn't want to hurt Chris by taking Charly to her apartment and leaving Chris. Vic didn't know if he knew. On the one hand, it seemed obvious; on the other hand, people routinely missed what was under their noses.

"Don't do that, Charly. We can work this out."

Chris sat up straight. Her robe opened again. "There's no point going back out again. You'll freeze."

He exhaled. "It is cold."

Chris, too, felt the tidal wave of sexual energy in the room. She was no fool. She knew in her heart that Vic had slept with Charly and was discreet enough to keep it from her. While that pained her, at this moment, seeing him, she felt heat rising up from her body. She wanted Vic. She wanted Charly, too. God knows, no one ever discussed this during sex education.

Vic felt Chris's desire. She had the advantage in that she'd slept with both of them. She could read them. They couldn't yet discern one another's moods.

Vic kissed Charly light on the lips as she reached for Chris's hand, pulling her closer. When she finished kissing Charly, she kissed Chris. The sight of two beautiful women kissing, one with her breast showing, sent all the blood in Charly's body straight to his dick. Beads of sweat dotted his forehead.

Chris, not quite sure of herself, but getting very excited, then kissed Charly.

Vic unzipped his pants, reaching in, packing her hand on his jockey shorts. Chris unbuckled his belt and opened the snap of his jeans. She lifted up his shirt, kissing his stomach.

Charly moaned.

Chris then kissed Vic, who moved her hand over his shaft to the tip of his penis. She took her hand and put Chris's on his dick.

Chris gently stroked him as Vic kissed Charly. Then Vic put her hand over Chris's, and they stroked him together.

"Come on," Vic whispered.

They floated into the bedroom. Chris dropped her robe on the floor. Charly sighed. Vic pulled off her shirt and jeans.

Chris thought he was the most beautiful man she had ever seen. She knew now that she was fundamentally gay, but Vic was excited, she was excited, Charly was excited. She could barely breathe.

Vic stood behind Charly, wrapping her arms around his waist. He closed his eyes, his hot dick pressed against Chris's stomach; she could feel his heartbeat in his penis. She kissed him as Vic ran her tongue down his backbone.

Then Chris stepped back, took his hand, and gently led him to the bed. He lay down as Chris got in the bed on the other side. She took her forefinger, tracing the outline of his lips, tracing between his pecs, down his stomach, tracing from the tip of his cock to his balls.

Vic was now on the other side of him. She kissed him; then with her tongue she retraced Chris's line. She put the tip of his dick in her mouth for just a moment, just enough to drive him crazy, and then she stopped, slid her crotch over his chest and grabbed Chris from behind.

She bit Chris's ear, the nape of her neck. She slid three fingers into her. Chris moaned, putting her left hand on Charly. Then Vic, who was incredibly strong, picked up Chris and sat her on Charly. She stayed behind Chris holding her as Chris carefully eased down on him. She whispered in Chris's ear, "Do it just for a little bit." Then she released her and returned to Charly to kiss him. "If you can, don't come."

In a few minutes, Vic straddled Charly, faced Chris, and kissed her.

"I love you," Chris whispered, holding her.

Vic kissed her hard, the sweat running down their bodies. "Don't come. Just wait." She lifted Chris up, who moved back between his legs as Vic slid off him. Chris moved up and down and then moved off.

"I could die right now." Charly's breathing came in gasps.

"Bend over, baby." Vic pushed pillows under Chris and motioned for Charly to enter her.

He held Chris's waist, slowly moving in and out until he couldn't help it, he had to pump it hard. Vic reached under Chris, touching her until both Chris and Charly came. He pulled out, still hard, and Vic pulled him on top of her. She came in about two seconds.

The three of them sprawled on the soaked bed, Chris's head on Vic's shoulder, Vic resting her head on Charly's shoulder.

"Thank you." Charly finally caught his breath.

"Thank you, too," Vic replied.

"Me, too."

"Aren't we polite?" Vic laughed.

"Jesus, if I don't play, this was worth it." He sighed.

"You'll play," Vic said encouragingly.

"Yeah," Chris agreed, and then looked up at Vic. "You are totally wild."

"You two inspired me." She threw her left leg between Charly's legs and her right leg between Chris's smooth legs. "You and the Blessed Virgin Mother."

24

A photograph of Our Lady of the Barbecue adorned the front page of the regional section of the newspaper. Monsignor Whitby complained bitterly of godless youth. High spirits never occurred to him. No suspects were in custody. No physical damage was reported, but the editorial page ran a column about the increased rowdiness of students, citing examples at other colleges as well as William and Mary.

Charly saw the newspaper as he took his seat in history class, pre-Revolutionary America. Chris didn't see it until after class. Vic read the story in class since she found concentration on the subject matter impossible.

After class she picked up Jinx, skipping out of the gym, her gym bag slung over her shoulder. As they strolled through the campus she told her everything.

"Wasn't it awkward?" Jinx asked.

"You mean more arms and legs to get tangled in?"

"No." Jinx moved her bag to her other shoulder. "This morning. What did you say to each other?"

"Oh, nothing. Everyone had to hurry to class. Neither of them seemed upset. They like each other."

"I hope so," Jinx said.

"Now what am I going to do?"

"Your life doesn't seem to be running according to plan."

"I never had a plan." Vic put her arm over Jinx's shoulder. "Mom and Dad, Aunt Bunny—maybe they have a plan for me, but I don't. I was ready to drop out of school and go to work, but Mom talked me out of it. I don't mind working. I just don't want to be stuck in an office."

"That severely limits your choices."

"Maybe I don't have to do anything."

"Possible."

"You don't sound convinced." Vic sighed, dropping her arm from Jinx's shoulders.

"I would imagine—and I have to imagine, since I don't know anyone in your circumstance and I think it is safe to say I will never be there—but I would imagine sooner or later Charly will want to marry you, and that will be the end of it. And who's to say he will want to sleep with both of you again? I mean it sounds great from a purely sexual point of view, but I don't know about it from an emotional point of view."

"Uh-huh."

They left campus, heading toward Jinx's apartment.

"So?" Jinx's eyebrow raised.

"So I don't know what I'm doing."

"That's obvious. Okay, what if I put a gun to your head and said, 'You have to choose.' What would you do? Don't think about it. Just react."

"Chris."

"Ah." Jinx dropped her head a moment and then lifted it. "Your life is going to be interesting."

"It already is. But that's what I feel. What I know is that it would be a lot easier to be with Charly for a million reasons."

"Does he know how you feel?"

"Of course not. I mean I love him. I do. How can I tell him something like that? Last night was spontaneous. I don't think he knew Chris and I are lovers. He didn't want to know."

"Well, girlfriend, how long can you keep both balls in the air—forgive the pun?"

"We could just go along." Vic shrugged.

"All three of you?" Jinx's voice rose.

"Well, not all three of us in bed all the time, Jinx. But . . . shit." Her stomach dropped; she felt a bolt of fear.

"Vic, if you can do it, do it. I'm not judge and jury. I just think the situation can last but so long. Sooner or later, one of them will start pulling on you. You're the one that's the monkey in the middle."

"That's such an awful phrase."

"Do you think Chris could live with a woman? It's one thing to have an affair, it's another thing to be a lesbian, I would guess."

"To come out?" Vic asked.

"No, not exactly. I mean to choose a woman and stick to it. She doesn't have to come out. Don't most gay people lie like rugs?"

"How the hell would I know?" A flash of irritation escaped Vic's lips. "I'm not lying."

"What if she wants to lie and you don't?"

"I don't know. I don't think of these things."

"That's obvious."

"Thanks."

"Someone has to think ahead, Vic. I'm not trying to ruin anything. I'm just asking questions." Jinx kicked some leaves out of her path. "You can't be in a relationship with a woman if she wants to hide and you don't, and does she even want to be in a relationship with you?"

"She does. I'm pretty sure she does."

"Does she know you've been sleeping with Charly?"

"We've never discussed it."

"That doesn't mean she doesn't know, for Christ sake."

"Yeah, I think she knows."

"Does he know you've been sleeping with her?"

Vic replied, "I told you. I don't think he knows."

"Think he'll get mad?" Jinx was glad she wasn't in Charly's shoes.

"No. He'd be hurt before he'd be mad."

"The longer he stays attached to you, the longer it takes him to find someone else."

"Bullshit. I can love him without marrying him."

"You can't sleep with him. I mean, you can, but Chris, who I happen to think is desperately in love with you, one woman's opinion, will

blow up before he will. He's a man, men don't take women's relationships seriously. If he puts two and two together, he'll discount it. He
wouldn't think he's sexist or anything, but men assume they come first.
He's no different."

They walked the rest of the way to Jinx's in silence.

As Jinx opened her front door, Vic finally said, "You're right. I
think you're right. Men believe they are first."

"As long as they're paid more, they will be. And who's going to
tell them they aren't?" Jinx said this as they walked into the kitchen.
"Hungry?"

"Starved."

"You butter the bread. I'll do the rest." Jinx tossed a package of
boiled ham and a cube of Swiss cheese on the counter; then she
grabbed a jar of hamburger pickles and a jar of mayonnaise. "Think
anyone at home knows about you and Chris?"

"No."

"Bunny will figure it out first. She's always looking, scanning the
radar," Jinx declared.

"She's scanning Don, not me."

"She scans everybody. It's like she has to know. Mom's like that. I
don't get it exactly. I'm too busy to care what anybody else is doing.
I'm putting pickles on, okay?"

"Lots."

Vic stepped out of the way as Jinx commandeered the buttered
bread. "Love must be a powerful thing. More powerful than—I suppose someday I'll know."

"It's wonderful and terrifying. You can't think. I will remember
until the day I die the first time I saw the light on Chris's cleavage. I
felt like I'd been blasted by a bolt of lightning. I had to have her. I
had to touch her and smell her. And then," she laughed, "song lyrics,
those stupid, vapid lyrics all sounded true and wise and God, it really is
horrible."

"And you truly don't feel that for Charly?"

"No. I love him. I like sex with him. I love being with him. We
know each other, through and through, but it's not the same."

"And it'd drive you insane to see him make love to Chris?"

"Just the reverse." She bit into the sandwich. "And I orchestrated it. You know what's really weird—I didn't know I had it in me. If you had told me in September that I'd go to bed with a woman and a man at the same time, I would have said you were certifiable."

"Would you do it again?"

"How do I know? It wasn't a rational event. It felt right at the time. I wanted to do it. And it was really, really exciting." She paused. "Maybe because we aren't supposed to do it or maybe because it's visual. You can watch."

"Pervert."

"So it would appear." Vic finished half her sandwich.

"I think I'd better make you another one."

"Finish yours first and let me finish mine. Then I'll know how hungry I am."

"I guess you are going to have to talk to each of them individually, don't you think?"

"Yes."

Jinx rose, made two more sandwiches, and then sat back down. "You need to keep your strength up, especially if you're going to keep up the recreational sex."

"I've been sleeping with him Wednesday afternoons because she's in class. And every night I've been with Chris." Vic's green eyes twinkled. "Maybe I need massive vitamin therapy."

"Bet you're glad Thanksgiving vacation starts in two days."

"Chris is coming home with me. She'll go home for Christmas, but we'll be together for Thanksgiving, my fave. And we'll go to the game, Charly's last. Got tickets for you, Mom, Dad, Mignon, Bunny, and Don. You should be proud of me. I really am organized."

"I am proud of you. I'll pay you for my ticket."

"No." Vic stopped and looked at Jinx's warm brown eyes. She felt as though she were seeing her dearest, oldest sister for the first time. She felt as though she could see straight through her. "Jinx, I don't know what I'd do without you." Tears rolled down Vic's cheeks.

Jinx got up, putting her arms around Vic. "You've bailed me out plenty of times."

"I love you. I'm so lucky to have you."

"I love you, too."

Vic pushed her chair back, stood up to hug Jinx with all her might. "I'm afraid I'm going to fuck up. I don't want to hurt anybody."

"I don't think we can go through life without hurting people, even when we don't want to, Vic. I don't know why it works that way, but I think it's the deal."

"There's got to be another way."

"Come on, finish your sandwich. Want another?"

"No, thank you."

They took their seats again. "Look, even if you are the best person in the world, people around you have expectations, right? Like my mother has expectations, and I don't fit them. I don't hate her. She makes me froth at the mouth, but I don't hate her. Still I can't be what my mother wants me to be, and I think that's just how it works whether it's parents or friends or lovers. They kind of invent you, and then one day they see the real you. And it's not the same person. So they either have to love the real you or find another invention. Of course, your parents are stuck with you, so they can ignore it or make up stories about how you're doing what they want. Mom does that. I hear her talking to her friends about how I'm dating this guy and that guy and I'm having the most fun any coed, her word, 'coed,' has ever had." Jinx sighed. "Fairy dust."

"Yeah. And when the fairy dust wears off, everyone feels betrayed."

"I haven't betrayed my mother. I don't think you've betrayed Charly. You never promised him marriage or fidelity, did you?"

"No."

"And what have you promised Chris?"

"Nothing. But I told her I loved her."

"Would you be faithful?"

"Yes. But you make me think, Jinx, you always do. If I marry Charly, the fairy dust will wear off. If I marry Chris, it will, too. Then what? Then I see her and she sees me and we either make it or break it."

"Yep. But any relationship that lasts is the same deal."

"Not us." Vic pointed at Jinx's heart.

"We've known one another all our lives. It's different when you grow up together. You see everything, pretty much. You can't hide anything."

"Not if you're true friends." Vic got up and opened a cupboard. "Mind if we eat up your chocolate chip cookies? I'll buy you more." Vic put the bag on the table and then started a pot of hot water for tea.

Vic fixed the tea, sat back down, and dunked cookies in her tea. "You know what I think? I think nobody wants you to be you. Your parents have this vision. Friends who aren't true friends have this vision or expectations, as you'd say. The church doesn't want you to be you. The government doesn't want you to be you. What people really want is obedience and conformity, even if it tears you in half."

"I agree." Jinx exhaled. "I don't know what to do about it except to be as true as I can to myself, to you, to the people who want me to be me."

"You know what Mom said to me once? I was in high school, and we were talking about the women's movement. There was a march or something like that, and I was full of questions and opinions and Mom said, 'I didn't conquer the world. I found a way to live in it.' It was so odd coming from her. It was like an explanation of why she wasn't marching, sort of, not that I ever thought she would. And I wonder if I will say that some day."

"It is odd, but I can hear your mother saying that. You know, Vic, maybe everyone who actually thinks for herself takes a step out of line. I kind of think it will happen to me some day, in a different way than it's happening to you, but I know I can't coast along. I can't go along. I can't. I mean, I'm not looking to be an obstructionist or anything, but I can't agree when I think something's not right or it's not going to work. Mom says men don't like women who think."

"Oh, they do. I mean a lot of them do. They just don't want you to disagree with them. But hey, women don't want you to disagree with them either."

"I don't know. Maybe we show it differently. I was just thinking, maybe it's easier to love a woman. For two women it's the same world. A woman and a man live in different worlds."

"Jinx, maybe we each live in a different world."

"And growing up is building bridges?" .

They sat there looking at one another, and Vic broke the silence. "I want to build bridges. I do. I don't want to be closed off from people, from life. I don't want to turn into a lot of what I see, closed and controlling. God, Jinx, I feel like I'm shedding my skin. I feel so raw, but I feel so alive. I have never felt this alive."

"Gotta shed your skin to get bigger."

I love you. Only you." Charly's voice sounded strong and clear.

"Where are you?" Vic had just walked into her apartment when the phone rang.

"Phone booth at Ewell Hall. I had a half hour before class. I had to call you. I want you to know I love you. I just want you."

"Hey, last night was my idea." She leaned against the kitchen counter.

"It's you, Vic. Last night was great, but I'm in love with you. I'll always be in love with you."

"I love you, too." She meant it, although that wasn't the whole story. Vic wished that she smoked. This would be a perfect time for a cigarette.

"Can I see you before you go home? I want to talk to you."

"Charly, let's do it after Thanksgiving. You have the game. Concentrate on that and—"

"You'll be there?" he interrupted.

"You know I will."

"Good." He was glad for the reassurance.

"And Mom and Dad and Mignon and Aunt Bunny and Uncle Don and Jinx and Chris. Aunt Bunny will be wearing her binoculars."

"Chris is going home with you?"

"Yes." She inhaled and then exhaled, concentrating on breathing.

"Last night was unique, but I'm still me and you're still you." She adroitly dropped Chris from the conversation.

"Uh, well, it was . . . unique." He hoped she believed he loved only her. He didn't really look at other women.

"That's the truth." She laughed and felt better when he did, too. "Charly, really, don't worry. I'm not worried about you. Things will all work out. They always do."

"Yeah, you're right."

"Guess you haven't been back to the dorm yet."

"No, after this class. I'm walking in like nothing happened. Why volunteer any information? No one may have noticed I wasn't in my room."

"Good idea. Let me know what happens. Well, I guess you can't because you'll be talking on the phone in the hall."

"I'll let you know. Hey, I've never missed a night, never missed a practice during the season since freshman year. They can stuff it."

"It will be your best game, Thanksgiving."

"Yeah?"

"Didn't I tell you I was clairvoyant?"

"I'm glad somebody is. Time to boogie. Vic, I love you. I want you to know I love you."

"I love you, too. Don't worry."

"Okay. Bye."

"Bye." She hung up the phone. A light breeze ruffled the leaves like feathers outside her window.

A few flaming maple leaves swirled to the green lawn, falling among the yellow oak and poplar leaves. She opened the window and let in the cool air filled with the fragrance of fall. Aunt Bunny bitterly complained about winter, comparing it to death, but Vic felt winter contained the beginning of life. Those beginnings were hidden from view, but they were there, waiting.

Being in college was a bit like being a seed in the ground during winter, Vic thought. Everyone watered you, put nutrients in the soil, waited for sunshine. At graduation you sent up your first shoot. It was a silly picture she had in her mind, all these seeds marching off the stage wearing mortarboards, tassels wiggling. Odd pictures often popped into her head. She wondered if other people's minds worked that way, too. She wasn't going to ask them in order to find out.

Maybe graduate school was a greenhouse. You could sit there for a few extra years before going out into the world. You still wouldn't need to fight the elements. But sooner or later, people did have to survive outside the university. If she married Charly, a burden would be lifted from her mind. She'd go where he'd go. His career, not hers, would be central. She didn't mind that, because in her fourth year she still had no pull in one direction or the other. She only knew she wanted to be outside.

And now, she knew she didn't want to marry Charly. Emotional truth was not something Vic avoided, but, like most people, it usually took her much longer to discover that emotional truth. She shrugged off the pressures from her family about marrying. To them it seemed a fait accompli. Everything was done except for the actual proposal, the actual ceremony. In their minds, she was already married—or so it seemed to her.

If Chris hadn't appeared, she probably would have married him. It was the right thing to do. She loved him. But somewhere, sometime a Chris would have walked into her life. What then?

Despite the tightening in her chest when she considered what she was going to have to do, she was grateful that Chris had appeared when she did. She was going to have to tell Charly that she wasn't going to marry him; tricky, since he hadn't formally proposed. She was going to have to tell her family that she wasn't getting married, and that if she could, she'd marry Chris. She wouldn't put it that way, exactly.

How do you do that? Tell people?

Jinx was right, Vic thought. People assume they know you. They create a future for you, and then are shocked when you have the audacity to create your own future.

Maybe life was one big curve ball, breaking high and outside. Vic folded her arms across her chest. Yes, maybe it was, but at least she was standing at the plate and not sitting in the stands. Better to strike out than to sit and watch. Better yet, hit the goddamned ball into the bleachers, curve ball or not.

A surge of energy flowed through her. It was her life.

A pounding in the stairwell diverted her eyes from the trees. The door flew open.

"Let's run away!" Chris announced as she entered, her lips glistening.

Vic hugged her. "Chris, I think we're going to have to face the music and dance."

"You lead, I'll follow," Chris answered with a kiss.

"How do you know I can lead?"

"I trust you."

Vic thought about that a moment and realized she trusted herself. She'd get through this. She'd get them both through it and Charly, too, she hoped. "The first thing I have to do is tell Charly I can't marry him. The second thing I have to do is tell my family I can't marry him. The third thing I have to do is tell them I'm in love with you."

Chris hugged her ever tighter. "They won't want to see me after that."

"Fine. Then they won't see me either." Vic kissed her cheek. "They'll be okay. At least, I think they will after the shock wears off. God, I hope so."

They both stared out the window. The wind blew a little stronger now.

"I don't especially like my family," Chris said. "I don't know when I'll tell them. I'm not being a chicken. I'll come out if that's what we're doing, but I don't know when I'll tell them. Is that cheating?"

"If you wait until I'm thirty, it is." Vic laughed.

Chris put her arm around her waist. A brilliant red leaf blew against the windowpane and remained there.

"About last night . . ."

"Uh-huh."

"Are you going to do it again? I know you've been sleeping with Charly. I never said anything. I wanted to, but, well, you know, he was first, I mean he knew you first, and you love him. But are you going to keep sleeping with him?"

"No."

Chris sagged with relief. "God, I am so glad." Then she stiffened a bit. "Will you miss it?"

"Sex with Charly?" Vic shrugged. "No. But if he walks out of my life—and I guess he'll have every reason to—I will miss him. I do love him, Chris, I really do. But not in the way he needs to be loved and not in the way I love you. I never felt for anyone what I feel for you. I didn't even know those feelings existed. It's kind of like . . . a tornado." She shrugged. "Not very original, but something powerful, uncontrollable, a force of nature."

"Me, too." She paused a long time. "It would kill me if you slept with him without me."

"Do you want us all to sleep together?"

An even longer pause followed. "You know, it was wild, just . . . wild. But I don't need to do it again." She held up her hand. "But I'm not sorry we did it. In a funny way, it makes me feel closer to you."

"Me, too." Vic had no desire to figure it out. Feeling it was enough.

"I wonder how it feels for him?"

"Confusing, maybe." Vic thought about his warm smile, his deep voice.

"Does he know about us?"

"I don't know." Vic thought he did, but the truth was she didn't know for certain.

"Poor guy." Chris watched as another leaf stuck to the window-pane, held there by the wind.

"He's very lovable, isn't he?" Vic said.

Chris nodded and then added, "But I have to admit that I want you for me even if he gets hurt. I don't want anyone to get hurt. I hate that, but it just happens."

"I'm starting to think that a lot of stuff just happens. People who think they can control life are full of bullshit. Major bullshit."

"When are you going to tell him?"

"After Thanksgiving. It'd be pretty shitty to screw around with his head before his last big game." Vic thought for a moment. "I hope it's the best game he ever plays. I hope he gets pro offers, you know. It would be great if something happened to kind of offset my telling him that we aren't going to ride off into the sunset."

Chris sighed. "I still wish we could run away."

"Maybe we will . . . afterward. Maybe they'll run us out of town.

Although I don't think I'd give people the pleasure of turning tail. I haven't done anything wrong. Neither have you."

"I'm a lover, not a fighter." Chris laughed.

"You might have to be both." Vic put her finger on the window-pane, as though touching the maple leaf. "You know, I never thought about being gay. I still don't really. But I've been thinking about my life—that it's my life, your life. Nobody is telling me what to do. It's funny, Chris, I never really had to fight. I'm white. We aren't poor. Well, we are now, but you know what I mean. I suppose being a woman imposes limitations on me, but I haven't run into them yet. Maybe that comes more when you're out there trying to get a job. I don't know. I never felt pressured to be anything but myself. I never felt out of step."

"We are now. We aren't dancing to their tune. You said face the music and dance, right? We aren't even on the same dance floor as most people."

Vic's face brightened. "I know and it's great. I feel so free. It's just great."

"You're great."

"Flatterer. I don't know why I feel this way, but I do. I feel like I could fly."

26

"I sn't your lavaliere getting heavy?" R. J. bemused, touched the heavy, powerful binoculars hanging around her sister's neck.

"Worth it. Look, we can get in and out of here." Bunny pointed to the slope of the pasture.

R. J. tapped the toe of her right boot against the ankle of her left, the sandy loam falling off. "Right. And there's plenty of shade over there. Be a good place for azaleas. They sell like hotcakes. Down by the water we can run willows. They love water. Redbuds, mmm, have to think about that. Got my soil map." She reached into her jacket pocket. "Bunny."

Bunny, binoculars to her eyes, was watching a red-tailed hawk. "You know, R. J., there's a whole world in the air." She dropped her binoculars, looking down at the earth. "And one down here, too."

"This is the one we have to work with." R. J. knelt down and pulled her pocketknife from her pocket, slipping the blade into the moist earth, cutting away the hay stubble. "See." Then she pointed to the spot on the map that Bunny had opened.

Both sisters hunkered down, studying the map. "Peters out if we get on higher ground."

"Yeah, but we can still use that soil. There's tough stuff that will grow in it or we can put pots in, you know, rich soil in the pots, the plants are already in the pots and when they're two or three years old, they're ready to go. We won't have to pot them."

"That's a good idea."

"The only problem is we have to buy the pots now. I was hoping not to lay out too much money. We need to buy seeds for the long haul. We'll make more money if we grow from seed. But we've got to get something going right off. We need saplings, small, but still, those plugs will run a couple of dollars each, depending on the type of brush or tree. And then we need a tractor, a fertilizer spreader. Big expense."

"I'll get the tractor. You're providing the land," Bunny said resolutely.

"Good." R. J. smiled and then returned her attention to the map. "Now here, all along the river except for in front of the house, I think we can use sod. There's a good return on sod farming. But the land is relatively level, soil's good from alluvial deposits. We'll have to pull it up in strips. Another expensive attachment for the tractor."

Bunny reviewed R. J.'s figures scribbled in pencil on the right side of the soil map. "You have been busy."

They both stood up. A half-mile walk would take them back home.

"I like to work. It's always better."

"Frank?"

R. J. shrugged. "He took his name off the deed. He rewrote his will. I am not responsible for his debts. Whatever he has in his portfolio will pay his debts. He says. Who knows? If there's a surplus, the girls get it, fifty-fifty. He signed everything last night in front of two witnesses."

"Discreet, I hope."

"Yes. Frank's depressed, of course." R. J. raised her voice. "But there's no other way. The leopard can't change his spots. You are what you are. You might be able to recognize a situation that will set you off, but if gambling's in your soul, it stays there."

"You don't think people can change?"

"Only so much. Look at us, Bunny. Have we changed?"

"The mirror tells me I have."

"That's superficial. Inside."

"Yes. You're a mother. That changed you. As for myself"—she

wrapped her forefingers around the binocular strap— "youth slips away and with it the idea that the future is exciting. I go from day to day."

They walked through the woods, the pine needles softening their tread.

"You can only live one day at a time," R. J. finally said. "And maybe what we lose are our illusions. Something better takes their place."

"I haven't found something better. You have the girls. Your hopes are in their future—don't you think?"

"Sure, but I have a future, too. Starting up our nursery." She jammed her hands in her pockets. "I don't know how we're going to do it, Bunny. It's hard, hard work and we can't afford to hire help, but dammit, we're going to do it."

"I'll do it to lose weight." Bunny could perform hard labor, which wasn't to say that she liked it. "And to make money. I don't feel that I have a place at the dealership anymore. Don asks my advice. He's good about that, but when I drive in, it's not like the old days. It's gotten so big, people have offices, and there's different departments, and I'm just Don's wife."

"Oh, sugar, they know you were the brains behind it. The Wallace girls came to you to find their Cadillacs. People know."

Bunny lifted her binoculars to inspect a huge nest in a tree. "Hmm, raptors, or could be a squirrel. Never saw so many squirrels as I have this year."

"Charly called Frank yesterday afternoon at the office."

"I knew it!"

R. J. smiled. "Now we don't know anything yet, but he made an appointment to talk to him first Saturday in December."

Bunny, binoculars now again on her chest, clapped her hands. "I knew it. A Christmas engagement."

"Don't put the cart before the horse." R. J. linked her arm with her sister's. "I reckon he will ask for our daughter's hand—but, oh, Bunny, she's young. They're both so young."

"Youth is wasted on the young. Who said that?"

"Most recently, you." R. J. pulled Bunny closer to her.

"Young but pliable. They'll grow together more easily, and they get along great. They're a good pair, and it is a brilliant match. That won't be lost on anybody."

"Least of all you."

Bunny laughed at herself. "When the money's gone love flies out the window. The money will never be gone for Vic if she marries that kind of wealth. A beautiful girl like that, my God, R. J., it's like seeing you at twenty-two all over again. Different haircut. Different clothes. It's eerie."

"My love didn't fly out the window."

"You're the exception that proves the rule. But for most people, money and love are intertwined. That's all." She paused. "But Vic and Charly are cute together. They just kind of fit."

"Seems like it."

"His family will set him up, you know."

"I hope so."

"It'll be less of a burden for you."

"Vic's not a burden."

"I didn't mean that. You know what I meant."

"I'd be a liar if I said I didn't wish for some help. Or at least, freedom from worry." R. J. stopped as they emerged from the woods, the late afternoon sun bright on the small, old peach orchard.

"Mom's peaches. Still producing," Bunny said in wonder.

"Got a lot up, too. The scarlet tanagers and orioles love what's left. Fruit trees just fascinate me."

"Lot of work."

"Bunny, everything's a lot of work."

"I suppose that's why it's important to do work you like."

They heard a horn toot in the distance, and Piper started barking.

"Bet the girls are back from college." R. J. quickened her step. "Vic said she'd drop off Jinx." R. J. smiled radiantly. "This is going to be a sumptuous Thanksgiving. I have so much to be thankful for."

"Let's start with good health. God, I sound like an old fart, and it used to drive me crazy when Mother would say that, but it's true." They stepped over the fallen peaches.

"It must be fun for Vic to have a close friend her own age," R. J.

thought aloud. "Mignon's so much younger. That always worried me. It was like having two kids who were not exactly sisters. Vic and Jinx were more like sisters than Vic and Mignon. Now she and Chris are like two peas in a pod. But I must say, Mignon has grown up so much in the last few months."

"You're a good mother, R. J.," Bunny said.

R. J. beamed. "Thanks, Bun."

"I envy you, and then sometimes I think, would I have wanted to get up three times during the night with an infant, and the measles, whooping cough, and mumps? And the back talk. I don't know if I could have done it."

"You could have. Are you kidding? Our mother raised us right."

They both laughed as they crested the last small rise before the house came into view. Then, like two college kids themselves, they raced back to the house, Bunny holding on to her binoculars.

Vic and Chris, petting an exuberant Piper, saw them running toward them.

"Girls, we're home!" R. J. laughed as she ran ahead, looking back over her shoulder.

"I'd win if I didn't have these binoculars!"

"The Bunny lavaliere," R. J. called as she reached her eldest daughter, giving her a bear hug. Then she gave one to Chris as well.

Bunny, a little out of breath, followed suit. "Happy Thanksgiving!"

27

There are times in life that are so radiant, so perfect, that they stay etched in the mind forever. We smile in remembrance, knowing that we can never fathom exactly why they were so great; they just were.

This Thanksgiving holiday at Surry Crossing was like that. R. J., Bunny, Vic, Mignon, and Chris laughed in the kitchen, at the table. Frank carved the turkey with coaching from Don. Jinx escaped her mother to join the Savedges. The Wallaces came over, providing their usual unrehearsed entertainment. Piper ate all the turkey scraps she could hold.

Everyone piled into three cars to go to the football game. At the old, brick stadium, the cool air accentuated the excitement. Cheerleaders worked the crowed into a frenzy, holding green-and-yellow pompons high in the air. The tribe fans waved pennants, their own pompons. Some wore green-and-yellow baseball hats, others wore green-and-yellow face paint. Bunny kept lending her binoculars to everyone until the last quarter. She couldn't bear to part with them then.

Charly scored the last touchdown. The stadium became a sea of green-and-yellow pompons; the screaming shook the foundations.

After the game, the Savedge party waited outside the locker room along with Charly's mother and father. He emerged to another chorus of triumph. He kissed his mother first, then Vic, then Mignon, then Bunny, and finally Chris. He hugged his father and shook hands with Frank and Don. He was leaving with his mother and father since they had yet to have their Thanksgiving dinner.

A glow of anticipation surrounded them all. Bunny couldn't stop smiling. The Harrisons fussed over Vic. Everyone knew, unspoken though it was, that Charly would soon be popping the question.

The only one not caught up in the anticipation was Vic. Even Chris anticipated it—although with dread. What if Vic changed her mind?

That night after everyone was asleep, Vic and Chris lay wrapped in one another's arms. A small pile of answered notes from Mignon rested on the nightstand.

"Vic, are you sure you can say no?"

"Hmm?" Vic nuzzled Chris's neck.

"It's going to be hard to refuse Charly's proposal when it comes."

"No, it won't. It will be hard to hurt him, but I can't lie. I can't do that."

"You sound so sure."

"Chris, don't worry. I can handle it. I'm not looking forward to it, but I'm not going to chicken out. I love you."

Somewhat relieved, Chris kissed Vic's cheek. "You know, I never thought about living my life with a woman. I kind of don't know what to expect. I mean, I know people will be upset, but knowing it and feeling it are two different things." She paused. "I guess we'll find out who our friends are."

"Being gay is a blessing. You weed out the trash early." Vic kissed her again. "I'm going to sleep. I'll wake up at five-thirty and go back to my room."

"I don't know how you can do that."

"Simple. The last thing you tell yourself before falling asleep is when you're going to wake up and then you do."

And she did. Chris was sound asleep as Vic tiptoed out of the room the next morning. She noticed another note had been slipped under the door and was about to ignore it, when she saw in the dim light that her own name was on the outside of it.

She picked it up, putting it in her robe pocket. When she reached her room she clicked on the night light.

The note read: *I know you're in there.*

A strong hand clasped Mignon's shoulder as she opened the door to the hallway at seven-thirty that morning.

"Come on. We're taking a walk," Vic commanded.

"Where?" Mignon apprehensively tried to wriggle away from her sister.

"Down to the mailbox and back or maybe we'll keep going to Richmond."

"Bet it's cold outside."

"That's what coats are for." Vic propelled her to the foot of the stairs, along the wide center hall, to the back room off the kitchen. She flipped a coat at Mignon and then grabbed one for herself.

Once out the door, Piper tagging along through the light mist, Mignon complained, "We can't be late for breakfast. Mom'll have a fit."

"She'll get over it. All right, Mignon, what's the deal?"

"What deal?"

Vic handed her the note. "Start here."

Shells crunching underfoot, Mignon glanced at the note and then shoved it in her plaid-lined barn jacket. "Nothing."

"You can do better than that."

"I don't care what you do."

"Oh, yes, you do, or you wouldn't have shoved the note under the door, Mignon. Let's just get it out and get it over with. Tell me what you're thinking."

A startled quail flew out of a hedge, a few throaty notes signifying its discomfort.

Mignon kicked a small stone with the tip of her shoe. "I don't think you and Chris are discussing astrophysics."

"Three points. Shoot again."

"Well . . . I don't care." She shrugged insouciantly. "I don't care what you do."

"Look, you want to know what I'm doing, you want to know why I'm doing it. You're the typical brat, worm, crud, nosy little sister." This was said with good humor.

"Want to hear what you are?"

"Queer. Is that what you're going to say? Go right ahead."

A hurt look crossed Mignon's face. "No, I wasn't going to say that. I would never say that. I don't care if you're queer. I mean that's not such a nice word, is it?"

"I don't know. I've never much thought about the words."

"Are you?"

"Queer?"

"Yeah."

"Always?"

"I don't know. I don't think so."

"Like, no kissing girls in high school?" Mignon hunched up her shoulders, a funny, elfin gesture.

"God, no." Vic laughed.

"So." Mignon breathed in the damp cool air, cool to the bone. "What happened?"

Vic slipped her arm through her sister's. "Don't know. I just looked at Chris one day, the sun fell like powdered gold on her, and I felt my heart thump. I couldn't exactly catch my breath and I—" She paused. "—I knew I loved her. And I lusted after her. I can't give you reasons. I don't have any. I just have feelings."

"Think that will happen to me?"

"Oh, Mignon, always back to you." Vic lowered her voice in mock frustration.

"I don't mean it like that. And anyway, what do you expect? I mean, were you just thinking about everyone else when you were fifteen? I bet you sat around and thought only about yourself. You just didn't say it. At least, I say it. But that's not what I meant."

"What do you mean then?"

"Will I fall in love like that some day?"

"How would I know?"

"You're my older sister. You're supposed to know everything. You're supposed to go first. That's the deal." Vic smiled as Mignon continued. "How do people fall in love? A brick hits you in the head? Your brains fall into your pants? What?"

"It's different for different people. I guess for me it was kind of love at first sight, but I didn't know it. For someone else, the person grows on them. Takes time. For other people, they start out just hating each other. That's what Aunt Bunny says. She thought Uncle Don was as attractive as dog breath. Sorry, Piper."

The golden retriever wagged her tail. No insult taken.

"They fought and insulted one another, and hey, somewhere along the way, I guess he started to look good to her. Who knows how it will happen to you?"

"If you're gay, maybe I'll be like that, too. Like maybe there's a gene or something. I could inherit it."

"You're so full of it. Jesus H. Christ on a raft. You are what you are. Whatever I am has nothing to do with you."

"Well, you didn't think you were gay when you were my age."

"I didn't think about anything except lacrosse and field hockey when I was your age, Mignon. I just wanted to play sports and pull my grades. We're very different."

"But how do you know?"

"You know when you need to know—about everything, not just being gay or falling in love. When you need to know something in life, it comes to you or you learn it or someone shows up and teaches you. That's as near as I can figure."

"I love you. You're my sister. I'd have to love you even if I didn't love you, but I don't want to be gay."

"You're not." Vic breathed in and then said, "I love you. I don't always know why. Seven years' difference is a lot. When we get older, it won't be such a gap, but when I was fourteen, you were seven and you were the biggest pest. I don't know why Mom and Dad waited so long to have you."

"I wasn't planned."

"But you know they wanted you more than anything."

"Now you can't have kids." Mignon thought about this as they reached the mailbox. She reached in and took out the *Richmond Times-Dispatch.*

"You're way ahead of me. I haven't thought that far."

"Vic, what about Charly?"

"I don't know." Vic draped her arm over the mailbox. "I have to do something. I have to do the right thing, but Jesus, I dread it." She looked straight at Mignon. "Are you going to run blabbing to Mom?"

"No," Mignon replied crossly, her voice rising.

"Guess that wasn't very fair of me. I'm sorry. I've got a lot to figure out."

They started back up the long drive.

"Couldn't you keep going out with Charly until I get big enough so that he might look at me? He is so totally cool."

Vic laughed. "No, I can't do that."

"But maybe if you kept going out with him you'd change your mind. You'd get tired of Chris."

"I'm not going to get tired of Chris, and even if I did, how do you know I wouldn't go out with another woman? Mignon, I'm not a faucet. I can't turn on and off."

"Yeah, but you went all this time without being gay."

"I can't explain it, but I swear to you, Mignon, it just is. It just is—like this mist burning off the river. It just is. I can't go back. I can't."

Mignon emitted a long, deep sigh. "It's going to be weird. Having a gay sister."

"Oh, just call me Twisted Sister. Sounds better than Queer Sister. And what? You're the only person in the world with a lesbian for a sister? Poor you."

"I don't care. I just said it will be weird. I'll get used to it."

"That's big of you."

"I have a generous disposition."

"Now are you going to act bizarre around Chris?"

"Nah. I'll try not to think of you kissing her."

"Mignon, you kill me. You really do. I'll try not to think of you kissing Buzz Schonfeld."

"I would never! Oh, how can you even say that?"

Vic whistled a few bars from "Dixie," which was another way of saying, Bullshit.

"Hey, it's Marjorie Solomon who wants to kiss him, not me. Oh, man." Mignon stopped for a moment. "She will make my life hell when she finds out I have a gay sister. Shit. Vic, don't come out until I graduate from high school."

"I doubt I will be the burning topic of the day at Surry High."

"No, but I will."

"That's right. I forgot. You're the most popular girl in the school."

"Asshole."

"Be more original."

"Dyke."

"That's interesting."

"Hey, it's not asshole."

"You're right." Vic watched a patch of ground fog in a hollow begin to disperse. "Let me tell Mom when I'm ready."

"Years."

"Not years, but when I'm ready. The first thing I have to do is talk to Charly."

"You fell out of love with him?"

"No. I loved him, but I didn't know what this kind of feeling was. It's kind of hard to know something when everything and everyone around you keeps you on a different track. Does that make sense? I didn't know any different, Mignon. I didn't know squat."

"So you are really and truly in love with Chris?"

"Yes, I am."

"Okay. What do you want me to do?"

"Nothing. Keep on keeping on, and don't drop the judicious hint. I know how you are. You've got a secret. It will kill you not to tell it."

"I might know more secrets than just yours," Mignon fired back.

"More power to you."

"Don't you want to try and get them out of me?"

"No, I don't. Right now I'm overwhelmed with my own life. When I get through all this I will beg you to tell me."

"You don't give me any credit."

"I do. I'm sure you have secrets."

"Not my secrets. Other people's secrets."

"Fine. Mignon, I'm on overload. Christ, I found out I'm gay. Or at least I'm in love with a woman, so everyone is going to call me gay. I might as well get used to it. I have this wonderful guy who's in love with me. I have to break up with him even though I really care about him. I do. Mom and Dad assume I'm going to marry him after college. I'm not. I have to contend with them. Dad's run us flat out of money. I can't walk off and leave Mom. And I can't leave you. You're going to college even if I have to pay for it."

Mignon leaned her shoulder next to Vic's for a few strides. "I do want to go to college."

"Well, baby cakes, you've got to work next summer. I've got to work."

"Dad might get the money back."

"Money and Dad are allergic to each other."

"Yeah. But why can't Mom borrow from Aunt Bunny?"

"Mmm, I don't think Uncle Don will go for it. If he lends us money, he probably won't get it back. That's the way he thinks. He won't do it."

"Why can't Aunt Bunny do it?"

"Because she feels the same way. She might not say it, but I don't think Aunt Bunny would give money to Dad."

"She's not giving it to Dad. She's giving it to Mom."

"Mignon, it's not going to happen. People are really weird about money. You think people are weird about sex . . ." She shook her head. "Doesn't matter. We'll get through it. But you've got to work next summer."

"I will. I'll work with Hojo."

"What's this with you and Hojo?"

"Nothing. I think she's funny."

"Funny enough to stick holes in your ears."

"Yeah. Guess I shouldn't work for Uncle Don."

Vic noticed the smoke from the chimney hanging over the roof. "Work for whoever you want who will hire you."

"Vic."

"What?"

"What if Chris gets tired of you? You ever think of that?"

"No."

"Maybe you should. You're going to dump Charly. What if you get dumped?"

"I can't change the way I feel. If I get dumped, hey, that's life."

"Maybe he'd take you back."

"Mignon, I can't go back to him. I'm not there." Vic blew air out her nostrils, two streams of condensation. "Is it that bad having a gay sister?"

"I don't know. I never had one before," Mignon replied saucily.

"Well, get used to it." She thought a moment. "When did you know?"

"Last visit."

"How?"

Mignon shrugged. "I just kind of did."

"You think Mom or Aunt Bunny knows? Dad wouldn't even think of it."

"No, but they'll figure it out eventually. Especially Aunt Bunny, sexual radar queen."

"Look who's talking."

"I don't really have a sexual radar. Last time, I snuck into your room in the middle of the night, and you weren't there. That's how I knew."

Piper lifted her head, sniffing the bacon odor escaping from the kitchen stove vent.

"Let's go in."

"Are you mad at me?" Mignon's voice wobbled a little.

"No. I just don't want to worry about you. I have enough to worry about."

"Are you scared?"

"No. I feel better in a way. But I have a shitload of stuff to deal with, you know."

"Everything's the same. Only you're different," Mignon said.

"Maybe I'm the same and everything else is different. Damned if I know."

29

Photographs of Charly filled the newspapers in Williamsburg and the surrounding counties. Clinging to the last days of Thanksgiving vacation, Vic didn't much notice. Monsignor Whitby certainly did.

When Charly showed up back at school that last Monday in November, he was whisked into the coach's office.

Coach Frascetti, a thickset man, drove straight to the point after showing him the complaint from Monsignor Whitby citing him and two unidentified women. "Charly, did you have anything to do with the statue of the Blessed Virgin Mother wearing, uh, cooking clothes?" Charly opened his mouth, but Coach held up his hand for silence. "Before you answer, consider this. You'll be hauled before the Dean of Men. Now if the season were still in full swing, I could bench you and everyone would be happy except for me, you, and the fans of Tribe football. Right? So the least that will happen is you'll listen to a harangue from Dean Hansen about responsibility, sensitivity to others. The worst that will happen is your ass will get kicked out of here, since the administration is extremely sensitive right now, but I think your father can fix that. Most likely you'll get some kind of suspension and you'll have to make it up to St. Bede's. I'm sure the monsignor will have a list of things for you to do. But there is another way. I've been talking to

Hap Stricker, our baseball coach." A gleam in Coach's eye indicated he thought he was quite creative. "He'll put you on his roster. Then he'll suspend you. You'll look crestfallen, and St. Bede's will be satisfied."

Charly sat facing his coach, his mind racing. He was not by nature a liar, nor did he want special treatment. On the other hand, the prospect of his father cutting a deal with the dean and making a sizable contribution to the alumni fund turned his stomach.

"Coach Frascetti, I was there. No sacrilege was intended."

"Okay. I'm proud of you for fessing up. Let me go talk to Hap."

"Sir, could I think about that? I appreciate all you've done for me, and I appreciate Coach Stricker thinking about this. I, well, if you could just give me until tonight. I want to make sure that what I'm doing is the right thing."

"Six o'clock. Call me by six." Coach Frascetti stood up from his desk chair. "I guess you weren't raised a Catholic."

"No, sir. Episcopalian."

"Well, I was. And the Blessed Virgin Mother finally looked like she was enjoying herself. Call me tonight, Charly. You let me take care of this."

"I'll call you, sir. Thank you."

Charly left the gym and reached Vic's apartment in twenty minutes. He told her about the meeting.

"I think I should go to Dean Hansen and get it over with," Charly concluded.

"It took three of us for that fashion show. Why should you go?"

"Your picture wasn't in the paper. The monsignor did say there were two girls, but Coach didn't push it. If I do penance, it'll blow over."

"Oh, Charly, let Coach Stricker put you on the baseball roster. Really. It's not worth suffering over because the old goat can't stand Mary with a barbecue apron on."

"I don't know."

"Three weeks, and we'll all be on Christmas vacation. The monsignor will be over it, too. At least wait until—what time do you have to call Coach Frascetti?"

"Six."

"Wait until then. You know, walk around, think it over, and call me before you call Coach."

"I thought I could stay here."

This wasn't in Vic's plan. "Sure. But I have to pick up Jinx. Here, you take my keys in case you want to go out. If something comes up, leave the keys over the doorjamb downstairs. But you wait right up until the deadline to talk again to Coach. It's a big decision, and there's no reason to be a hero about it. I mean, really, Charly, it's not like we did something all that wrong. Promise?"

"Yeah, okay." He kissed her on the lips.

"Help yourself to Coke and crackers. Sorry, it's all I've got," she called as she opened the front door.

"God, Vic, I'm going to have to make enough money to hire us a cook."

"That's right," she sang back as she headed down the steps.

Hearing Charly speak of the future knotted up her stomach. She'd think about that later. As Vic cranked up the Impala, she wished she had time to talk to Chris, but she was in class. Better get on with what she'd decided to do.

After Mary received her makeover, Monsignor Whitby had called the police, and then he called the papers. He wasn't likely to let this blow over now that he had identified Charly. No, it was glaringly obvious that the monsignor believed in punishment.

Charly, being a star athlete, could expect one of two things: to get let off the hook or to be made an example. Football season was over; Charly was expendable, and the administration would look good if they took a hard line. Coach Frascetti knew this but chose to keep it to himself. Luckily, he genuinely liked Charly, and his plan with Coach Stricker was a good one. It would appear that Charly was being punished, the administration would look good, the athletic department would appear morally responsive, the newspaper would have a story, and the monsignor could gloat.

If Charly's father tried to buy off the administration, that, too, could leak its way into the papers, causing new embarrassment.

Vic pulled into the parking lot behind the administration building.

She walked determinedly up the stairs and down the polished hall to Greg Hansen's office.

The secretary waffled when she asked to see the dean, but Vic persuaded her by explaining it was about the incident at St. Bede's.

She was soon ushered into a paneled office complete with leather chairs, diplomas on the wall, and one Greg Hansen, a thin man of around forty who approached his job with utter seriousness.

"Dean Hansen, I appreciate your seeing me on such short notice."

"Not at all, Victoria. This is a delicate situation with the community. As you know, these tensions between the college and the town are part and parcel of university life. Since the Middle Ages, actually." He smiled broadly. Formerly a history professor, he relished any chance to impress a listener with some arcane historical fact.

"I can solve your problems, sir, with Monsignor Whitby. I know that he's identified Charly Harrison from a photograph in the sports page. It's true that Charly was there, but he never touched the statue. I talked him into being my lookout. I did it, and he shouldn't have to be punished for my behavior."

Dean Hansen looked grave. He brought his hands together so that his fingertips touched, making a little tent. "I see."

"So I should be the one punished."

"The monsignor said there was another girl."

"She didn't do anything either, but when the monsignor came out the front door and yelled we all ran. If you'd seen him, Dean Hansen, you'd have run, too. But really, it was all me."

Dean Hansen appraised Vic. He had heard that Charly had a girlfriend, the most beautiful girl on campus, and he had to agree with that assessment. She was one of the most beautiful women he'd ever seen in his life. If her career at William and Mary was botched, it wouldn't be so bad. She'd marry Charly or someone else.

"Well now, Victoria, you know that this could get you expelled. We can't treat a matter of religion with insensitivity, and Monsignor Whitby feels that a desecration has taken place. I've been in touch with the Cardinal Newman group here on campus and they, too, are deeply disturbed. I think you should know what might be ahead."

"I do. But I can't let Charly pay for what I've done. He'll say he did it to protect me. Dean Hansen, I can't see that it's good for William and Mary to darken the reputation of one of its best students. I just have to face the music."

"I can appreciate that. Well, I'll call the monsignor," he said as he flipped over his day calendar pages. "I'll let you know what the disciplinary committee decides on Wednesday."

"Should I report to the Dean of Women?"

"No." He shook his head. "I'll take care of that. Leave your phone number with my secretary on the way out."

She found Jinx at her apartment planting bulbs in the front flower beds. The temperature had warmed up to the low sixties.

"Let me help you." Vic knelt down beside her.

"My landlady likes tulips, so I thought I'd put a bunch in for her. She's a sweet lady." Jinx appreciated her landlady's kind treatment.

"I think my ass is grass."

"There's a poetic turn of phrase." Jinx carefully pulled earth over a bulb shaped like the top of a Russian Orthodox church.

"Monsignor Whitby knows Charly was at the BVM and—"

"Back up."

"Charly's picture was all over the sports page."

"Ah."

"Yeah. So I just told Dean Hansen that I did the deed and talked Charly into being my lookout. It's the truth, pretty much. I did organize it."

Jinx had laid out the bags of bulbs according to color. She reached for a bulb that would bloom sunburst yellow. "Do you know what you're doing?"

"I owe Charly something, Jinx. The least I can do is take the blame."

"You really are going to leave him, aren't you?"

Vic swallowed hard. "I can't seem to work up my nerve to tell him."

"Jesus, Vic, you do lead an interesting life." Jinx plunked a bulb in the hole. "What if you get thrown out?"

"Then, I go." Vic felt the thin paperlike skin on the bulb.

"If you do get kicked out, what are you going to do about Chris? Your parents? Your future?"

"Get a job. Work until Chris graduates and then take it from there. Mom and Dad will be pretty upset."

"What kind of job?"

"I don't know, Jinx. Anything that will bring in money. Mom told me she and Aunt Bunny might be going into the nursery business. I don't know if they can hire me, but I'd really like that kind of work."

"Isn't this a grand sacrifice?"

"If I want my degree later, I can get it. One semester left. Big deal." Vic sounded stronger than she felt.

"It will be a big deal if they pass a flame thrower over your records."

"They can't do anything about my grades. I can finish at a community college."

"William and Mary looks better on a diploma."

"It will be on yours," Vic said with a smile, although she, too, thought the name "William and Mary" would be perfect on a diploma.

Jinx smiled back. "Do you think your Mom and Bunny really will go into business?"

"Yeah." She reached for another bulb. "Mom's mentioned it in passing a couple of times, but last visit she showed me soil maps, where she wants to put willows and stuff. I think she's serious. Oh, yeah—I forgot to tell you. Mignon knows about me and Chris."

Jinx stabbed into the earth with her trowel. "Jesus."

"She was pretty cool."

"For how long?" Jinx's brow wrinkled. "She won't be able to keep her mouth shut. This is just too good, and she's the first to know."

"She won't say anything."

"Wanna bet?"

"Five bucks."

"You're on."

"Time?"

"Six months. I mean, you'll have to tell your mom and dad by then." Jinx flicked dirt off her thigh.

"Before."

"What are you going to tell them about this?"

"The truth." Vic checked her watch. "I need to get back to the house. I left Charly there and told him not to do anything." Vic stood up, brushing off her jeans. "You know what?"

"What?"

"I'm not the least bit sorry I updated Mary's wardrobe."

Charly wasn't at her apartment. He left a note that he'd gone out to eat. He called just before six. She told him what she'd done. He argued with her, but she insisted what was done was done and there was no point in both of them getting into more trouble. He finally gave in.

Then she walked next door and told Chris everything.

"I hope you don't live to regret this," Chris said, worried.

"I won't."

"Is Charly coming back now that he doesn't have curfew?" she asked nervously.

"No, I talked him out of it."

Chris relaxed. "This is all so wild."

"At least we're not bored."

30

T he rising winter sun washed the bowl of the football stadium in scarlet.

Having kissed a sleeping Chris, Vic left her a note on the kitchen table. She needed to burn off energy; she needed to think. Running the stadium steps would do her a world of good.

She'd already trotted to the top and back ten times and intended to complete the process twenty more times when a figure in dark green sweats appeared on the track, running toward her with a familiar grace peculiarly his own.

Wordlessly he fell in next to her, and they ran the last sets of stadium steps together. By the time they'd finished, the frost was turning into glistening dew.

They walked around the track to cool down.

"Change your mind?"

"I thought I had you organized on that."

"Vic, you could get bounced right out of here."

"I'll get slapped on the wrist or forced to write 'I will not dress or undress the Blessed Virgin Mother' on the blackboard one thousand and one times."

"After Alpha Tau's disgrace, I think it's going to be more than a slap on the wrist."

"Charly, don't worry about me. If I'm out of here tomorrow, I'll survive, you know."

"Yeah, but come on, what's one more semester?"

"I can finish it up later, somewhere else, some other time. We went through all this last night."

"Oh, the phone. I want face-to-face, baby." He slapped her butt. "I thought maybe I could talk you out of this. I don't mind taking my licks."

"There's absolutely no point. None."

"What if I go to Dean Hansen and confess? Then we both get the proverbial boot. We'll be together."

"No."

"Or I could march in there and say you were covering my ass."

"Forget it. No one wants you out of William and Mary, including Dean Hansen. Why do you think Coach went to so much trouble? Just finish up. Then if you get drafted into the pros—"

"First of all, I'd be a last pick. This isn't a football powerhouse."

"But you are."

"Thanks." He paused. "I'll end up a stock broker. No one's going to draft me."

"Law school?"

"There are too many lawyers in the world." He laughed. "Actually I'm pretty psyched about learning the stock market."

She reached for his hand. "Don't rule anything out. It's a long way from here to graduation. And you will get drafted. Scouts have come to see you play. You know Coach has had calls. Just wait. You don't have to take any job offered you, but wouldn't it be fun to know? Just for the hell of it?"

He pulled her hand to his lips, kissing the cool flesh. "And what if I said yes, and got drafted by, um, Green Bay? Would you live in the frozen tundra?"

She swallowed hard. "It's not about what I want, it's about chances that come to few people. The stock market will always be there. You can study the market—maybe even work at a brokerage house in the off season. You can make a lot of money in football, a lot of money to invest."

"I'll make money no matter what I do." He grinned, exuding self-confidence.

"I've never heard you say that before."

"Money is the last thing people should talk about."

"Well . . . I guess if you have enough, it's not such a sore subject. I think Mom only talked about it to me because she was still pretty beat up by everything."

"I didn't mean that, honey."

"Oh, I know. I'm thinking out loud. I probably shouldn't. I do talk about money more than I should. It's been on my mind."

"You'll never have to work. You'll never have to worry about money. I promise."

"Charly, I want to work."

"Sure. I know you can't just sit around, but you will never, ever have to worry. I'll take care of everything." He put his arms around her.

She hugged him then, her arms around his waist. How was she ever going to let him go? Couldn't they stay close but forget marriage? She wondered if she was selfish in being able to enjoy them both physically or if it was just human. Love is love, sexual pleasure is sexual pleasure, she told herself. You're going to be dead a long time, so get a lot of both while you can.

"If I confessed and got thrown out with you, we could get married right away." His eyes sparkled.

Thinking fast, Vic replied, "And your mother and father would hate me. I'd much rather have them on my side than against me. Why make things difficult?"

"They'd get over it." But he knew she was right.

"Fat chance. I'd have to present them with four of the most perfect blond children in the world for them to forgive me."

"Blond?"

"Right. And they'd have to have names like Nigel and Clarissa." Vic burst out laughing—she couldn't help it. She didn't dislike Charly's parents, but they could be such awfully squeaky WASPs. Not that she wasn't a WASP, but the Savedges set less stock in it.

He laughed, too. "Dad would love it even more than Mom." He

stopped, reached for her hand, and kissed her. "Vic, let's go back to your place."

She wanted to make love to him. Even though she knew it was good-bye to that part of them, she wanted to make him happy one more time.

Vic drove them to Jinx's knowing she would be in class. Charly didn't ask any questions. Vic said this would be exciting, since it was kind of forbidden.

She pulled off his sweatshirt and then the T-shirt underneath. She ran her tongue from the waist of his sweatpants, up between his pecs, up to his Adam's apple, and to his lips.

She put her hands around his tight rear end, feeling the muscles, feeling him get very hard, very fast, next to her. She kept kissing him as she slid her left hand around and rested it on his jock strap, letting the heat from her hand make him crazy. Then she stripped off his sweatpants and jockstrap in one clean motion. She felt the smooth skin of his penis, the heat, the head. He kissed her forehead, her nose, her lips.

They launched themselves onto Jinx's unmade bed, coupled in seconds, came in minutes.

Charly rested on his elbows, over her, breathing hard. His penis softened for a moment and then stiffened again.

"Can men have multiple orgasms?" he whispered, quite thrilled with the possibility.

"Why not?" She moved herself under him. This time it took longer but was no less pleasurable.

Afterward, he rolled over on his side.

"For my first million, I'll write a book about multiorgasmic men." He stroked her stomach. He loved her washboard abs. "All they need is you."

They showered. Vic left Jinx a note, said she'd explain everything and that she owed her a dinner and a clean set of sheets. She did strip the bed and put on new sheets with Charly's help. She dropped him off at the dorm so he could change for class.

She drove out to the discount stores and bought a new set of white cotton sheets for Jinx and a reduced maroon blanket for herself.

She wasn't going to tell Chris. It would serve no purpose other than to hurt her. She probably should have ended it with Charly this morning, but she couldn't quite bring herself to say the words. Still, she knew that as good as sex with Charly felt, Chris's love was like a firebomb. Maybe she had needed one last time with Charly to be sure of where she stood.

She told herself it was nobody's business but her own, but a wave of guilt and confusion washed over her. She felt guilty because she had betrayed Chris, guilty because she was going to hurt Charly, guilty because she was going to let her parents down.

She fought back tears. Maybe the only way anyone learns anything is to make a mess, she thought. Well, she'd made quite a mess.

31

The monsignor, at first suspicious of Vic's confession as relayed by Dean Hansen, soon seized upon it with enthusiasm. Punishing a beautiful woman somehow provided more of an emotional reward than punishing a man.

Monsignor Whitby had graciously offered sherry to Dean Hansen and the two other college officials accompanying him.

The first step the monsignor wanted to take was to call a newspaper reporter with the story. Dean Hansen suggested that enough negative publicity for the college had been generated this year. Better to forgive and forget.

The monsignor resisted. Young people needed to be held accountable for their misdeeds.

As the discussion rolled into a monologue from the monsignor, the dean and his colleagues realized the only way to satisfy him while protecting the college would be to punish Victoria Savedge. Though none of them especially wished to do this since her record was spotless and her grades high, the needs of the whole had to take precedence over any of its parts.

After two hours of reaching for the decanter by the monsignor, the meeting concluded. The clergyman agreed not to call the local newspaper, radio, or TV stations with the story or tell anyone Vic's name. Dean Hansen would expel her from William and Mary. Of course, the

Cardinal Newman group on campus would be honored to receive a lecture from the monsignor on the Scripture mandates concerning relationships between men and women. The monsignor felt the college Catholic group had been avoiding him. He was assured that the campus church groups were all very busy. No slight was intended. The semester passes in the blink of an eye.

A mollified monsignor, all smiles, closed the doors to his office. The three less-than-thrilled university administration members walked back to the campus. Their compromise was that the school would not cite this on Vic's record. She would have to leave the college, but there would be no mention of it in her file.

When Dean Hansen called Vic into his office late Wednesday morning, he was impressed with her calm. But then, he'd been impressed when she'd confessed to the prank in the first place. She thanked him for keeping her record clean.

She asked if she would lose the work she'd completed to date, which would mean that wherever she'd transfer she'd have to complete one year instead of one semester. He said unfortunately she would lose the work she had completed to date; there was no other way since she couldn't take final exams.

Vic asked the dean to wait until Friday to call her parents. She wanted to go home and talk to them herself.

He agreed.

Vic shook his hand, walked out, and took a deep breath of clear, fall air. A profound sense of resolution filled her. She didn't exactly know why she felt so good, but she did.

She left a note at the dorm for Charly, promising to call him that night, telling him she'd be going home to break the news to her Mom and Dad tomorrow.

Jinx was in class so Vic walked to her house and left her a similar note.

She walked back through campus and noticed how the symmetry of the elegant brick buildings suggested order. And conformity. Rigidity. She felt as if she were seeing William and Mary, her Alma Mater, in a new way for the first time.

Chris discovered Vic waiting in the hall outside her American poetry seminar. "Hello."

"Hello."

They walked silently down the steps and out onto the grass.

"You look happy, Vic."

"I am. I'm a free woman," Vic said with a quiet smile.

"Oh, no." Chris didn't share Vic's happiness. She was afraid that in a year or two, Vic would regret this. Even more, she felt guilty that she didn't confess, too.

"I feel . . . clean."

"I feel kind of bad that I didn't own up to it."

"You need to get your degree and I don't. Anyway, it was my idea."

"I went along with it."

"Oh, you sound just like Charly."

"He's right." Chris always felt a pang of fear when Charly's name was mentioned.

"I know what I'm doing. Now let's go home and celebrate." She whispered in her ear. "I'm going to make you so hot you'll beg me for it."

Chris blushed. "Vic, just seeing you makes me hot."

"Even hotter, then." Vic wanted to kiss her ear. "Let's make love and make love and make love. Then I've got to go home and get it over with." She sighed.

"Tonight?"

Vic paused. "Tomorrow morning. But you might have to tie me up to keep me tonight." She winked.

"How do you think of these things?" Chris marveled at Vic's indefatigable sexual energy and imagination.

"I don't know. But I never thought of them until I met you."

32

Whitecaps frothed the top of the James due to a stiff wind blowing up from the southeast, not the usual direction. Small-craft warning flags flapped in the wind at boathouses and yacht clubs up and down the river, the metal bits on the ropes clanging insistently against the flag poles.

Charly borrowed a buddy's car to get to his appointment with Mr. Savedge. As the Jamestown ferry docked at Scotland Wharf, he was heartened as always at how agricultural Surry County remained. Southside Virginia existed in a time apart from the rest of the state. He liked that.

Ever since the night he'd gone to bed with both Vic and Chris, he'd obsessively thought about them, alternating between heightened sexual desire, at the idea of the two women making love to one another, and terror. Women finding one another sexually desirable seemed reasonable to him. Women were sex, the center of all desire. He didn't think that he was sharing Vic with Chris. He thought of their relationship as a friendship with something extra.

He wondered if he should talk to Vic about her friendship with Chris.

He liked Chris. She was pleasant and pretty. Making love to her had been no chore, but he couldn't honestly say he was sexually

attracted to her. Vic was always the center of his attention. He was like
a tuning fork. When she came near him, he vibrated.

Surely, she felt that way about him. Her kisses were passionate, her
body turned hot under his touch, she wanted him inside her. They belonged together.

The town of Surry came into view. He drove down Main Street,
turned at the alley behind Frank's office, and parked. He stepped out
into the wind, better than brisk, closed his eyes, and breathed deeply.

Just as he reached the front door, Sissy Wallace opened it from the
inside.

"Why, I thought it was you. I haven't seen you for too long." Sissy
beamed. She'd grown fond of Charly over the previous summer.

"Hello, Miss Wallace. Good to see you."

"You come on in here this minute. We're going to get a terrible
blow. Maybe it will do some of my pruning for me. I have to do all the
yard work now that Poppy's old and Georgia might break one of her
precious nails." She closed the door behind him. "I was just leaving,
you see. Frank's our lawyer, and I so enjoy talking to him, but today it
was a business call, not social. Poppy has let Yolanda in the kitchen.
She lives in the kitchen. This just won't do. Georgia indulges him. Says
Yolanda makes him happy. Well, I say she's a cow and Poppy can find
his happiness elsewhere."

"Uh, I'm sorry to hear that, Miss Wallace," Charly replied, surprised that Sissy would call another woman a cow. Perhaps a few margaritas were behind her.

"If I put up with her, I'll go mad. If I don't, he'll cut me out of the
will again. It's tiresome." Her lower lip, bright red, jutted out petu-
lantly. " 'Course, Georgia will indulge him morning, noon, and night.
She's banking on my losing my temper somewhere along the way so
he'll tear up the will and me with it. I know how she thinks, the snake."

"I'm sorry you're unhappy, Miss Wallace."

Charly hoped Frank would come out of his office as they stood in
the front hall. He didn't know if Frank's secretary had heard him, but
he knew how Sissy could talk.

"Well, I'm not wretchedly unhappy, Charly, not throw-myself-on-
the-ground-and-eat-dirt kind of unhappy." She brightened. "A Cadil-

lac would restore my spirits considerably, and you know, Bunny says she will help me get one wholesale. I want a cream-colored Cadillac with a sea foam interior, I do. I'll wear a scarf to match the interior . . . brings out the color of my eyes, although you're used to looking into Vic's eyes. Now aren't they the brightest green you've ever seen? Like a cat. Her mother, too. Maybe they're both cats. Graceful as cats. Land sakes, here I am talking about me and you played that wonderful football game, why, we are all so proud of you, Charly Harrison. Proud as punch."

Finally, Frank's secretary, Mildred, appeared. She winked at Charly. "Mr. Savedge is expecting you."

"Well, let me hurry before this storm breaks. I suppose I'll have to tolerate Yolanda. I can't turn her out in a hurricane." She laughed. "Maybe I could turn out Poppy instead." She opened the door, the wind pulling it closed with a bang.

Frank walked out and shook Charly's hand. "Sorry, I didn't know Sissy Wallace had given you the benefit of her person."

Frank's office was clean and spare. A threadbare dark blue Chinese rug covered the floor and two brown leather wing chairs, as worn as the rug, faced his desk.

Frank sat in one and invited Charly to take the other.

"Would you like a drink?"

"No, sir, thank you."

"I suppose you heard all about Yolanda."

Charly laughed. "Poppy Wallace is really something, keeping a woman in the kitchen."

"Actually Yolanda is a cow."

Charly burst out laughing. "I thought Sissy was joking when she called Yolanda a cow."

"No. Yolanda really is a cow. The last of his old Jersey herd and Edward decided she shouldn't live outside anymore. She can stay in the kitchen when the weather's bad. He says it's a linoleum floor and she won't hurt anything."

"Is he . . . you know." Charly touched his temple with his forefinger.

Frank leaned back in the chair, crossing one leg over the other. "No, I don't think so. I think he's reached that age when anything or anyone that's still around from his glory days is now very dear to him. She's the last of that bloodline from his big herd. Each year he'd breed less and less. In his prime, he ran three successful businesses simultaneously. The dairy was just one. Had a lot of pride in that." Frank rolled a pencil to his telephone and then stopped it. "Well, I don't reckon you're here to talk about cattle and the Wallaces."

"No, sir, although the Wallaces are unique."

"Charly, every damned resident of Surry County is unique."

"Yes, sir." Charly smiled, breathed deeply, and said with great confidence, "I am here to ask for the hand of your daughter, sir. I love her. I will provide for her and I will do everything in my power to make her happy."

This came as no surprise to Frank. "I believe you will."

"I love her, Mr. Savedge. I don't think I could live without her."

"I want her husband to be a gentleman, a man who will cherish her, support her, respect her. I believe you will do that, and I grant you permission to ask for her hand."

"Thank you, sir."

"I assume you haven't asked her yet."

"No, sir. I had to speak to you first."

"Have you planned anything?" Frank smiled. "I guess I'm curious, though perhaps it's none of my business. I took R. J. fishing and waited for the sun to rise over the James, when I proposed. I put the ring in her tackle box." He smiled again, remembering how fast his heart had thumped, how he had almost forgotten to breathe and became light-headed. "Vic loves the river, you know."

He smiled broadly. "Part of me wants to race back to school and ask her right now and part of me wants to plan it. I'd like to ask her Christmas Eve. I was thinking I'd tie a red ribbon through the ring and hang it from a branch of the tree or maybe from the mistletoe. I haven't made up my mind."

"You'll figure it out splendidly. I have no doubt of that." Frank stood up to shake Charly's hand.

Charly rose. "Thank you, sir. Thank you so much."

Frank clapped him on the back. "Come on. We'd better go home to R. J. You can't drive back to Williamsburg now. It's really going to be a big one."

They reached Surry Crossing just as the heavens opened.

Frank said nothing to his wife. Mignon stayed glued to Charly, and Frank didn't want to break the news with his youngest there. Charly called Vic and told her he wasn't in the dorm. If she guessed why he was at Surry Crossing, she didn't let on.

Finally Frank told Mignon to go to her room and study. He and R. J. had some business to discuss with Charly. When they told R. J. the news, she cried, hugging Charly and kissing Frank. She said she was happy that Vic had such a good young man. Yet she thought to herself that Vic was so young and the world so big. Couldn't they wait a year or two? But she kept these thoughts inside. After all, she had married at twenty.

H ow could you?" R. J. was so upset she whipped the kitchen
counter with her dish towel.

"Mom, it's not all that bad." Vic faced her mother.

Both women were standing at the kitchen sink. Piper sat between
them, intently watching the exchange.

Outside, tree limbs lay scattered over the lawn. The storm that had
roared through Surry Crossing the night before was now worrying
ships on the Atlantic. Charly had returned to William and Mary early
in the morning, so Vic had missed him.

"People are sensitive to things like this, Victoria. You don't just go
around dressing up a religious icon like the Virgin Mary."

"Everything was really okay. Her barbecue apron was clean, her
chef's hat perfect, and all her cooking utensils were clean, too. You
would have been pleased at her turnout." Vic's green eyes lit up as she
described the statue. "She looked just like one of the girls. I even
thought I'd change her outfit to go with the season. You know, a William and Mary sweatshirt for football games, a pennant, maybe a wrap-
around skirt and a TriDelt pen for rush week."

R. J. laughed. She couldn't help herself. "Honey, the Virgin Mary
would be a Kappa Kappa Gamma."

"Without a doubt."

R. J. leaned forward and kissed her daughter on the cheek. "Oh, well—no harm done, I guess."

"Uh, that's not exactly all that happened."

R. J. straightened her shoulders. "Oh?"

"The monsignor saw me. Anyway, he went to the dean." She paused. "And to make a long story short, I'm expelled."

"What? Oh, Vic, you can't be." R. J.'s dismay was palpable. Piper licked her hand.

"I suppose I could have lied my way out of it, but that didn't seem right. I did it."

"But it's such an extreme punishment."

"Yeah, it is. But after the Alpha Tau stuff, I guess they figured they had to crack down. So . . ." She shrugged.

R. J. leaned against the sink. "This is just terrible. Your father and I will go right down there. We'll talk to the dean. We'll talk to the president if we have to. You are so close to graduating and . . ."

"Don't. Mom, please don't."

"Listen, young lady, in the state of Virginia there are only two diplomas that matter, William and Mary or the University of Virginia. I guess we can haul you over to Charlottesville."

"No. I'll figure this out. If I had to go somewhere else, I'd rather it be Tech."

"Tech? What in the world are you thinking?" R. J.'s face turned red. "Next you'll tell me you want to go to VMI!" R. J. sat down and put her head in her hands. "What are we going to tell your father?"

"The truth." Vic stood behind her mother, her hand on her shoulder.

"Of course, we'll tell him the truth, dammit, it's just how we'll tell him. And Bunny. Lord, it will be all over town. I suppose Jinx knows everything."

"Yes."

"Regina will worm it out of her. We might as well put an advertisement in the Norfolk paper." A hint of sarcasm flickered from R. J.

"It's not like I've killed anyone. All I did was create Mary's barbecue."

R. J. swiveled around, looking up at her daughter. "I guess that's how we know Mary is Catholic. If she were an Episcopalian, she'd be wearing a pink and green dress with three strands of pearls and matching earrings, and she'd be holding a cocktail." She let out a small laugh. "Which reminds me, you'll have to talk to Father Dermott about this."

"Mom, we're Episcopalians. Why do I have to talk to him?"

"Because we live here and because the word will fly around this country like a balloon with the wind escaping. You don't want the good father to think you're sacrilegious."

"I am sacrilegious, sort of."

"You can keep that to yourself."

"You really think I have to call on him?"

"Of course you do."

"Couldn't we send all the Catholics back to Maryland?"

R. J. pulled Vic into a kitchen chair. "You're being a bad girl."

"Yes." Vic showed no sign of remorse.

R. J. grew solemn. "Honey, you have to finish college."

"No."

R. J. folded her hands together. "What has gotten into you?"

"I don't know exactly. Just let me find a job."

"Here?"

"Well, I could look in Williamsburg." Vic was trying to find the right way to approach her mother about what she really wanted to do.

"To be close to Charly?"

"That wouldn't hurt," Vic mumbled unconvincingly. "I don't suppose you're going to tell me why he was here?"

"To pay a call. And have you considered that you might not get a job in town after your escapade?"

"No one knows about it other than the monsignor and the dean."

"I see." She drew a deep breath. "And what does Charly say about this?"

"He's upset."

"I would expect that Jinx is upset, too."

"She thinks I'm bone stupid."

"Yes, well, she has a point there." R. J. leaned toward Vic. "Were you alone in this achievement?"

"Sure. Who else would be so dumb?"

"I can think of at least two other people and given your power of persuasion, probably more."

"It was just me."

"What on earth got into you?"

"You already asked me that, and I said I didn't know."

"Oh, Victoria Vance, you don't just go out and tape barbecue forks to the Virgin Mother's hands."

"Didn't you ever just do something for the hell of it? You were bored or you were full of yourself or the moon was full? I don't have a reason. I wasn't an abused child. My parents weren't alcoholic. I just took a notion," Vic said firmly.

R. J. studied her eldest, noting the strong jaw, the determination underlying her beauty. "Actually, dear, I have taken few notions in my life, and I think I'm the poorer for it. I have tried to be logical, efficient, and organized. There have been times when I've bored myself silly."

"You've never bored anyone else."

"Thank you, dear, that's a pretty thing to say." R. J. leaned back in her chair with a flop. "Your father is going to be fit to be tied. And your sister will think it's too, too divine." She looked out the window; the river was still stirred up. "Are you in love with Charly?"

"Where did that come from?"

"From the heart." R. J. knew in her bones that something was different. When she and Frank were first together they were besotted with one another. She hadn't observed that in Vic. She had observed it in Charly.

"I thought you liked him."

"I do. It's just—oh, I don't know." R. J. reached for her Lucky Strikes.

"I know why he came over, Mom."

"Did he tell you?"

"No, he didn't."

"Then maybe you don't know why he paid a call."

"I'm not stupid."

"That, from a girl who's just gotten herself thrown out of college in her senior year over a prank. You might want to revise your statement."

"Yes, well . . . Look, do you think if I marry Charly, his family will settle money on us?"

"Yes," R. J. stated flatly.

"Would my marrying him help you?"

"I don't know. I don't know what you two will do with your money."

"Aunt Bunny always implied that it would help the family."

A flash of irritation crossed R. J.'s face. "She doesn't know what she's talking about. And since when have you listened to Bunny?"

"I'm worried about money. I'm worried about Surry Crossing."

"Don't. I told you to get through school. It's not your concern." R. J.'s voice rose.

"It is if you're going to kill yourself worrying and working." Vic's tone matched her mother's.

"Do I look like I'm at death's door?"

"No."

"All right, then."

"Mom, do you want me to get married?"

A long silence followed.

"I want you to be happy. He's a wonderful young man. When you're young, a husband seems easy to find, but as you go along in life you discover there aren't that many people who will go the distance. So many things go into the equation: physical attraction and ethics and temperament and sense of humor and well, so many things."

"Is marriage important to you?"

"For you?"

"For me and in general, I suppose." Vic folded her hands.

Another long silence followed, finally broken by R. J. after she exhaled a plume of smoke. "I think it's important to be married if one is going to have children. After that, I don't know. I used to be quite sure of all these things, but having seen some ugly, ugly divorces among my friends . . . all I can say is if children are part of your dream, then it is important. I suppose my advice is, look before you leap. But then, you know Charly. You've been dating him for over a year, you worked together last summer. You say you love him. And I assume you want children some day."

"If they turn out like Mignon, I'm not so sure."

"She's a good kid."

"Yeah," Vic grudgingly replied. "Actually, she's grown up a lot lately."

"It comes in fits and starts. I'm still growing. I think you never stop if you're lucky."

"Why did you want to know if I love Charly?"

"I've known you longer than anyone on earth, honey. I became acquainted with you in the womb." She smiled. "Correct me if I'm wrong, but I don't think you love him quite as much as he loves you."

Vic's heart thumped against her rib cage. Was this the time to tell her mother? Did she have the courage? She'd just told R. J. she'd gotten her ass kicked out of school. It would be a lot at one time. "Mother, I think women love differently than men."

R. J. appraised Vic. "You're very diplomatic."

"Don't you think it's true?"

"No. Love is love, and it may never be in an equal balance between people. I don't think men love more or women love more. I love your father, for instance, and I know he loves me. Sometimes he loves more and sometimes I love more. There's no rhyme or reason to it that I can fathom. Men and women may show their love differently. Men want to provide, want to be heroes, but then I've seen plenty of women be heroes, too. But you know if there is that rolling passion like the tide, you can feel it. I don't feel that from you."

Vic closed her eyes and then slowly opened them. "Because it's not there."

"I see."

"But I do love him, Mother, I do. I love who he is. I love his body. I love his mind."

"But you're always in control of your own emotions."

"Yes."

"Love and reason aren't compatible." R. J. reached for her pack of Luckies, tapping out another one, lighting it with the stub of her first cigarette. "Honey, maybe if we were reasonable, no two people would ever get together. If you think about the demands of marriage, of a close relationship, I don't know if anyone would ever enter into it. Love is blind. It has to be."

"I don't know."

"Can you be a wife?"

"No, Mom, I can't. I can be a partner, I can be a friend, but I don't think I can be a wife."

R. J. smiled. "Sometimes I think you have an old head on those beautiful shoulders and then other times, like upon hearing that you've been expelled from school, I wonder what's up there."

"Me, too." She paused. "You're worried about me getting married."

"Of course I am. Any mother would worry. I want you to be happy, and you can't be happy being second fiddle. You need to be in charge, to some extent you need to be the center of attention. You don't ask for it, honey, it just comes to you. I don't know how happy you'd be otherwise."

"So you don't think I'd be a good wife, either?"

"You could, but you'll pay a high price. I sometimes think your generation is different from mine, like night and day. You girls aren't going to fulfill yourself by comparing notes about your children. You all want to be out and doing, out in the world."

"If I marry Charly you think I'll be towed along behind him?" she questioned, interested in her mother's perspective.

"Inevitably, because of who he is. You're both stars in your own ways, but it's still a man's world."

"I always thought you wanted me to get married."

"I do. When you're ready and to the right man, of course, I do. There's a great joy in a strong marriage, a joy without substitute."

"You know a lot, Mom."

"When you get as old as I am, you're bound to have learned a little something."

"You're not old."

"Yes, well, I'm not young."

"If it will make you feel better, Charly hasn't asked me to marry him."

"What makes me feel better is that we've had this talk." She rose. "All right, let's go to town. We might as well talk to your father and get it over with. He should be in a good mood, and that's in your favor."

"I'm glad to hear that."

"He's dealing with the Wallaces again. That always perks him up."

"Ratshot again?"

"No. This time it's Yolanda."

"God, she must be the oldest living cow in the universe."

"She's the oldest living cow in the Wallace's kitchen now."

"Mom, there's something else I'd like to talk about."

R. J., who had stood up to grab her purse off the counter, turned around, "Shoot."

"You said you and Aunt Bunny might start a nursery."

"We're making progress."

"That's what I would love to do. Mom, let me work for you. I'll work cheap. I'd love to start a business like that."

R. J. put her purse back on the counter. "Do you really think, if you marry him, Charly would live here?"

"Mom, we just sat here and both agreed I wouldn't make a good wife."

"A traditional wife," R. J. added as a modification.

"Some people are afraid of life, they're afraid to leave home and go out into the world." Vic rose and walked over to her mother to look her straight in the eye. "I'm not like that. But Surry Crossing is exactly where I want to be. Working with living things is exactly what I want to do."

"You don't really expect me to agree to your not finishing college, do you?"

"Mom, I do. I finally found what I want to do."

R. J. glanced out the window at the river, at the pale winter light. "Well, I didn't finish college either. I'd be very pleased if you did."

"Mignon can finish for both of us."

A long silence followed. Even Piper was quiet, waiting for R. J. to speak.

"All right. I'll talk to Bunny. I can't make a decision without her."

34

While not pleased, Frank took the news better than either
R. J. or Vic had anticipated. R. J. decided to stay in town to
run a few errands and then come home with Frank. She
asked Vic to pick up Mignon from school.

As the aqua-and-white Impala idled in front of Surry High, Vic
watched the cirrus clouds turn to ruddy gold. A large wreath hung over
the main door to the school, a reminder that she hadn't bought a single
Christmas present. A leather bomber jacket would be just right for
Charly, but they were so expensive. She would have to think of something else. She wanted to buy a ring for Chris and then thought that
might best be given on graduation day. Maybe a necklace or something for Christmas, depending on the cost.

A small Ranger truck pulled up behind her and the driver honked
the horn. Vic twisted around to see Teeney Rendell.

Vic cut her motor, got out, and walked to the Ranger. "Hey, what
are you doing home?"

"Holyoke lets us out early. I'm here to pick up Walter. You look
good, as always."

"You do, too." Vic noticed Teeney's seal-brown eyes and hair.
"Last time I saw you was summer."

"This summer I'm getting a job on Cape Cod. The pay's better
than around here. I guess you'll be looking for a real job soon."

"Yeah."

"You'll find a good one. I just know it." A flicker of recognition lit up Teeney's eyes.

Vic, too, recognized it, an unspoken sense. She knew without being told that Teeney was gay.

The school bell rang, sounding oddly like the bell at a boxing match.

"You know, there are times when I miss this place. Miss being in high school without a thought in my head." Vic pushed away from the truck.

"You always had thoughts in your head."

Vic laughed. "If I don't see you, have a Merry Christmas."

"You, too, Vic."

Vic walked over to the Impala, leaning against the passenger door. She didn't want being gay to become the center of her existence, but she had to look at herself in a new way. After all, she only knew how to be straight; that's what she was trained to be. She would have to change her expectations of herself. Maybe it was like learning a new language.

"Vic!" Mignon waved, skipping toward her. When she reached her, she threw her arms around her sister, giving her a big hug. "What are you doing here?"

"Being your chauffeur. Mom's busy."

"See you, Walter." Mignon waved at the best-looking guy in the senior class. She whispered, "Makes me hurt to look at him." She raised her voice when she recognized Teeney in the Ranger. "Hey, Teeney."

"Hey, Mignon." Teeney waved as she fired up the Ford truck and pulled away from the curb.

As students walked by, Mignon nodded or called out. She'd become a popular girl. Vic noticed she even said something nice to Marjorie Solomon.

"Such discipline."

Mignon wrinkled her nose. " 'Cause you and Mom beat me black and blue." She hopped in the car, bouncing on the seat. "When are you going to let me drive this 'chine?"

"When you get your first gray hair." Vic cranked the motor, gunning it down the road just to hear Mignon squeal.

"Hey, where are we going?"

"Uncle Don's. I want to make a phone call without Mom and Dad around. Uncle Don will let me use the phone in his office."

"Oh, baby." Mignon rolled her eyes and then made kissing sounds.

"Creep."

"Queer."

"Mignon, give me a break."

"How come you're home? I didn't think you got break until next week, speaking of breaks." Mignon smiled, finding herself clever.

"I'm home in disgrace."

Mignon turned to face her sister, her body rigid with expectation. "They find out?"

"No."

"You know Charly was here?"

"I know."

"That why you're home?"

"I'm home because I got thrown out of school and I had to tell Mom and Dad."

"No!"

"Yes."

"They throw you out because you're queer?"

"No, dammit, nobody knows but you, unless you've blabbed your big mouth."

"Thanks." Mignon dropped back on the seat.

"Sorry, Mignon, it's been exhausting. Mom was really upset. Then she and I drove down to tell Dad. He was okay. I mean, he wasn't blessing me, you know, but he wasn't condemning me either. I thought I'd sail right through this, but I guess I was more scared than I knew. God, I hate to disappoint Mom and Dad."

Mignon rapped her finger against her school books. "Jeez, then how are you going to tell them about Chris?"

"I don't know, but it's going to have to wait a bit. One thing at a time."

"What'd you do?"

"Huh?"

"What'd you do to get kicked out of William and Mary?"

"Oh, I went over to the Catholic Church and put a barbecue apron on the statue of the Blessed Virgin Mother, and I gave her a chef's hat and cooking utensils and a grill."

"That's so cool!" Mignon clapped her hands. "Too cool."

Vic laughed. "It was pretty funny, but I got caught, and that's that."

"Are you upset?"

"I didn't think I was, but I guess I am a little bit. I'm going back tomorrow, pack up, try to work out my rent, and I'm out of there."

"What about Chris?"

"It's not like she's in Tunis, Mignon."

"She wants to live with you?"

"After she graduates . . . yes, she does."

Red and gold metallic streamers were wound all around the light poles at the car dealership. A giant Christmas tree took place of pride behind the huge plate-glass window, almost but not totally obscuring Hojo at her command post.

They parked.

"Aunt Bunny's here," Mignon warned. "Wearing her binocs. Does she think it's, like, a fashion accessory or something?"

"Uncle Don's her most perfect fashion accessory." Vic knew she was going to have to tell Bunny about events but hoped she could just squeeze by today without having to spill the beans.

"Mignon, let me see," Hojo squealed as the sisters came into the display room.

Mignon trotted over. "Hoops. Finally." She noticed Hojo's nails. "Oh, Hojo, that is so cool."

Each nail was painted a different color, and each nail had a star, a sun, a moon, Saturn, or some other planet on it.

Hojo rolled her fingers in front of her. "The solar system. I got tired of moons. Took me four hours!"

"That is so cool!" Mignon repeated, with slightly less enthusiasm. Vic headed toward Bunny.

"What a surprise. You finish classes early?"

"Yes." Vic didn't lie.

Bunny fingered her binoculars. "I can see the expression on drivers' faces when they drive by, and I can tell who's going to come onto the lot and who isn't. I swear." She smoothed out her skirt. "Had to help with the books today. Lottie, Don's bookkeeper, took to her bed with the flu. I think it was the flu. With Lottie, you never know. She's the only nymphomaniac hypochondriac I know."

"Where's Uncle Don?"

"Service."

"Do you think he'd mind if I used his office phone?"

"No. Go right ahead." Bunny waved her toward Don's office, a cubicle with glass partitions halfway up.

Vic sat down and dialed Chris.

"Hello."

"You're home. I'm so glad." Vic breathed out.

"What happened?"

"Everything's okay. They aren't thrilled, but it's okay."

"I've been so worried." Chris's soothing voice sounded deeper.

"I think I was a little more worried than even I knew. Hey, I'll come back over tomorrow. It will be our last weekend until after Christmas. It'd be kind of nice to spend it with you in the apartment, but after dropping the bomb on Mom and Dad I think I should be here this weekend. Come home with me. It's kind of corny, but everyone decorates and I don't know, it's just fun."

"Sure it's okay? Your mom and dad aren't too upset to have a visitor?"

"It will be fine. I'll get you at two unless you cut your last class. I'm not suggesting that you do."

"Two." Chris waited a moment. "I've been thinking about you every minute. Really, Vic, I was so worried. I wish I could have done the deed for you, but, well, I can't. I love you."

"I love you, too."

They said their good-byes. Vic pressed the disconnect button and then called Charly's dorm. After going through three different guys picking up the receiver, which was now off the hook, she finally reached Charly.

"Hey, handsome."

"Vic, what happened?"

"It's okay. They're upset, but it's okay."

"I still think I should . . ."

"Don't. Now, come on. It's done. I called to tell you I'm staying home over the weekend to kind of keep things cool and to Christmas-shop. I don't want you hanging around because I'll never be able to get your present."

"The only present I want is you."

A little pang rippled through her chest. "Well, you're getting something else, too."

He replied, "Guess I'd better do some shopping, too, huh? I'll miss you. I hate being without you. I am so glad the season is over. You don't know."

"I'll call you over the weekend—that is, if I can get through."

"I'll call you. You okay, for real?"

"For real. I feel bad for Mom and Dad, but it's okay."

"This will all work out. I promise."

"I know."

"Well, I feel like a heel."

"Charly, forget it. This just works out better for everyone."

"I love you, Vic."

"I love you, too, Charly."

He lowered his voice, a light note creeping into the tone. "You know I can't even think of you without my dick standing straight up. You make me crazy."

"Charly, if I had a dick, it would be stiff, too." She laughed.

"That's a really weird thought." He sucked in his breath. "But I love you."

"Love you, too. See you Monday."

"Okay. Bye."

"Bye." She hung up the receiver and walked out, nearly bumping into Georgia Wallace, who had just come onto the floor. "Miss Wallace, I'm sorry. I wasn't looking where I was going."

"Young people never do." She smiled. "You're always in a hurry to go somewhere, and then you discover there's nothing there."

"Hey," Hojo called out, dispensing with the formality of calling the older woman by her last name.

"That Hojo" —Georgia shook her head— "up to no good and loving it. Oh, for a little bit of that energy. I am just ragged out because Poppy's going senile. Yolanda's in the kitchen, Sissy's being a real pissant about it" —the corner of her mouth turned up— "and I told her, 'Leave Yolanda alone. It makes him happy. How much longer are we going to have him with us?' And I can scoop up cow dung with the best of them. Sissy is so spoiled." Her voice dropped an octave on "so."

Hojo flashed her fingers. "Do you love it?"

Both Vic and Georgia studied the fingernails now drooped over the side of the command post. Mignon was next to Hojo, fiddling with the computer.

"Hojo, sugar, you are celestial," Georgia intoned.

"Got my nails done, got my push-up bra, Georgia, I'm ready for life. Let's go out tonight."

"Hojo darlin', you're too wild for me. You're more Sissy's cup of tea."

"Oh, come on, Georgia, you can't be but so good," Hojo wheedled.

"Well . . . not tonight, but I'll go out with you sometime. You know, I'll have to get my hair done, and I'll have to lock Sissy in the basement. She'd kill me if I went somewhere fun and she had to stay home."

"Lock her up, then." Hojo threw up her hands, her many bracelets sounding like castanets.

"Mignon, what are you doing?" Vic asked.

"Pulling up inventory, see?"

Vic stepped onto the dais. "Which car do you want?"

"Yours. I just like playing with the computer."

"Come on. Hey, let's get some takeout so Mom doesn't have to cook." They drove to a nearby Chinese restaurant.

As they waited for their order, Mignon inquired, "Are the Wallaces mental?"

"Not in Surry County."

She whispered, "Do you think there are a lot of gay people in Surry County?"

"I don't know. Why?"

"Well, you'll find out. I mean when you come out, won't they tell you who they are?"

"I don't know. Mignon, I don't think of these things."

"When they tell you, tell me."

"Why?"

"Because it's exciting."

"For Christ's sake." Vic grabbed her by the back of the neck with one hand. "Gossip queen."

"I didn't say I'd tell, I just want you to tell me."

"Maybe I will and maybe I won't."

Mignon poked her finger in Vic's ribs, making her release her neck. "If you don't, I'll bring a cow in the kitchen."

"That's a moo-t point."

"Oh, lame!" Mignon switched back to wanting to know who was gay. "Really though, tell me."

"Mignon, that is a confidence. A person might be scared. I can't violate a confidence."

"You're not scared." Mignon said as they carried the white cartons in a cardboard box out to the car.

"I haven't told anyone yet but you. I didn't exactly tell you; you figured it out. And I am scared. I just don't think too much about it, that's all."

"Are you really afraid?" Mignon couldn't imagine her big beautiful sister being afraid of much.

"Of course, I am."

Mignon grew solemn. "I don't want you to shut me out."

Vic opened the back door, Mignon put the cardboard box on the floor of the car and then Vic hugged her. "You're my sister, I'm not going to shut you out."

"I don't want things to be different. Like you're moving to a different world and I'm not."

"Ah, honey, that's not going to happen. It's not like I'm on a different planet." She then opened the passenger door for Mignon. "I don't know what's going to happen, but no one does . . . about tomorrow, I mean."

"Think there are books about what you do if you have a gay sister?"

Vic shook her head, shutting the door, and then walked around to her side, getting in the car. "No. Know what I think?"

"What?"

"All those books about controlling this or understanding that— it's all crap. There are no rules. Think about it. The rules we're told to live by were all made up by dead people. People we'll never know and people who don't know us. Like America. All written up by white men with property. I'm not saying it's all bad, I'm just saying no one thought of us."

"Women?"

"Kind of. But mostly what I wonder is why everyone is so ready to believe dead people."

Mignon gave this her ripe consideration as they drove home. "What about the wisdom of the centuries?"

"Okay, there is wisdom, there is stuff that needs to be passed along, but my point, if I have one" —she laughed— "is that every single person has to examine everything. You can't just believe something because someone tells you to. Hell, what do they know? It's not their life."

"Yeah."

"Yeah, what?"

"I see your point. Do you see mine?"

"Which is?"

"I don't want to be left out of your life."

"You won't be left out."

Vic thought for a while as they passed Boonie Ashley's store. "When you think about what a needy mess the human animal is for such a long time, it's a wonder anyone has children."

"It's all that poop, puke, and pee." Mignon wrinkled her nose in disgust. "If God were so smart, you think he'd have come up with a better solution."

"Men don't think of those things." Vic laughed. "Maybe God is a man, after all."

"That's why people pray to the Virgin Mary." Mignon folded her arms across her chest.

"Look what happened to her . . . Mary's barbecue."

In Williamsburg, candles glowed in every window, garlands adorned the horns of the much photographed oxen down in the historic area, mistletoe hung over doorways, and trees filled the big shop windows. The *tramp tramp* of tourist feet reminded each resident what side his or her bread was buttered on, too. Despite the constant traffic, shopkeepers and shoppers smiled, doing their best to please.

A frazzled Vic was also doing her best to please. Packing up her apartment didn't take much time. She'd never advanced beyond the bed and the kitchen table. She left the bed, moved the kitchen table to Chris's, sold her textbooks with a twinge of sadness, and paid her landlord, whom she liked, an extra month's rent.

Charly, overflowing with energy, was as happy as she'd ever seen him. She thought no longer having her apartment would end the possibility of making love with him. But he wanted to find another place. She put him off, felt terrible, and drove over to see Jinx.

Jinx sipped from her steaming mug of hot chocolate. "Whoever invented this stuff should be sitting at the right hand of God." The steam rising from the drink made her blink. "Sorry, no religious talk around you."

"Hail Mary, Mother of . . ." Vic blew over her own cocoa.

"You haven't told him."

"Oh, Jinx, he's so happy except for the fact that I wouldn't sleep with him today. It's almost Christmas. I feel like a total shit."

"The longer you wait, the worse it gets, unless you're changing your mind." Jinx swallowed a little of her drink.

"No, but come on, we're all out of here on Friday. It can wait. I know you think I'm a wimp, but I'm not." She sighed. "Except it is harder than I thought. I really do love him."

"Why can't you just marry him and keep Chris as your mistress? He'll never know." A devilish gleam sparkled in Jinx's eyes.

"She'd never put up with it. Don't think I could do it. I couldn't lie to him."

"You're lying to him now. Omission is a form of lie."

"Goddammit, Jinx, you're supposed to be my best friend. You're not making this any easier."

"I am your best friend, and you're lying to him."

Vic was about as steamed as her hot chocolate; then she cooled down. "Can't we compromise and say I'm easing him down?"

"Don't you think he knows? Come on, you all went to bed together."

"If a guy's getting good sex, it wouldn't begin to occur to him that you're also having great sex with a woman."

"I still think he knows," Jinx declared.

"Then why is he putting up with it?"

"Because he loves you, idiot. And like anyone in love, he can't allow himself to think of losing the person that he loves. So maybe he just thinks it's a fad."

"Haven't told Mom and Dad either. I've got to work up for the next major emotional event. Details at eleven." Vic ruefully smiled.

"Yeah, the main attraction starts in three minutes." Jinx took a big swallow. "How do you know you won't miss him when he's gone?"

"I will."

"Sex, too?"

She turned the cup around in her hands. "Maybe sometimes I'll think of him like that, but what I'll miss is him."

"How do you know you won't pick up guys on the side? You know, later on."

"No."

"Okay. Let's try another scenario. Suppose for some inexplicable reason"—Jinx held up her hands palms outward, a pacifying gesture—"you and Chris broke up. Would you go back to Charly?"

"No."

"Another man?"

"No. I'm not saying I wouldn't go to bed with another man. Look, I'm discovering that I'm incredibly sexual, but he wouldn't be my first choice."

"You'd look for another woman?"

"Yes."

Jinx drained her cup, setting it back on the table. "You won't have to look far. People will always find you."

"Are you surprised at how I feel?"

"Not now. I was in the beginning, but if you believe this is your path, I believe it, too. And I hope it all works out. I'm sorry for Charly, but you are what you are."

"The person who has surprised me the most is Mignon. She knows. She's actually kept her mouth shut. And she said to me over the weekend that she didn't want me to shut her out of my life. I nearly fell over."

"She's incredibly smart."

"She is, but she's been such a pain in the ass for the last couple of years I haven't noticed. She's grown up, sort of all at once. I don't remember doing it that way. Guess I'm still growing up."

"I don't think it's supposed to stop."

"Sure has for Edward Wallace."

"Oh, that."

"Yolanda's living in the kitchen."

"God."

"You know, I had a thought while I was cleaning. It's a terrible, terrible thought, and I should have my face slapped."

"Oh?"

"It's Christmas. The Blessed Virgin Mother should have a pretty new red satin dress, a glass of eggnog, a reindeer pin, and a Santa hat."

"Don't you dare!"

36

Vic drove Chris to the Norfolk airport Friday morning. They spent the hour-long trip planning their reunion.

They exchanged their gifts sitting in the car in the parking lot. Each one promised not to open the other's present until Christmas morning. The kissed, left the car, and made their way to the gate.

"Oh, honey, I don't want to go."

Vic hugged her. "Won't be too long before I'm right back here picking you up, but I'll miss you. I hate being without you."

"Me, too." Chris wiped her eyes, sniffled a little, kissed Vic on the cheek, and then hurried down the runway.

Vic watched from the huge windows until the silver airplane lifted off. Chris would fly to Baltimore and from there catch a commuter to York.

From Norfolk, Vic drove home. She motored along back roads, through the hamlets festooned with Christmas decorations, everything red, green, and gold. Elves cavorted on the lawns, Santa and his reindeer appeared to land at county courthouses, churches put their crèches out front, and town squares boasted large trees draped with lights and ornaments. She thought about the work total strangers had put into these displays, and she was suddenly deeply grateful. Everywhere around her people tried to make things beautiful, festive. And when it wasn't Christmas, they cut lawns, trimmed fence lines, painted fences, barns, and houses, and planted gardens of flowers and vegetables. She was the beneficiary of this labor, if only for a fleeting moment.

She wanted to stop the Impala at the next courthouse, push through the old double doors, and thank everyone. But instead she knew it was time to contribute her own labor, great or small. It really was time to grow up.

Rather than making her feel solemn and sober, her sudden lack of structure made her feel wonderful. College now seemed to her a holding pen. She had charged out of the pen. She'd make her way in the world as best she could and do what she could for others.

One for all and all for one. Alexandre Dumas was right, she mused, as she pulled into McKenna's, the sun high overhead. She planned to ask Uncle Don what Bunny wanted for Christmas. Something to watch with her binoculars, probably.

She was no sooner out of her car when Hojo flew out of the display and called to her, "Vic, come in here!"

Vic hurried in, pushed a little by the wind at her tail. "What?"

"You aren't gonna believe this. Come here." Hojo grabbed her by the wrist, her tight sweater revealing breasts in perfect proportion to the rest of her body. Hojo dragged her to the spotless garage area. "Can you fucking believe it?"

In the garage sat a brand-new blue-and-silver three-quarter-ton Dodge Ram truck. Welders were working on it, orange sparks flying upward.

"What's going on?" Vic asked.

"Old man Wallace marched in here today, bought the truck, and then paid for the modifications. He's putting in a ramp that won't hurt his back to raise and lower . . . it's got a hydraulic lift, and you know how expensive something like that can be, and then he had these thin metal bars put across his back window, although I don't know why. And he's putting on steel sides welded right onto the bed, can't ever remove them."

"Kind of like a small hay wagon."

"He's throwing another five thousand dollars into this truck, and honey, it ain't cheap to begin with—plus, plus, he's putting in a phone. A phone in his truck. He's going to have an aerial as long as a fishing rod, swaying every time he goes over ten miles an hour."

"Guess he's going back into business. Retirement is killing him." Vic wished that lovely truck were her Christmas present.

"Hell, no. He's doing it for Yolanda. She can walk up and down the ramp. He says that if she wants to go for a spin, he'll take her."

"Holy cow." Vic laughed, winking.

"You got that right." Hojo laughed along with her. "If he wants to haul his cow around Surry County, what do I care? But you'd better believe that Georgia and Sissy will care, 'cause this rig costs as much as a brand-new Cadillac. They'll kill him, I swear they will."

"That's a possibility."

"Not when I'm working. I don't want to clean up all that blood."

"Vic!" Bunny called from the doorway of the garage.

"She's like a tick," Hojo grunted. "I know she's your aunt and all, but the last week it's like she's painted on the floors. And on my ass. I do my job. I earn my paycheck."

"Vic! I want to talk to you right this instant."

Hojo looked sympathetically at Vic. "Sounds like she's going to tear you a new one."

"It kind of does, doesn't it?"

"Sorry." Hojo slapped her five, low and inside.

"Thanks." Vic, head up, smiling, approached her aunt.

Bunny grasped Vic's elbow and pulled her into the narrow hallway between Parts and Service. "Just what are you doing, and why didn't you tell me? You could have said something when you were here yesterday. I am so upset with you I could spit."

"It didn't seem like the right time."

"It was." Bunny pressed her lips together.

"Not in front of Hojo and Georgia and—well, Aunt Bunny, I was worn out from telling Mom and Dad. I didn't mean any disrespect."

"I would have heard you out."

"I'm sorry."

"Sorry? I'm sick. How could you do such a foolish, stupid, childish thing? And so close to graduation. I ought to hit you over the head with my binoculars and knock some sense into you."

"Yes, ma'am."

"This is just killing your mother."

Vic flared up. "No, it's not. Come on, Aunt Bunny, don't make it worse than it is. Mom and I talked it through, and she may not be real proud of me right this minute, but she's not wretched."

"She's damned upset!"

"You're more upset than she is."

"I am upset. I can't believe you'd be that dumb, to do it in the first place—and then to get caught!"

"There's nothing I can do about it now."

"Well, you'll finish up somewhere else. That you can do. After that, you'll be gone who knows where."

"I'm not going anywhere. I'm going to work."

She threw up one hand. "Oh, la! You'll be married in no time, and who knows where you'll land."

"I don't want to land anywhere. I want to stay right here. I've thought a lot about it. I love Surry County. I don't know if Mom has talked to you, but I'd like to work in your nursery. I'd love to learn the business from the ground up, forgive the pun. And . . . this is my home."

"Your home is where your husband is."

"Aunt Bunny, my home is where I say it is." A flash of fire came from Vic.

This stopped Bunny for a minute. "The jobs aren't here, and men make more money than women."

"I don't give a damn. I'm living in Surry County."

"Vic, you surprise me sometimes. I believe you mean it."

"I do." Her anger ebbed, and she joked. "Maybe I'll set up a rival dealership. Cadillacs. I can sell them to the Wallaces."

"The way they drive, you'd have steady customers."

Bunny's mood lightened. "Pushing metal . . . tough business. And I have called every damn dealer in Virginia trying to get those two birds Cadillacs cheap. I'm telling you . . . tough business."

"Has Mom spoken to you?" Vic returned to the subject close to her heart.

"Yes. We're getting together to thoroughly discuss it after Christmas. There's too much to do right now, and this deserves our full attention." Bunny paused. "What have you bought Charly?"

"Nothing yet. I want to get him a bomber jacket, but I don't have the money. Tell me, what would Uncle Don like?"

"Vitamins."

"Really?"

"That man needs help." Bunny tossed her head to the side. "Buy him B-vitamins and ginseng, and anything that restores vigor."

"If you say so. What do you want?"

"A husband with restored vigor."

Vic smiled. "I'll think of something."

Bunny reached into the deep pocket of her skirt and pulled out a wad of twenties. "Here. Buy that jacket for your boyfriend."

"Aunt Bunny . . . thanks. But I can't take it."

"Get your degree."

"I can't promise that either."

Thwarted, Bunny finally said, "Take the money anyway. Get him his bomber jacket. By the way, did you read the Williamsburg paper today?"

"No. I got up early to take Chris to the Norfolk airport."

"Well, there's a photo of the Virgin Mary statue. And she's dressed like Santa Claus. Did you strike again?"

"No. Honest."

"I'm glad to hear that. At least you learned something. And it appears you started a tradition."

"Think I'd better get the paper."

"Have it in the office."

They trooped back to Don's office, past Hojo who was ensconced once more in her command post. Vic flashed the okay sign to her behind Bunny's back as she passed.

When she saw the photograph in the paper, Vic snickered, then giggled, and then laughed out loud. "I would have put her in a cocktail party dress."

"Tsk, tsk," Bunny scolded her, but obviously enjoyed the idea.

37

Vic called Chris every day. Chris couldn't wait to get out of there, for Christmas to be over and to be back in Vic's arms. Her mother, committed to perfection and therefore eternally disappointed, was going crazy over the holidays, and driving everyone else nuts, too. Other than that, life was peachy.

Once R. J. walked by just as Vic was signing off, saying, "I love you."

"Charly?" she asked, after Vic hung up the phone.

"No."

Her mother paused a minute, the dish towel she'd been using to polish silver flapping from her waistband. "A rival?"

"Mother."

"Well, darling, one doesn't tell people one loves them unless one does."

"I love you," Vic mischievously replied.

"I love you, too. Shall I assume you aren't going to tell me?"

"Yes."

R. J. grabbed her dish towel to throw it at Vic when the phone rang again in the kitchen. She reached past her daughter to pick it up. "Hello?"

"Merry Christmas, Mrs. Savedge." Charly's deep voice wished her well.

"Merry Christmas to you. I'll bet you want your girl, and she's right here."

"Thank you."

She handed her daughter the phone, walked over to the now sparkling silver tray, and put the teapot, coffeemaker, creamer, and sugar bowl on it, carrying all of it into the dining room.

Vic called out, "Mom, Charly wants to come over later—is that okay?"

R. J. called back, "Of course."

Mignon joined her mother in the dining room. "Mom, make Daddy put together the base for the tree. I can't do it."

"I'll just bet that you can."

"Oh, Mom."

"Mignon, there's a lot to do. Now just reach down into your very depths and summon up the courage to tackle this most arduous task."

Mignon's eyes narrowed. "You can be so mean sometimes."

"Mothers are supposed to be mean."

Vic entered the dining room. "All right, what next?"

"Bring the tree in. But you can't do that until your little sister here, I amend that to your *afflicted* little sister, puts together the base."

"Make you a deal," Vic spoke to Mignon. "I'll do the base if you put on the lights."

"I hate that job."

"You hate every job. Take your pick."

"If we did the lights together, it would take half the time," Mignon bargained.

"If we did the lights together, I'd wind up doing them all."

"No. We'd divide the strands up. You take half, and I take half. I'll have to finish my half no matter what. Now that's fair."

"All right."

R. J. laughed, "Mignon, you'll wind up in politics."

Three hours later, the huge Douglas fir, sturdy in its base, lit by strands of colored lights, dominated the corner of the living room farthest from the fireplace. Piper had already made a bed under it.

R. J., Vic, and Mignon carried out the boxes of Christmas balls, stored in the basement in a huge wooden chest. A few of the ornaments dated from the late 1800s, and one was from 1861 and was dubbed "the war ball." Most were from the 1950s when R. J.'s mother had gone on a Christmas buying spree.

They started with the inside of the tree limbs and worked their way out. That's how Vic and Mignon had put on the lights. Doing it this way created depth, fullness. R. J. allowed no shortcuts.

After all the balls were in place, the process would be repeated with icicles. Then the golden garlands would be wound around the outside, top to bottom, and finally the large gold star would be placed on the top.

The mantelpieces were draped in pine garlands studded with holly and shiny red and gold Christmas balls.

In the wide center hall, also adorned with garlands, mistletoe hung from the beautiful, hand-blown nineteenth-century light fixture. A children's sleigh, filled with teddy bears, sat at the end of the hall.

Just as the setting sun turned the James as red as a holly berry, the three women finished the tree.

R. J. took a step back. "Ladies, what do you think?"

"The best, really, Mom, the best tree we've ever had," Vic said.

Mignon walked around it. "Piper thinks so, too."

The *thump thump* of a dog tail punctuated Mignon's observation.

R. J. walked to the long windows overlooking the river. The hand-blown glass in the small square panes was a little wavy in places. "The winter solstice. Always brings a mixture of melancholy and hope."

Mignon, now standing next to her mother, said, " 'Cause we get a minute more of daylight each day after today?"

"Yes, but the worst part of winter is still ahead of us, so the melancholy." She put her arm around Mignon's waist. "I'm lucky to have such wonderful daughters."

"Oh, Mom." Mignon hugged her.

"You're looking so beautiful these days, Mignon." R. J. hugged her back.

"My sister, the movie star," Vic called out as she stacked up the empty boxes to take them back to the basement.

"You two put those away, and I'll make us some mulled wine. We've earned it."

Vic and Mignon were still in the basement when Charly arrived. When R. J. opened the front door, he presented her with an enormous floral centerpiece for the hall. He dashed back to the car and returned with his arms filled with presents. R. J. led him into the living room, where she took the presents out of his arms, one by one, putting them under the tree, where Piper sniffed each one.

"Why, it's Santa Claus." She kissed him on the cheek. "Here, let me take your coat, come on in the kitchen."

They both heard the two sisters thunking up the wooden stairs, laughing uproariously about the Virgin Mary's latest transformation.

"Charly!" Vic hurried over and gave him a big hug and a kiss.

"Merry Christmas, beautiful." He kissed her back, then he released her and gave Mignon a hug and kiss on the cheek. "Merry Christmas to you, Mignon. Another beautiful Savedge to kiss."

"No wonder you like coming here." Vic pulled out a chair for him.

"No, no, let's sit in the living room like civilized people," R. J. said. She glanced out the kitchen windows. "God, look at that sky, will you? What a show."

Flames of scarlet, orange, and melon curled high in the sky, the place on the horizon where the sun had set vibrating a deep red. At the edges of this wide expanse, the clouds tinged with pink would soon be scarlet, too.

"Let me run upstairs and get Charly's present." Vic dashed up the stairs.

"Me, too." Mignon followed.

They fetched the present and then hurried down the wide front staircase to meet Charly and R. J., who had carried the warm wine into the living room.

"I'll just put this under the tree until you go. You can't open it until Christmas morning." Vic knelt down, placing a large silver package with a red ribbon under the tree.

"Mine, too." Mignon did the same.

Charly sat on the sofa so Vic could sit next to him. R. J. and Mignon nestled in the large chairs opposite them. Outside the whole western sky was on fire.

"What a solstice!" R. J. exclaimed. "I just can't get over it."

They drank their wine and chatted about their holiday plans.

"Mom, when's Dad coming home?" Mignon asked.

"Why, are you hungry?"

"I'm getting there."

"He'll be home in about a half an hour, unless someone detains him at the office. Charly, you'll stay and have dinner with us, won't you? Actually, you must. Having you here is the best present." She smiled her dazzling smile.

"He will." Vic squeezed his hand.

"Yay!" Mignon reluctantly followed her mother into the kitchen. R. J. was giving her the high sign.

"Outnumbered," Charly sighed in mock defeat.

R. J. stuck her head back in the living room. "Are you starved, or can you hold out for a little bit?"

"Hold out," Charly called back.

When R. J. returned to the kitchen and Charly felt secure that Mignon wouldn't pop back in or spy on them, he wrapped his arms around Vic, giving her a long kiss. "Merry Christmas, baby."

"Merry Christmas to you, too."

"Okay, you have to open one present now. The others can wait until Christmas morning." He rose and walked to the tree.

"Others, Charly?"

"Beautiful women need to be spoiled." He beckoned her to the tree. "You have to open this one now." He pointed to a small, dark green velvet box, silver icicles glittering over it.

Hesitantly, she untied the thin red satin ribbon. She opened the box. Nestled in black velvet a five-carat marquise diamond glistened in a platinum setting, the cold light almost blue in its pure brilliance.

"Oh, my God!" Vic almost dropped the box, then juggled it to her breast safely.

"It was my grandmother's."

"Charly, this is the most beautiful thing I have ever seen. My God. I don't know what to say. I, oh . . ." She couldn't help herself. She slipped it on her finger, and it fit perfectly. "I cannot believe it." She threw her arms around his neck, kissing him passionately. "I cannot believe it. Oh, Charly, it really is the most beautiful thing."

He laughed. "I don't think I've ever seen you this way."

"Oh, I don't know what to say."

Gracefully, for he was so graceful, he dropped to his right knee, took her right hand, and kissed it. "Will you do me the honor of being my wife?"

Vic froze. The tears spilled out of her eyes. She couldn't stop them as she struggled to speak. "Oh, Charly, let's get through your last semester."

"Is that a yes?"

"That's a delay." She removed the ring and pressed it back in his palm.

"Victoria, I love you. I will always love you until the day I die. The ring is yours. You come to me when you're ready."

"Honey." She knelt down, facing him, throwing her arms around his neck. "You are the best man in the world. You are the only man I would ever marry. It's just well, I've gotten thrown out of school. I need to get a job."

"I'll take care of you." He kissed her again. "I've told you that. You just need to believe me."

"I want to take care of myself. I don't want to be a burden."

"You could never be a burden."

"Well, I want to earn my keep. I can't live the life that your mother lived or mine even."

"I know that."

"Let me work this semester. When you graduate, then we'll do the right thing."

He placed the ring back on her finger. "I can't live without you."

"I love you. Whatever happens in our lives, just know that I love you."

Outside a truck horn sounded.

"I'll get it," Mignon called from the kitchen, and dashed through the hall and out the front door.

Charly and Vic got to their feet. She wrapped her arms around his neck, pressing her body to his, and kissed him. "I will never forget this Christmas."

"Well, since you haven't given me a clear yes, may I assume it's a clear maybe?"

"Sure." She shuddered at her own cowardice.

"Mom, Vic!" Mignon yelled from the front yard. "Hurry up!"

Vic hurried out of the living room and down the hall. Mignon had left the front door open. "Mignon, what—?"

Charly came up behind her. They both walked outside to join R. J. and Mignon and beheld Edward Wallace behind the wheel of his new truck. Yolanda was in the back, looking festive in a little elf hat. She was munching on alfalfa, the best of the best, and as happy as she could be.

Edward, at his most expansive, stepped out of his truck, handing R. J. a very expensive bottle of brandy. "You deserve the best, R. J. A Merry Christmas to you. Oh, and a little something for the girls." He handed Vic and Mignon each a bar of milk soap, wrapped with a red gingham ribbon.

"Edward, you come right on in now because we have a little something for you." R. J. put her arm around his shoulder.

"Poppy will be right back," Edward called to Yolanda, who paid no attention at all.

Piper, awake at last, dashed out, saw Yolanda, and set to barking.

"That's enough out of you," Vic told her.

The excited dog stopped barking but decided to sit there and give Yolanda the evil eye.

Just as Vic was closing the door, she saw a pair of headlights speeding down the driveway. "Charly, I think it's Sissy."

It was, and she was hauling ass, too. She slowed a bit at the wide curve in the driveway, then straightened out, heading directly toward the side of her father's gorgeous blue-and-silver truck.

"Sissy, *slow down!*" Vic hollered.

Sissy, eyes straight ahead, rammed the truck so hard that Yolanda fell to her knees.

"Jesus Christ." Charly sprinted to Sissy.

"I'm fine. It's that goddamned cow I want to kill." Sissy pushed Charly in the chest. "Hamburger. Do you hear me, Poppy? Hamburger."

Vic swung up on the pickup and examined Yolanda, finding only a little scrape on her right front knee. "There, Yolanda, it's a long way from your heart."

Edward, glass in hand, for he'd been sampling his own brandy, charged outside. "You dipshit! You hear me, Sissy? Oh, Yolanda, how is my baby?"

"She's just fine, Mr. Wallace," Vic reassured him. "Scraped her knee."

He climbed up pretty fast for an old man. He ran his hands over her legs. "You're all right, sugarpie." Then he jumped off the truck like a man half his age. He pointed to Sissy, as R. J. bent down to pick up the brandy glass he'd thrown to the side. "Out of my will. This does it!"

"Who you calling a dipshit, you old windbag? You're too god-damned mean to die. You can take your will and shove it where the sun don't shine!" Clearly, Sissy was filled with holiday spirits of the liquid variety.

Edward ignored her. "R. J., do you have a place where I could leave my Yolanda? I don't feel I should drive her home under the circumstances. Someplace warm?"

R. J. thought. "You know, I think the girls could clear out the garden shed. There's a fence around it, Edward. She'll be tidy. I can throw a blanket over her. Girls." R. J.'s voice had the tone of command.

"Let me help." Charly hurried off with them.

Vic dashed back in the house and grabbed a jacket and gloves. It took them twenty minutes, but they got the garden shed in pretty good shape, making sure there would be nothing for Yolanda to step on, rub against, or eat.

R. J.—now helped by Frank, who had come home—kept the two warring Wallaces apart.

With gentleness, the gentleness of Joseph leading Mary toward the stable, Edward coaxed Yolanda toward the gardening shed. Charly and Frank both carried her alfalfa.

Yolanda settled right in. Mignon brought an old blanket, which they rigged up for her with a little rope that crossed over her chest and another one around her large middle. Yolanda might have been old, but she was a very well-fed animal. A large bucket of fresh water was placed in the corner.

"Now, Edward, don't you worry about a thing. We'll crack the ice in her bucket in the morning. She'll have everything she needs," R. J. soothed him.

"If this truck can drive, I'm dumping it at Don's door. Frank, will you follow me?"

"I can follow you," Sissy suddenly offered.

"You can follow me to hell is what you can do." He turned his back to his youngest. "No Cadillac for you!"

This stung more than the threat of being cut out of the will. After being used so many times, that one had grown stale.

"Isn't that hydraulic lift the prettiest piece of work you've ever seen?" The old man pressed the button, and the lift miraculously slid back up in place.

Luckily, Sissy's savagery had damaged the side of the truck, not the rear.

"Folks, you go on and eat. I'll eat when I get home." Frank kissed R. J. on the cheek, climbed back in his car, and followed Edward down the driveway—the Dodge ran pretty well, all things considered.

Sissy stood in the middle of the driveway, her lower lip about to drag the ground. "I hate him. You just don't know how much I hate him and Georgia, too, the flaming hypocrite! Georgia has sex with young men. She pays them. I, at least, get volunteers!"

"Now, Sissy, let's discuss this later." R. J. blushed. "Would you like supper?"

"No, I want a new father and a new Cadillac and a handsome man to pay attention to me. If there's no handsome man, I'll settle for an ugly one with a big cock." She slammed her car door and backed down the driveway.

"Did she say what I thought she said?" Mignon's mouth hung wide open.

"You can catch flies that way." Vic laughed so hard her sides hurt.

"She did." Charly wiped his brow more out of nervousness than overexertion.

"Well, darlings, suppertime," R. J. sang out. "Suppertime."

It wasn't until they were all seated that Mignon noticed the marquise diamond. "What a rock!"

R. J. put down the serving fork and reached for her daughter's hand. "Honey, that is beautiful, stunning. That is the most beautiful diamond I have ever seen." Her eyes moistened. "Does this mean what I think it means?"

Vic cleared her throat. "Not exactly. It means we'll figure all this out when Charly graduates."

For a moment everyone was silent. Then Yolanda from the garden shed let out a glorious, happy "Moo."

38

The phone rang at ten-thirty on December 22. Until then it had been blissfully quiet . . . except for Yolanda. Vic and Mignon were out on a trip to the feed store. They bought a sack of high protein mix, some corn, molasses, other grains, and asked GooGoo (so named because he ate GooGoo Clusters morning, noon, and night) to drop off a round bale for Yolanda. She wouldn't be going home anytime soon with Edward fearing for her life.

When Vic rolled back down the driveway an hour later, her mother opened the back door and said, "Vic, call Chris. She says it's important. I've got to run over to Regina Baptista's. Lisa has been picked up for shoplifting."

"What?" Vic was surprised, but Mignon, who remained silent, was not.

"I don't know how long I'll be. First order of business is settling down Regina, who is awash in an extravaganza of emotion. Then I'll carry mother and daughter down to your father. He'll do what's necessary."

Vic and Mignon hurried through the back door.

"Anything we can do?"

"No, not really. If there's a problem, I'll call. Did you get the food for Yolanda?"

"She'll be very happy. GooGoo's dropping off some hay later."

"When I get home we might consider fixing up the old tobacco shed. The gardening shed is a little small for her. However, she seems quite happy. We'll figure it out. I know what you two can do." They looked at her expectantly. "Mark out a little pasture. We've enough odds and ends lying about, I bet we can rig up a snake fence. If that doesn't work, Edward can bring over some wood for a slip fence."

"Can't dig post holes if the ground is frozen." Mignon had no intention of digging holes.

"Only freezing at night, dear." R. J. smiled at her with exaggerated sweetness. "All right, hold down the fort."

"Mom, if Jinx wants to come back with you, will you bring her?" Vic, who had planned to see Jinx today, felt she shouldn't drive over to the Baptistas under the circumstances.

"Jinx needs to stay home and go through this with her family." She kissed each daughter on the cheek and left.

Vic turned to Mignon. "You knew."

"Uh-huh."

"You *can* keep secrets."

"The shit's hit the Baptista fan." Mignon shrugged.

"Happy holidays," Vic sarcastically said.

"You know, I could wear your ring for you if your hand gets tired."

"Get out of here!" Vic pushed her away. "No eavesdropping. I'm calling my girlfriend."

"Bet she won't give you a five-carat diamond. You'll have to give him back the ring."

"If she had one, she'd give it to me. And, smart-ass, I tried to give him back the ring. I did."

"See, that's the real problem with being gay, Vic. No engagement ring. No wedding presents. No honeymoon."

"Every day's a honeymoon. Scram. I'll find you when I'm done, so we can mark out the pasture for Yolanda."

Mignon trudged up the stairs. She still had packages to wrap, and she figured Vic would be on the phone for a while, especially since R. J. wasn't around.

Vic dialed the 717 area code and Chris's number. Chris picked up the phone. "Vic, thank God it's you."

"I was out this morning getting cow feed and—"

Chris interrupted, "Pick me up at the Norfolk airport at two-thirty. Can you?"

"Chris, what's wrong?"

A strangled silence followed, then a deep breath. "I'm pregnant."

Chris hurled herself down the runway and into Vic's arms. Since other people were hugging and kissing, home for Christmas, their reunion didn't seem as peculiar as it might have to those people not used to seeing women embracing.

They had to walk a mile to the Impala, since the parking lot was full. Once free of airport traffic they both started talking.

"It's not what you think," Chris said.

"What do you mean?"

"I didn't go to bed with anyone but you. I mean, I didn't go to bed with men. It was that one time with Charly." She was determined not to cry.

"The other thought never crossed my mind," Vic truthfully replied. "When did you know?"

"I didn't. I skipped my period, but I don't keep very good count anyway. But more time went by, and I felt good but different. I can't explain it, but I kind of knew something was different. So I went to my doctor at home, a lady I adore. And yes, I am pregnant."

"I'm too young to be a father." Vic reached for Chris's hand.

Chris smiled weakly. "If only you were the father, Vic, if only you were."

"Do you want to have the baby?"

Chris squeezed Vic's hand. "I wouldn't put it like that. I know I don't want an abortion. I can't do it, Vic. I just can't."

"Okay, okay. I'm not suggesting that you do. Just asking. It's not my body. I can't make the decision."

"Would you marry me if you could?"

"You know I would. Jesus, we have a lot of decisions to make. You can finish out this year, but I don't know how you can get through your senior year with a newborn baby."

"I'll finish later." A sad silence followed. "Do you know any children raised by two women?"

"You mean lovers?"

"Yes."

"No, but how would I know? People don't tell you those things." Vic squeezed Chris's hand and then realized she needed both hands on the wheel for a curve ahead.

"My parents will kill me." Chris teared up for a moment and then lifted her head slightly. "You know what? I don't really give a shit about what they think. My mother wants perfection, and she isn't going to get it. I don't even know if I'll tell her. I'm not going back there."

"We're going to have to tell mine." Vic braked slightly for the curve.

"That could wait a little bit. I won't show for a while, and I'll still be in school." A shadow of panic crossed Chris's face. "I won't be able to teach."

"Why not?"

"First of all, I'll have a child and I won't be married. That's a career killer. And then, sooner or later, people will find out that I'm gay. Goddammit!"

"What if you married a man? Someone you know?"

"Vic, who?"

Vic shrugged. "I don't know."

"Charly? Well, that's not going to work since he wants to marry you. A gay guy?" Chris turned to look at Vic. "I'm not doing it. I'm not doing any of it."

"Okay."

"Do you want me to do something like that?"

"No. I was thinking about your teaching, that's all."

Chris, wrapped up in her emotions, at that moment noticed the diamond on Vic's finger. "Vic." She pointed to the glittering ring.

"He asked me to marry him. I put him off. I gave him the ring right back, but he said he wanted me to have it, no matter what."

Chris slunk down in her seat. "Oh, marry him, Vic. Your life will be so much easier."

Vic pulled off the road. "Look, I don't know what to do. I've never been gay before. I've never been in love before, and now I'm, I'm going to be a father, a mother—is there a name for this? I don't know what to do, but getting all emotional about it isn't going to solve anything. Isn't going to make me feel better either. So, shut up. I'm not marrying Charly. We'll get through this somehow. Christ, it's not like the world is ending." She reached over, put her hand behind Chris's neck, pulled her close, and gave her a big kiss.

Chris caught her breath after that. "You're right. I'm just . . . scared."

"So am I. But you know what? A column of German panzers and tiger tanks aren't bearing down on us." She smiled. "We'll figure it out." She drove back onto the road.

"This is probably a good thing. Like the ugly duckling turning into the swan. A crisis sometimes makes things better, forces you to find what you've wanted all along. What is that expression, I can't remember it, but it's something like crisis is opportunity in disguise."

"At the moment, it's certainly effectively disguised," Vic replied, her voice calm.

"Funny, I always thought I would teach. I mean, what else do you do? Nursing? Teaching? Be a secretary?"

"We've got more choices than that."

"Maybe they do in New York City, but in the rest of the country it's the same old, same old. And I figured teaching would be okay—I'd get vacations. I'd be around other teachers. I mean, at least people would read." She lapsed into silence.

"Are you sure you want the baby?"

"I am absolutely sure. I just wish he or she will look like you."

"Okay. So you'll have the baby."

"What would you do if the shoe were on the other foot?"

"Pregnant?"

"Yes."

"I don't know." Vic struggled. "I can see both sides of the issue."

"It's not an issue. It's your body, it's your future, it's somebody else's future."

"You're right. I'd hope I'd be happy. It's just trying to figure it out and the money and the practicalities. I'd hope I'd be as strong as you."

"I'm not so strong. I know what you said about us facing tanks is true. Our lives aren't in danger, but, but I won't be a kid anymore when the baby comes. You know? I've only had to think about myself, I'm going to have to grow up. I'm bringing another life into the world."

Vic smiled. "It's the Virgin Mary. You probably wouldn't have this attitude if you hadn't spent quality time with the Blessed Virgin Mother."

"Vic." Chris rolled her eyes and then laughed.

They were glad to laugh. It drew them closer together, banishing the gloom.

"If you can be brave, I'd better catch up. I'm always putting stuff off. Actually, I like to think of it as weighing my options. I'm going to pull into this filling station. We need gas anyway. I'm going to call Charly and hope he's home. And, if you agree, we should go tell him what's going on. This affects him, too. If I wait, I think I'll backslide."

Chris closed her eyes for a moment. "Right. Let's do it."

The Texaco station, old but clean, had a phone booth outside. Vic called Charly while Chris pumped gas.

"Charly, I'm glad you're home."

"Hey, what's up. I'm on duty tonight, but I thought I'd come over tomorrow. Mom's got the house on the Candlelight Christmas Tour."

Vic checked her watch. "Can you get away for a little bit? I could meet you, um, wherever."

"Come here."

"Uh, I've got Chris with me."

"I thought she was back home."

"She was. We'd both like to see you, but coming to your house might not be the best idea."

He was quiet for a moment. "The Episcopal church. You know where it is, and it's always unlocked." He paused. "Are you all right?"

"I'm fine. We can be there in thirty minutes."

"Okay."

The white clapboard building, constructed before the Revolutionary War, had the strength and simplicity necessary to sustain its parishioners throughout the centuries.

The three of them greeted one another; then Charly opened the shining black door, and they entered the unheated church, the winter light filtering through the long, clear windows. They sat in a back pew.

"This must be pretty important." Charly picked up a hymnal from its resting place.

"It is." Vic wondered how she could say what she had to say. "I have never lied to you, Charly, but I haven't been honest either. I keep thinking I'll find the right time or the right place or something."

His face remained impassive as he fought back his fear. "This is a pretty good place."

"I guess for the three of us, important things happen at churches." She smiled sadly. "I love you. You are a special person but . . . I can't marry you." She put her right hand on her left ring finger.

He reached over and stopped her from slipping off the ring. "Don't."

"I know, too, it might seem kind of insensitive to have Chris here for this but you see, she's part of it. We're all in this together, I guess that's the best way to put it."

Charly looked from Vic to Chris and then back again. "I don't follow you."

Vic inhaled deeply. "I'm in love with Chris. I can't marry you."

Charly felt a flash of aching desperation. "But you love me. I know you love me."

"I do, Charly, I do, but it's not the same."

"So marry me anyway. You can still see Chris." His voice shook a little as he said it.

"I can't do that. It's not fair to anyone."

"You mean you want to be with Chris? *Be* with her."

"Let me put it this way . . . if I could marry her, I would."

He leaned against the hard back of the pew. "Why?"

"I don't know why. It just is."

"I'm sorry." Chris meant it, too.

Charly looked at her pretty face. "You didn't have to be here."

"She does. I'm not finished." Vic's voice was steady. This wasn't easy, but she was becoming more clear, more steady by the moment. "She's going to have your child."

Charly's mouth opened, but no sound escaped his lips.

"Things will work out, Charly. It was a shock to me, too, when I found out." Chris hoped to console him.

"You could have an abortion," he said flatly. "I'll arrange everything."

"No," Chris replied firmly.

He rubbed his forehead. "Okay, okay, do you want me to marry you? Is that where we're heading?"

"No." Chris's voice was quieter this time.

"Why can't I marry Vic and we'll raise the child as our own? Who would know?"

"Charly, that won't work."

"Why not? She can live next door if you have to be close." His face reddened.

"I'm not going to marry you. I'm not going to live a lie. I love you, Charly, but not the way you want to be loved, the way you deserve to be loved."

"What the hell can she give you that I can't? I can give you every-thing. I will give you everything. I'll live my life for you."

"I know you would. But I don't love you that way."

He directed his anger at Chris. "What can you give her?"

"Me."

"Vic, you'd never have to worry for the rest of your life. I mean it. I'll marry you. I'll raise the child with you. No one will ever know. My parents won't know. Your parents won't know. I'll learn to live with your relationship with Chris. I don't know how, but I will."

"It won't work."

"Why won't it work?" he shouted.

"Because I don't love you that way, Charly. Because it's not fair."

"I told you, I'll . . ."

"You said you'd learn to accept Chris. That's a wonderful gift, I know that, but I can't accept it just like I can't accept your ring."

"Keep the ring, goddammit!" This was the first time Charly had ever sworn at Vic.

"Chris and I will raise the child. She wants to have the baby."

"Vic, you've gotten thrown out of school. How can you support a child? You, too, Chris. You need me."

The three said nothing for a minute; then Charly repeated, "You need me."

"Charly, there's nothing you can do. You have your own life to live."

"It's my child, too."

"Are you willing to have your name on the birth certificate?" Chris asked.

"Are you sure it's mine?" Another surge of anger shot through him.

"Given that I have never slept with any man but you, unless a star rises in the east, it's yours." Chris gave as good as she got.

"So you're gay. You seduced Vic."

"Oh, bullshit. She did not seduce me," Vic said.

"You just woke up and decided you were in love with a woman?" Charly shook his head.

"In a funny way, yes. I am in love with her, Charly, and no matter how painful that is to hear, it is the truth. Now I can't pretend to love you in that way. If I did, you'd always wonder. You'd be miserable. You'd be wondering did I sleep with her that day or whatever. Men seem to focus on the sex part an awful lot."

"As if you don't." He nearly called her a hypocrite.

"This isn't going to get us anywhere," Chris interjected sensibly. "Charly, I did not seduce Vic. Our attraction was spontaneous. And I am in love with her. No, I can't give her money, social prestige, anything like that. I wish I could. I don't know what we're going to do. I don't know how we can support a baby, much less one another. But, for what it's worth, I love her, and I'll do my best for her."

"That's easy to say. She's making a lot bigger sacrifice than you are."

"Charly, that's unfair. Her body is on the line. Mine isn't."

"Why can't you have an abortion?" Charly, exasperated, threw his hands in the air.

"I can't take the life of this baby." Chris hastily added, "For me, it's not an option. What another woman does is her business."

"God, if only it were you." Charly wanted to put his hands over his eyes and cry. He wouldn't, though.

"What would that change?" Vic touched his forearm.

"You'd marry me."

"No. I would still marry Chris."

"You can't be serious."

"I am."

"I don't get it. I just don't get it." He stared at her beautiful face.

"I'm sorry. I never wanted to hurt you. I don't blame you if you hate me, but maybe someday you'll understand."

"All I understand is that you won't marry me and you're ruining your life. I don't understand that you want Chris."

"Would it be any easier if she were a man?"

"Yes. I'd know how to fight another man."

"But if I left you for another man, fight or no fight, I don't know if the pain would be much different."

"Okay." He took a deep, deep breath. "All this is happening at once. It's a lot. Why don't we let everything alone? Let's talk after Christmas. You don't know what will happen." He paused. "Do your parents know?"

"About Chris being pregnant?"

"No. About you and Chris."

"No."

"Vic, they might not take this as well as you think."

"It isn't going to change what Chris and I are going to do. We are going to live together. We are going to raise the child together."

"All right. All right." He held up his hands. "But time does some-times sort things out."

"Charly, what I hope for, what I pray for, is that you'll be my friend and that you'll learn to be a friend to Chris."

Chris, thinking along different lines, said, "We're all upset. This really is a shock. And I don't want to hurt you either, Charly. I wouldn't want to lose Vic. And I hope time will help, but how do I know that time won't only make you angry? How do I know you won't someday try to take the baby away from us?"

Vic hadn't thought of this. She wouldn't have. Her mind didn't work that way.

"If Vic and I got married, the baby would be safe."

"But I'm the mother."

"How do I know you won't take the baby away from Vic? What if you leave her?"

"I won't leave her." Color rose in Chris's cheeks.

"How do you know? What chance do two women have in the world? Two unemployed women with a kid?"

"What chance does anyone have when they start out? All we've got is love. All anyone's got. Maybe the difference is that we know up front how unfair the world is," Vic replied.

"Vic, you're willing to ruin your life?"

"I'd ruin my life if I married you, and I'd ruin yours, too."

This finally got through.

"Jesus." Charly had to fight back the tears.

"I'm sorry." Vic wished to her core that she had had the guts to tell him before now. The pain wouldn't have been so great. She swore she'd never be an emotional coward like that again. She never wanted to hurt anyone the way she was hurting Charly now.

He shut his eyes and then opened them. "I won't try to take away the baby. But don't you take the baby away from me."

"What do you mean?" Chris said this calmly.

"I'm the father. I expect to pay child support, and I expect to see my child."

"You just want to see Vic."

"Of course, I do. But it is my baby, and Chris, like it or not, you two are going to need all the help you can get."

"And when you marry?" Chris could have left that unsaid, but she wanted things out in the open.

"I only want Vic."

"Charly, I think what she's getting at is, would you and your wife try to take the baby away?"

"I told you I won't do that. I give you my word."

"Thank you." Vic took his hand and squeezed it; then she let go.

It wasn't until Vic and Chris left him that Charly finally cried.

40

The crackling emotions between Vic and Chris did not go unnoticed, but neither R. J. nor her husband could have imagined their real source. The Savedges, ever generous, were happy to include Chris in their holidays. Jinx and other young people not getting along with their parents had often found their way to Surry Crossing over the years.

Christmas Eve dinner was planned for seven o'clock with the McKennas.

At half past four, the sun dipped below the horizon. Bunny had been helping R. J. cook all day. As the sun's last rays bathed the landscape, Don called her and said he was running a little behind, but he was finally home. He'd shower, shave, change, and be over at the Savedges' on time.

At six Edward Wallace rolled down the drive in a brand-new red Cadillac, Georgia behind the wheel. He brought Yolanda a salt block and some sliced apples, which he mixed into her feed.

As he was leaving, Bunny stepped out for another armful of wood.

"Merry Christmas, Edward. When will your truck be ready?"

"Don't know. Georgia drove me by the shop, and everyone's gone, I think, but Don."

"You must be mistaken. He's at home."

"No, saw his car parked on the side and a new Dodge Ram."

"Nora Schonfeld," Bunny hissed under her breath.

R. J. jumped when Bunny roared back into the kitchen, dumping the wood by the kitchen fireplace. "Bunny!"

Bunny ignored the pile of wood she had just dropped. "That son of a bitch! He's with Nora Schonfeld at the office. Edward saw her truck."

"He's an old man. Surely he's mistaken."

"Edward is an old man but he doesn't miss a trick. I am going to nail Don. This will be a Christmas he never forgets!" She tore off her apron.

"Vic!" R. J. called.

"Mom?" Vic came into the kitchen.

"Go with your Aunt Bunny, will you? She'll explain, and you, well, just go."

"I don't need a keeper!" Bunny glared.

"Murder on Christmas Eve . . . Bunny, count to ten. The old man is probably wrong."

Vic threw on her down jacket and ran back to the living room to tell Chris and Mignon she'd be out for a while. Then she sprinted to the car because Bunny was likely to take off without her.

"Goddamn his eyes!" Bunny took the left turn out of the driveway so sharply that her binoculars would have slid onto the floor if Vic hadn't grabbed them.

"Yes, ma'am."

"He's down there with that bitch. Edward Wallace saw his car and her truck parked back by Service. I will kill him. No, death is too good for him. I'll make him suffer first."

"He could have used another car. It's not like he doesn't have a lot of choices."

"I know him!"

"Aunt Bunny, slow down."

"It's good that you see this. Men are all the same, Vic. Conniving, lying, cheating bastards. Just remember when you walk down the aisle."

"No time soon."

"That ring on your finger says different." She hung another curve too fast.

"Aunt Bunny, slow down now."

"Don't be reasonable! You're like your mother!"

"I'd like to live to be as old as my mother."

Bunny slowed slightly. "It's not like I don't give him what he wants. He wants sex, I am always available. Remember that. Don't refuse Charly sex. If you do, he'll find it with someone else. Men regard sex as a right, not a privilege."

"Don't we?"

"Oh, don't get philosophical! Women are better than men, and that's the end of it!"

"Yes, ma'am."

"God, I never realized this place was so damn far away."

"Aunt Bunny, it's only fifteen minutes away. You're upset. Everything seems, uh, tilted."

"Don't tell me what's wrong. You're my niece, not my guru."

"Yes, ma'am." Vic feared for the safety of the other cars on the road.

"Think twice about getting married. I mean it."

Vic flatly said, "Slow down."

"If I don't kill him, I might practice on you!"

The glittering red and gold ribbons of McKenna Dodge waved in the wind as Bunny slowed, sneaking onto the parking lot through the service entrance. Sure enough, Don's car of the moment was sitting next to a 1980 new Ram . . . but it wasn't Nora Schonfeld's.

She picked up her newest, most expensive binoculars, training them on Don's office. She could easily see through the many windows.

"See him?"

"No." She scanned and then stopped abruptly. A sharp intake of breath announced she had found her target.

Vic reached for the binoculars. Bunny, stunned, let her take them. Vic was greeted with the spectacle of Hojo in her command post, hands gripping the edge, legs apart, skirt hiked high up, and Don pumping away from behind. It appeared to be a very merry Christmas Eve at McKenna Dodge.

"Oh, shit. I'm sorry, Aunt Bunny."

Bunny snapped to attention, her mental clarity returned. "Get out of the car."

"Now, Aunt Bunny . . ."

"Vic, get out of the car."

"No."

"Then fasten your seat belt. It's going to be a bumpy ride." She laughed hollowly. "Always wanted to say that line."

Vic fastened her seat belt, frantically trying to think of something to say. Bunny swung around to the front of the dealership, turned on her bright lights to add to the terror, gunned the motor, and drove straight through the plate-glass window into the command center.

Glass shattered everywhere. Hojo, when she saw the lights, uncoupled herself from Don, scrambling over the top of the command post. She ran like hell for the side door and made it to her truck.

Don, a step slower and somewhat hampered by his erection, the head of his cock as red as Santa's suit, managed to get down behind the command post as the car hit it.

Motor still running, Bunny rolled down her window. "The divorce papers will be on your desk tomorrow. Merry Christmas." She backed out over the crunching glass.

"Aunt Bunny," Vic gasped. "We'll never make it back home. Your tires are punctured."

"You're right. Go grab a set of keys. In fact, let's take the big black truck out front. I own half of the dealership now . . . independent of that bastard! It's my Christmas present to you." She slammed the door, grabbing her beloved binoculars as Vic sprinted to the key board. She scanned the keys, found the set for the black 1980 Ram half ton, and hurried back, taking Bunny by the elbow. She didn't want Don to come out from wherever he was hiding and inspire Bunny to do God knows what.

They heard Hojo floor her red truck as it careened around the front of the dealership.

"I'll attend to that filthy whore later."

"Good idea. Come on, Aunt Bunny. Do you have your purse? Everything you need from your car?"

Bunny turned back and grabbed her purse. Then, her emotions fluctuating between battle euphoria and an impending sense of dread, she allowed Vic to lead her out to the new truck.

They drove back to Surry Crossing in silence. They had no sooner stepped through the back door than Bunny, on sight of her sister, burst into heart-wrenching sobs. Frank, Mignon, and Chris came into the kitchen to see if they could help.

R. J., her arms around Bunny, said to her husband, "Maybe a Scotch would help settle her nerves." She turned to Mignon. "Honey, bring Aunt Bunny some cheese and crackers . . . and a Scotch on the rocks."

"I never want to see him again!" Bunny raged.

"Come on, let's go to the living room." R. J. guided Bunny.

Piper, under the tree, thumped her tail in greeting.

Mignon put a plate of cheese and crackers on the coffee table and handed Bunny her drink. A fire filled the room with dancing light, the cheery wood releasing its intoxicating aroma.

R. J. put Bunny on the sofa and sat next to her. Frank stood, not sure what else to do. Mignon plopped in a wing chair, as did Chris. Vic stood next to her father.

"Frank, draw up divorce papers."

"Let's wait a day or two," he advised, his voice soothing.

"No. Give me those divorce papers as a Christmas present. I'm not backing down, and I'm not changing my mind. He's had one woman too many. And I'm giving the truck outside to Vic."

"Aunt Bunny, I don't . . ."

Bunny cut Vic off. "I could have hurt you. I know what I did was foolish but" —she laughed bitterly— "it was worth it."

R. J. wrinkled her nose for a minute, her eyebrows darted upward, then she composed herself. "Bunny, what did you do?"

"Drove through the plate-glass window. Caught them in the act on that damned command center—which I designed."

R. J. looked at Vic.

"She did drive through the window. We left the car there because of the glass. I guess Uncle Don will come up with some explanation for the police and the insurance company."

" 'I was fucking my receptionist when my wife drove through the plate-glass window.' Bet the claims adjustor would love that." Bunny laughed and cried simultaneously.

"Have a sip, honey." R. J. held the glass up for Bunny.

"I don't want a drink. I want a divorce." She pointed her finger at Vic. "Think twice, Victoria, think twice. Charly may be wonderful now, but in middle age, men just . . . unravel."

Frank ignored this. "Would you like me to go down to the dealership and see if I can find Don?"

Bunny, red-eyed, thought about this. "I don't care if he's dead."

Frank stared at R. J. for a minute. "You know, we don't want this getting in the papers in the wrong way. Girls, don't wait supper on me."

"If you see my sorry husband, my soon-to-be ex-husband, tell him I never want to see his face again and that next time I'll kill him."

Frank didn't respond. He left the room, put on his long Brooks Brothers camel-hair coat, worn thin at the elbows, and opened the back door, letting in a blast of cold air.

"Dad." Vic followed him into the hall. "Do you think Uncle Don will rat on her to the sheriff?"

"No, but if the sheriff should swing by, do not under any circumstances let Bunny talk to him. But I think your Uncle Don is probably glad to be alive at this point." He clapped on his hat and left.

Mignon came up behind Vic. "Bad, huh?"

"Not good."

"That was pretty cool, though."

"Not if you were sitting next to her." Vic shook her head.

"I knew."

"Knew what?"

"That Uncle Don was banging Hojo."

"Jesus, Mignon, why didn't you say something?"

"Because I can keep a secret," she replied with pride. "I caught them kissing once."

"So that's why Hojo pierced your ears even though she knew damn well Mom would have a fit."

"It's not like I blackmailed her." Mignon closed the front door. The cold was making her shiver.

"I forgot I left it open." Vic wondered where her mind was. "You did the right thing, not to tell. There wasn't anything Mom could have done about it or me. And no one wants to tell anyone their husband is sleeping with someone else. You know what happens to the messenger who brings bad tidings." She ran her forefinger across her throat. "Come on, we'd better get back in there."

The two sisters returned in the middle of another one of Bunny's impassioned attacks.

The stricken woman fixed on Vic as she entered the room. "Mark my words. You get a prenuptial. Every piece of jewelry he gives you during the marriage is yours. Every piece of property, stocks, bonds, anything of value, half because you earned half of it. I know you're in love, but you do this. Now." She pointed to the big ring on Vic's finger.

Tears slid down Chris's face. Vic walked over, sat on the edge of the chair. "It's okay. Come on, Chris, it's okay."

All of the day's emotions were catching up to Chris.

Bewildered, Mignon sat down in the other wing chair.

Bunny slowed down her own crying for a moment. "You, too, Chris. Mark my words!"

Chris reached up for Vic's hand.

"It's been a wild day." Vic held Chris's hand.

"What do you have to cry about?" Bunny thought perhaps her behavior had triggered Chris.

"Here." Mignon, trying to be helpful, had fixed Chris a Scotch.

"I suppose seeing me doesn't make marriage look appetizing." Bunny wiped her eyes with the tissue R. J. handed her. "But you must draw up the proper papers. I don't give a damn how much you love him now."

Vic breathed in and then exhaled slowly. "Mom, Aunt Bunny, Mignon, I'm not going to marry Charly Harrison."

Even Bunny stopped crying to stare.

R. J. picked up Bunny's Scotch for a sip and then handed it back to her sister, who thought another blast was not such a bad idea.

"Wow." Mignon blinked.

"I'm sorry. I'm so sorry," Chris said as she cried anew.

Vic patted her back again. "There's nothing to be sorry about. It's all settled."

Bunny asked the obvious question. "Just what the hell is going on?"

"I'm pregnant," Chris simply stated, drying her eyes.

R. J., puzzled, tried to soothe Chris. "These things happen, dear—we'll help you. But what does this have to do with Vic and Charly?"

"Charly is the father," Vic calmly explained.

"I told you men were shits!" Bunny fumed. "I'll kill him, too." Then she turned on Chris. "How could you betray your friend like that? And this whole family, which has only shown you hospitality?"

"Aunt Bunny, stop. It's not like that." Vic's voice was like ice.

As she had never spoken in such a tone to her aunt, it guaranteed silence. But only for a moment. Bunny couldn't stop herself.

"What else could it be? They both betrayed you!" Bunny practically shrieked.

"No, they didn't."

R. J., very quietly, suggested, "Perhaps you can enlighten us."

Mignon got out of the wing chair to stand next to Vic. She didn't know what was coming, but she knew she wanted to back her sister.

Vic stood up, too, but kept a hand on Chris's shoulder. "It was a twist of fate."

"In my limited experience," Bunny sarcastically said, "pregnancy is not caused by a twist of fate."

"In this case, it was." Vic breathed in again and then exhaled. "We all went to bed together. No one betrayed anyone."

"Wow." Mignon's eyes grew as big as the Christmas balls.

"You all?" Bunny was trying to compute this, but her mind was muddled.

"Charly, Chris, and myself."

"Victoria." R. J. reached for the Scotch again.

"Mother, it wasn't a bad thing. In fact, it was a beautiful thing. It just happened. We were happy. We were in love."

"Love?" Bunny cast a jaundiced eye. "Men don't sleep with other women when they're in love with you."

"But they do," Vic quietly asserted. "I instigated it. It was all about love."

"I see," R. J. said simply.

"Get rid of the baby," Bunny spat out. "Don't ruin three lives."

"No." Chris found her voice.

"She's not ruining three lives. Charly, Chris, and I talked it over. Chris and I will raise the baby."

"What?" R. J. nearly choked then started crying.

Vic went to her mother. "Mom, it's all right. Don't cry. Please don't cry."

"Honey, I'm just so sorry for you. I know you love Charly and he loves you. You don't have to give him up and well, I just don't understand this."

"She'll find another rich one. With Vic's beauty, she could marry a goddamned Arab sheik and own half the world's oil."

"Aunt Bunny, I'm not going to marry."

"You say that now. It will pass."

"Mom, would you like another drink?" Vic handed her the glass.

"That depends." R. J.'s green eyes sought out her daughter's.

"I love Charly, but I'm in love with Chris. So you see, this is the right thing to do."

Mignon stood stock still.

"What are you talking about?" Bunny crossly said.

"I'm gay."

"Then I want my truck back!"

R. J. put her glass on the coffee table and gathered her composure. "This must be very painful for you, for both of you." She looked at Chris.

"Jesus, R. J., slap her face." Bunny stood up, but R. J. pulled her back down. "Vic, you need a vacation from yourself. You'll come to your senses," Bunny continued.

"But I have. I'm glad I realized this before I . . . Well, it doesn't matter now. The three of us have made our decision, and it's a good one."

"I don't see how telling us that you're a lesbian can be a good decision."

"That part's not a decision, Aunt Bunny," Mignon said, taking up for Vic.

"You shut up," Bunny growled at her.

"No, Vic is Vic. She didn't decide to be gay."

"It will pass." Bunny crossed her arms.

"It won't pass. I love Chris, and she loves me." Vic refused to cry, despite the lump in her throat.

"I do," Chris said.

"Did you always feel this way, dear?" R. J. asked her daughter.

"I did what was expected of me. I went through the motions. I didn't ask questions. It's not like I grew up knowing there was another way or that I'd go that way."

"Well—" R. J. thought awhile. "—the three of you have put the child first, and that speaks well for all of you. I can imagine this is extremely difficult." She looked at Chris. "I'm glad you're having the baby." She looked back to Vic. "I think it will take me awhile to get used to this. Is this why you were kicked out of school?"

"No, that really was over the BVM."

"She took the blame for Charly and me." Chris reached for another tissue.

"I see."

A silence followed that was finally broken by a wail from Bunny. "But what about me!"

Epilogue

People have always known that time flies. The Romans famously said, *"Tempus fugit."* Yet, it's one of those realizations that startles each person as they feel it happening in their own lives.

The image of Father Time as a white bearded man, bent over with years, isn't quite correct. Time is an imp, a little devil who kicks over the hourglass. By the time you right it, half the sand has run out and you can't find the rest of it, the grains have scattered to the winds.

So it was at Surry Crossing. The shock of Vic's declaration, Chris's pregnancy, and Bunny's discovery yielded to the details of daily life. Tempests occurred most notably with Bunny. She sued for divorce and won. For a while she argued that bringing Vic into the new business was just endorsing her lesbianism.

This argument was quickly dropped when Chris was delivered of a beautiful blond boy whom she named Victor, in honor of Vic.

Much as Bunny fumed about the social disgrace of lesbianism, she couldn't resist Victor. Neither could anyone else, most especially Piper.

Chris's family cut her off. Her brothers sporadically kept in touch with her, but she never heard from her mother or father again, and she never attempted to contact them. Her view, often declared, was that your family is made of the people who love you for you.

R. J. saw that Vic was happy and so she accepted the relationship.

But then R. J. always did believe in love. She loved Frank in spite of everything. Why shouldn't Victoria have her chance?

If Frank didn't understand the relationship, he kept it to himself. He was never critical. He remained what he always had been, a Virginia gentleman. He liked Chris. He loved Victor.

Once Bunny got off her high horse, she and Chris became friends. Both of them suffered a streak of perfectionism, which drew them together since they were lightning fast to see the tiniest flaw in anyone else's personality, plans, or performance. Chris kept the books for the nursery. Bunny couldn't find one single thing wrong. Then the two decided the nursery could expand and sell outdoor furniture, sculpture, and trellises. That sideline became very successful.

Charly, true to his word, visited Victor when he could and each month he sent money. He had entered the draft after graduating from William and Mary and was picked by the Kansas City Chiefs in the last round as an afterthought. He worked hard and beat out guys who had played for powerhouse schools like Ohio State, Notre Dame, and Nebraska. By the second season he was a starter. He set up a college fund for his son.

He also married a beautiful woman. Her physical resemblance to Vic escaped no one—especially his wife. The marriage was wretched. He paid through the nose to divorce her.

He'd call Vic once a week and talk to her about his life. He'd talk to Chris about their son. He was now famous, handsomely paid for being able to run around with a pigskin tucked under his arm. And he was just miserable.

Vic gave Jinx, Charly's number. She had graduated from the University of Virginia Law School and was working for a high-powered firm in Washington. She specialized in tax law, which seemed boring to everyone else, but Jinx, always looking ahead, realized it was a powerful political lever. She had a conference in Kansas City and she called Charly. She was attractive, brilliant, kind, and she had that self-confidence that attends people who love their work. They married two years later. This marriage was a success.

When Charly retired from football at age thirty-four, before his knees were totally destroyed, he moved to Washington, took a job in a brokerage house, and found he loved his work as much as Jinx loved hers. He grew closer to his father, too, now that they shared a common profession.

Don continued to run the dealership. He owned half of it, but he was surprised to learn he couldn't really live without Bunny. He begged her to take him back. She was in no hurry to do so since she liked being free, as she put it. His entreaties finally wore her down. But Bunny, being Bunny, cut a tough deal. He could run the Dodge/Toyota dealership, but she was going to get the Mercedes and Nissan dealerships, which she would run herself. He agreed. They remarried.

Bunny sold her half of the nursery business to Vic and Chris, who had formerly been paid employees. She gave them good terms, and Chris figured they would pay off the debt in eight years.

Mignon sailed through William and Mary, then attended New York University's Medical School. She specialized in plastic surgery, lived in New York City, and made boatloads of money. She married a teammate of Charly's. Mignon blossomed into a most delightful woman. She and Vic adored one another.

Edward Wallace hung on to eighty-eight. Yolanda succumbed long before the old man did. In his grief when she died, he marched out and bought a few more Jerseys, which put Sissy right over the edge. More visits to Frank Savedge finally straightened it out, but the old man did break down and buy her a cream-colored Cadillac with a sea foam interior, which Bunny, after hundreds of phone calls, got for a great price. Then he had to turn around and buy a black one, for Georgia. They became a three-Cadillac family.

When Edward went to his reward, he willed his cattle as well as all his farm equipment to Vic and R. J. Mother and daughter cried when they found out. Edward had been a true friend to the Savedges through all their struggles. He shut up Georgia and Sissy when they pitched a fit over Vic and Chris. He shut up a few other people, as well. He, too, was a Virginia gentleman, the type that confused people because on the outside he could seem prejudiced and sly, but on the inside he was always fair. In that sense, he truly was a gentleman be-cause he did not see the world in terms of groups or causes. He took the world one person at a time.

Hojo moved to Charlotte, North Carolina, and enrolled in the University of North Carolina. Determined to make something of herself, she majored in business and then returned to Surry County. She took a job at the Chevy dealership, eventually buying out the owner, an aging and alcoholic relative of Boonie Ashley's. Hojo became the McKennas' fiercest competitor, taking over the GM dealership in the process. She never married, contenting herself with a string of men whom she could dismiss at will. Which she did. She became something of an expert consumer in that respect.

Vic worked morning, noon, and night when she was an employee of Surry Crossing Nursery. Once she became a partner, she worked even harder, but she was still outside most of the time, so she was happy.

She loved Chris and Victor. Children force you to do a lot of things you'd never do otherwise. In a way, she was grateful because Victor probably saved her from becoming self-centered or too focused on the business. Still, Chris was better suited for motherhood than Vic was. Vic always worried Chris protected Victor too much.

When Chris wanted to have a second baby, Vic argued they couldn't support a second baby. Victor was two years old then. R. J. understood Chris's desire much better than Vic did, and she brought Vic around to the idea. Thanks to artificial insemination, a little girl was born, whom Chris named Sean, which provoked another fight since Vic said Sean was a boy's name. However, Sean worked her way into everyone's heart, and Little Vic became a big brother, a job that was quite important to him.

One hot July day, Vic was having a beer with Don as her truck was being serviced. She said, "Christ, women are a pain in the ass." She'd had a knock-down fight with Chris that morning. He just laughed sympathetically.

Still, she and Chris stuck together. Like most couples, as time goes by, they were bound by money, by possessions, and above all, by the children. Vic sometimes wished Chris weren't so damned picky, and she really wished Chris were more sexual. For most people, that wildness wears off, but it never did for Vic. As the years rolled along she recognized she didn't have a sex drive, she had a sex overdrive. She had a few affairs but she was lucky. She never got caught. Sometimes she thought she was in bed with another woman because she needed more sex. Other times she thought she was there just to get some positive energy, just to take a vacation. Her Uncle Don's former behavior made a lot more sense to her now.

She loved Charly, but not once did she regret not marrying him. He couldn't have found a better partner than Jinx, with whom she stayed best friends.

Piper died of old age. Within a year another golden retriever joined Surry Crossing.

Frank died of a massive heart attack on the courthouse steps in 1996. He was given a funeral with full military honors. At the end of his life he had stopped reading even the *Wall Street Journal*. He accepted that he wasn't ever going to make up the money he lost and redeem himself. He didn't really need to, of course, because the love he gave others, quietly, generously, was redemption enough.

Don McKenna gave the funeral oration and said something that stayed in Vic's mind. It became her mantra.

He said, "Most people believe in 'Live and Let Live,' but Frank believed in 'Live, Let Live, and Help to Live.' "

Tempus fugit.

When Victor Carter graduated from William and Mary, one year early in 2001, thanks to his advanced studies, the Savedges, Harrisons, Wallaces, and McKennas proudly attended. He was a great-looking kid, a terrific athlete, and he was going on to attend Auburn Veterinary College.

After graduation he led them all to St. Bede's. There waiting for them was the Blessed Virgin Mary, appropriately dressed for the occasion in a graduation robe and mortar board. Vic thought her expression was unusually serene.

RITA MAE BROWN brings you more
of the fascinating and clever world of
foxhunting in the fourth book in the
New York Times bestselling
OUTFOXED series

THE HUNT BALL

Tension stirs over the local prep school's controversial collection of historical artifacts made by slaves. When a faculty member turns up dead, Sister sets her mind to find the killer—with help from her furry mystery-solving friends—and is led directly to the foxhunting crowd.

The Hunt Ball, written with Rita Mae's signature humor, is steeped in tradition, lush landscapes, and the thrill of the hunt. This year's Hunt Ball will prove to be the most spectacular yet . . . at least for those who live long enough to get there!

Read each volume in the Outfoxed series
OUTFOXED • HOTSPUR
FULL CRY • THE HUNT BALL

 Ballantine Books • www.ballantinebooks.com

© Bernard Vidal

Rita Mae Brown is the bestselling author of *Rubyfruit Jungle, In Her Day, Six of One, Southern Discomfort, Sudden Death, High Hearts, Bingo, Starting from Scratch: A Different Kind of Writer's Manual, Venus Envy, Dolley: A Novel of Dolley Madison in Love and War, Riding Shotgun, Loose Lips, Outfoxed,* and a memoir, *Rita Will.* With her tiger cat, Sneaky Pie, she also collaborates on the *New York Times* bestselling Mrs. Murphy mystery series, including *Claws and Effect.* An Emmy-nominated screenwriter and a poet, she lives in Charlottesville, Virginia.